WHEN THE DEAD

A zombie novel by Michelle Kilmer

WtD BOOKS

Book design and formatting by KILMERHANSEN

ISBN: 0988252244
ISBN-13: 978-0-9882522-4-0

DEDICATED TO . . .

the first type of person
who will do anything to survive,

my family and friends for the love and support,

my editors Rachel and Rebecca Hansen and
Kevin D. Looney for helping the dead walk,

To my father who, in his time with his children,
encouraged us to be creative, unique and intrepid,

and to my wonderful husband
who doesn't like zombies at all

TABLE OF CONTENTS

WHEN THE DEAD

A zombie novel by Michelle Kilmer

THE INFECTION

It starts with a cold sweat then a swift drop in body temperature that makes the teeth chatter. The skin feels itchy and hot but the insides are dying from the cold.

Then the numbness starts in the extremities. Finger tips, toes, up through the feet and hands into the legs and arms and finally the core. It cannot be rubbed out as the hands do not work anymore.

It reaches the chest and the ability to control the breathing is lost. Just before the last breath of air escapes the lungs, numbness reaches the head.

The eyes go crazy, the tongue limp. One cannot call out for help as the head falls on the chest. There is but a single moment for the dying self to think a final thought . . .

Why me?

But then . . . you aren't you anymore.

FUCKED

"I can't understand what they're saying," Edward said as he slammed a fist down on the radio.

"You could try another station. That sounds like French they're speaking," his wife Moira suggested. She had wanted a television for a long time but Edward preferred the way the voices came floating from the speakers into the apartment. This meant that in the current situation though, they had to rely on the radio show hosts' graphic descriptions to give them any idea of what was going on in cities across the globe.

"The other stations keep replaying the same stuff. It's not getting any better; only worse," Edward grumbled.

"Then there's nothing we can do but make some tea and wait to see what happens next."

"It's happening everywhere," Isobel said to her mother over the phone. She had spent the morning reading news articles online. She had watched a clip of someone succumb to the infection on a CDC table, surrounded by plastic and strapped down like a criminal or lunatic.

"Things will be ok, Isobel! They have a carrier. It really is only a matter of time. If they can study it, they can find a cure or at least a vaccine. Try to keep this thing from spreading any further."

"It's too big already. The world is fucked. I've got to go." She hung up the phone not knowing it would be the last time she'd speak to her mother.

"On and on for three days, man; can't they talk about something else?" Vaughn turned off his television angrily. "Could have been aliens, maybe the government, maybe bio-terrorists? Shut up." He chucked a drained beer can at the black screen. "Just fix it and forget it!"

Vaughn was alone, as he often was, unless he paid for company. He was talking to himself. He probably couldn't even pay someone to listen to him. Especially when he was drunk and that was most of the time.

"Couldn't be bio-terrorists, they'd a laid claim to it. Been proud of the trouble they were causing. Pretty fancy stuff making dead people come back to life. It has to be the government; only group with enough funding and closed doors to pull this shit off."

The infection was quickly spreading. It had reached terrorist groups and government groups alike. It lay in thousands of sickbeds, it rode the bus, and it lived next door to many already. No one was immune from this unstoppable plague.

The number one cause for the spread of the disease was denial. It made no *sense* to anyone. News media could be blamed for the lies with headlines like *It's impossible! Death is death, the final breath*, and *People Don't Come Back. They stay wherever it is that they went.*

the infection does not discriminate in human hosts. sex, race and religious conviction no longer divide the population.

WILLOW BROOK APARTMENTS

Willow Brook is a three-story building, four if you count the basement. Each floor has six two-bedroom apartments with identical floor plans.

The kitchen is to the left of the entry. It has an island that looks out on the dining room and living room. The first room on the right down the hallway is a second bedroom. Next is the laundry closet with a stacking washer/dryer unit. The last room on the right is the bathroom. At the end of the hall is a closet and the master bedroom is on the left.

All of the apartments look more or less like this save for differences in décor and varying levels of tidiness. The Willow Brook building is controlled access, meaning that if you don't have a key, someone has to buzz you in, or not.

THE FIRST DAY

On the morning of the first day, the day that things would start to change for the residents of Willow Brook Apartments, things looked normal. When Isobel Shiffman looked outside it was almost too normal, right down to the happy thieving squirrel in the tree nearest her living room window.

Northgate is at the northern edge of Seattle and the nearest reports of the disease were further north in Everett and south in Tacoma, still far enough away for Isobel to brave the outdoors. Her mother had told her to stock up on food just in case things didn't clear up as quickly as she hoped. Isobel had gone shopping on Sunday and it was only Tuesday but her mother insisted.

Like Isobel, the rest of the city driven by nagging mothers, packed into the grocery stores and left them in such a state of disarray that it was hard for her to navigate. The cart, even without the help of the wobbly right front wheel, kept running into things: cans of food, a bag of chips, some nylons, and other items strewn about. All of which were displaced far from their original aisle and shelf. She struggled with it until she found the secret to making the cart move was to put pressure on the left side of it with her foot. She went for some of the fresh food that everyone else was ignoring, figuring it could be eaten first and when it ran out or started to rot, whichever happened first, she'd break into the non-perishables (of which she had a lot).

She made it up to the only open checkout lane.

"How long did you buy for?" the nervous cashier asked.

"Um . . . I don't know. A week?" Isobel wasn't good at estimation or small talk. Her cart was full with what she knew was affordable for her budget and, more importantly, what she could carry up to her second floor apartment on her own. She hadn't been thinking about timelines.

"That won't be enough. The world is coming to an end."

"Ok. Well how long do you buy for when the world is coming to an end?" Isobel snapped at the cashier.

"Don't know," the cashier shrugged. "Do you want your receipt?"

"Sure."

On the way back home, the radio still reporting news from all over, documented the plague's movement. It crept slowly closer. Isobel turned the radio up and listened.

"Early this morning, a ferry full of people trying to get home to their families left Whidbey Island alive and well and arrived at the Edmonds ferry dock infected with the mysterious disease we've been seeing. They had somehow contracted the disease on the passage over the Puget Sound. Ferry officials at the Edmonds Pier heard no reports from the captain of the vessel that anything was wrong on the boat. The captain routinely steered the ship into port and the infected disembarked and started attacking people in the parking lot. It is suspected that at least twenty of the infected passengers made it out of the ferry terminal and into downtown Edmonds. Efforts to locate and apprehend them in order to contain the spread of the infection have been unsuccessful. Several injured passengers made it safely onto lifeboats before the ferry made it

ashore, but they did not survive their wounds. The captain of the vessel has been detained for questioning at this time."

The program switched to weather and Isobel changed the station, desperate to find out just how close it had become.

"- determined that the perpetrator of a street fight in downtown Seattle, described by witnesses as a "drunken transient", was actually a person suffering from the infection. Police shot the man after he attempted to attack them. It is unknown how he came into contact with the disease. Attempts to identify the individual are ongoing, as his body appeared to be in a state of decomposition. The flesh of his fingertips was gone, rendering fingerprinting useless. Investigators are working with dental records -"

Isobel changed it again, looking for another news story and its location.

"A group of students started a riot on University Avenue in the U-District just after eleven a.m. Over fifty college students were injured in the event, four fatally. The group seemed to have no agenda and was only intent on causing destruction and harm to individuals. Sources at the scene noted that the group was not involved in looting or property damage. Most of the students fled the scene before they could be arrested and interrogated. Campus police had great difficulty dealing with the problem and are not commenting at this time. It is still unknown whether the perpetrators were rioting in response to the disease, or as a result of being infected with it."

Isobel's heart beat faster.

"A bloody scene at the Helene Madison Pool greeted Shoreline Police investigators midday today. A lifeguard interviewed said that a man had emerged from the men's locker room at the start of Public Swim and started attacking children in the shallow end of the pool. It

took two lifeguards on staff to remove the man from the water and hold him while a third employee called the police. All of the children involved suffered only minor injuries. The pool has been shut down for investigation and sanitation reasons and will remain closed until further notice."

"That's just up the road," she said to herself.

Initial reports thought the disease spread and made people psychotic and violent; that the infected were living people with altered minds and an inability to differentiate right from wrong. Whatever the process, it only took one infected person to ruin everybody's day.

Approaching from all directions, the disease was soon upon Isobel's neighborhood and suddenly it was right in front of her in the form of a traffic accident. Someone had destroyed a bicyclist with an SUV. A deep cut in his abdomen sat open, displaying his intestines. One of his legs had been almost completely severed near the hip joint. He had not survived his injuries. The driver of the vehicle, a pale young woman in hysterics and leggings, was leaning over the dead man when he sat back up, guts spilling from his body, and bit her face, taking a chunk out of her cheek as she screamed for help. Isobel wasn't the only driver that swerved around the mess. She could still hear the woman's yelling as she sped the last three blocks home. *There was nothing I could do to help the man or the woman,* she thought over and over again, trying to calm her nerves and her conscience. The world was feeling much smaller to her; the troubles of it more her own now.

She pulled her car into the parking lot of Willow Brook and quickly lugged her two bags of groceries from the lot to the front door.

"Whroah roah wroooah! Roah!" A giant black poodle jumped into her making her scream and drop her food.

"Kiki, no! Get down! Bad dog, BAD DOG!" Sheila Brown from apartment 201 yelled, tugging roughly on her dog's leash and dragging it up the stairs.

"Oh, it's ok. I can pick it all up myself. Really, don't worry about it!" Isobel said to Sheila who was already out of earshot. "Thanks for the apology too, bitch."

Upstairs she put the groceries away with what was already in the cupboards. Her food situation looked much better to her now so for the rest of the first day she sat alone in the living room in front of the television, eyes glued to news report after bloody news report; ears listening intently to the speculation. Several times she hopped up to check that the door was locked. She was still having trouble mentally digesting what she'd seen on the road earlier. *Maybe the bicyclist wasn't dead? Perhaps he was just knocked unconscious and when he came to, in all his pain and bewilderment, he lashed out?* No story she made up explained how the man could be alive after suffering wounds so horrific, nor why he would want to bite the driver who shattered and shredded his body.

His guts were on the road, she kept coming back to this single sight, this undeniable fact. *No one sits up with his guts on the road.*

S.O.S.-LESS

Many people still had a very strong sense that things would be ok because they had no contact with the disease yet. They were viewing the plague on televisions and computer screens, not in person. Their faith in the police force, that the uniformed men and women in affected areas could get things under control, was strong. Stronger still was the idea that all of the world's best scientists would be gathering in a sterile room at an undisclosed location, working day and night until they found the cause and then the cure. Hollywood had showed the citizens this response so this is what they demanded; what their minds had decided would happen - *was* happening. The population waited for quarantines and white-suited specialists with giant mobile labs but they didn't come. Many CDC labs had already been overrun with the dead.

As the day disappeared and night came, things were falling apart fast as the spread of the infection continued from one complacent and unprepared house to another. In Northgate strange noises filled the air, mixed with relentless emergency response sirens. Isobel turned off the television, filled the bathtub with water just in case it stopped running, cooked some pork chops and drowned out the horrible cacophony with her mp3 player.

Slowly she fell asleep. Around one in the morning the gunshots picked up and tore her from her rest. Unable to regain unconsciousness over the noise, Isobel turned the television back on. The dead weren't just coming back; they were definitely coming back hungry. Her mind returned to the bicyclist. *He wasn't lashing out in anger; he was* trying *to bite her!* The confirmation was terrifying. The attacks had spread so quickly that the infection had reached uncontainable levels. With one eye open, Isobel barely slept at all the rest of the first night.

THE SECOND DAY

The second day of the plague was noisy. *All this death is so much nosier than the daily grind of life,* Rob Pace thought. Midday brought a motorcycle accident in the street out front of the building. He heard the bike speeding up the street, then a horn honk, some metal crashing on metal, and then yelling.

Rob looked outside. He saw the motorcyclist lying on the ground a few yards from his bike. He was dragging himself along the ground; his legs made useless in the crash. Rob noticed he wasn't yelling from the pain. The dead people that had appeared on the street overnight were slowly moving towards the maimed man.

"Get away! Stay back!" Rob heard him yell. "I have a gun!" And he did. The biker pulled it from inside his jacket and started recklessly shooting into the growing crowd. He took two down easily but he realized he wouldn't have enough bullets to kill them all. He turned the gun on himself.

"No!" Rob yelled from his apartment balcony. The man pulled the trigger before he was killed by one of the undead.

"What is it Dad?" Gabe, his seven-year-old son, had run to his side. Rob quickly threw a hand over his eyes.

"Something you shouldn't see."

"But I want to see it."

"You are only saying that because you don't know what it is."

"Well . . . yeah."

"And you'll never know."

Rob found it within himself to laugh as he pulled his son away from the window.

TISSUE THIN

It was easy to stay inside if you were anyone other than Jeff Brown. He hadn't been out of the apartment for almost a week due to the combination of a nasty cold he'd caught and then the infection that everyone else was catching. His desk job, providing technical support for a major software company, always drained his energy. He should have felt rested from the time off but he was tired.

His marriage to Sheila was crumbling; if you could call it a marriage to start with. She'd forced him into it ten years ago and he'd regretted that every day since. There was no communication and his wife loved her dog more than him. All this he was ok with though. The issue lay with being stuck inside with her for a week and for an indefinite length of time to come. He blew his nose into one of the last tissues they had in the house.

"Do you have to blow your nose so loud? It's disgusting!" Sheila yelled from the other room.

He could feel his patience grow thinner with every remark she made and every tense conversation they had; thoughts tugging at his brain of leaving or asking her to go instead. *She could take her untrained dog with her,* he fell asleep on the couch dreaming of it, used tissues scattered across his sick body.

THE DEVIL'S WORK

"We just have to survive this. Please be patient, Edward. Life has thrown us more difficult things in the past," Moira tried to comfort her husband who had been pacing their first floor apartment for two days.

"Have you looked outside today? There's blood on the street and people everywhere."

"They aren't people anymore. Maybe you should stop looking if you don't like what you see."

"Folks on the radio are saying we should try to get somewhere safe."

"No place is safe! The army bases started turning people away and now they are dying at the closed front gates. The mega churches asked their congregations to gather for mass prayer in order to cast out the demons that possess everyone. Then they all got trapped in the buildings with the infection. The pews are covered in blood just like the street. NPR said the best course of action is to stay inside and lock the doors."

"That isn't action; that is *inaction*."

"So we don't change a thing then. Sit down and read your book."

A PROMISE

Ben had been waiting for his girlfriend since yesterday. She lived a few cities away and he'd asked her to stay with him. He waited to hear the front door buzzer all day. He heard it a lot but when he answered the phone to see if it was Anna it was someone else. Today, all he heard was growling.

He waited without hearing from her the entire day. The sirens grew further and further apart. How many ambulances were still capable of responding? How many paramedics now needed medical help themselves? Ben imagined a lone ambulance racing from incident to incident; brave medics fighting to save lives and to stay alive themselves but eventually even that siren stopped wailing.

He hoped Anna made it safely to him. He had insisted that she come. She had made him promise that everything would be fine. He had.

COPING MECHANISM

Molly Mathay was out of the program. She'd completed it and was eating healthily for almost six months. But she was still on probation in a sense. A mentor would come by once a week to check on her. Now things were getting more difficult than she'd ever imagined they could. The treatment center staff hadn't trained her how to handle apocalyptic situations and she knew that her mentor wouldn't be able to come by with the plague that was spreading.

She was alone with it and the thought of losing easy access to food made her anxious. Her anxiety made her more food obsessed. She started to binge and purge again to cope.

Her apartment wasn't stockpiled with food; she wasn't allowed to shop for more than one normal week at a time. She wanted to ask for help but she barely knew anyone in the building. She'd spent a small amount of time with Rob Pace and his son but that was an awkward situation for other reasons.

It would be difficult if not impossible in the new world to find either enough support or food to settle the urge.

THE PLAGUE IN PIXELS

Markus was left with his mind, filled with endless questions, all of the second day. He sat around and browsed the Internet to try to distract his busy brain. The infection was everywhere though and he couldn't escape it. YouTube had terrifying first-hand accounts:

A father's hands trembled as he recorded his wife eating their son in the backyard. Two minutes passed by and his wife started to come straight at the sliding glass door for him. The double-paned glass protected him and she could only paw at the slider, desperate for her next meal. The video ended with a tribute to the consumed child: "R.I.P. Elijah." Comments showed that viewers were touched by the heartache, others disgusted that the man posted such a violent video detailing the death of his child.

A video shot from a high window showing a street in Everett full of bodies. Someone with a sniper rifle across the street was taking out the infected as they wandered into the area. Markus watched the video until the end where he saw that the shooter didn't discriminate between infected and uninfected people. Trigger Happy was the video's name. A comment listed the street address of the shooter and a warning: "Don't travel this street unless you want to die." Comments included minute markers in the video for viewers' favorite kills, mostly the headshots.

One of the last videos Markus watched was of two teenage boys, both around 15 years old, looking for the infected and then messing around with them. Pouring soda on them, taunting them to chase after one of the boys, tripping them, etc . . . It was kind of funny to him - almost like a prank show he'd seen on MTV- until the taller boy recognizes his mom in a nearby group of infected and the recording ends. Comments listed request after request for more "episodes" of "They've Got No Brains!" (Which Markus thought was a clever title they'd given the video). Many offered suggestions for content.

Twitter too had been infected. It was full of sad stories, told in snippets. Never before had 140 characters or less been so depressing, so full of the woes of a nation and world.

Markus didn't feel so lonely and he felt much better off when he read what others were tweeting.

@ncallaway: My dad's got a fever and his feet are numb. I looked it up on WebM.D. and it says he might have lupus. Anyone dealt with anything like that?

@Jen_is_Twenty: I went to class yesterday but half the kids stayed home. I wonder if anyone will come back? Should I even go in tomorrow?

@heismine43: stay away from the hospitals. My husband contracted the infection at one and never came home. It was a madhouse.

@lordLover2010: Jesus will come for me and my fellow Christians. Fear the rapture, praise the Lord! Your time is now, you sinners, burn in hell!

@margareet: I have a few extra swords and weapons if anybody needs them. I'm in McMahon Hall at the University. Safest place I know. Stay safe friends.

@haro_kitei: Trapped in my room because my sister is trying to kill me. I don't know what to do. Can any of you guys send help? I can pay you.

How could anyone help? No one even knew where she lived, what her house looked like, who her sister was. And pretty soon, no one would care.

Twitter was full of tweets with the simple words: *the infection is here*. With a search for '#infection' one could track its spread and if you really paid attention, you could tell when someone was exposed to it. They would tweet less and less, perhaps more desperately. Some would say their goodbyes and most would say their "fuck yous". They'd end up typing gibberish as their hands went numb and then they'd disappear. The last tweet gathering digital dust as time continued without them.

BEN ON THE THIRD DAY

The phone lines cut in and out on the third day or *maybe*, Ben thought, *they were just flooded with calls.* Ben had tried to reach emergency services off and on all day but he either got a busy tone or nothing.

Anna had made it to him in the late afternoon but she'd been attacked along the way and had a wound on her leg. She needed help but due to the spotty phone connection and his anguish at seeing her hurt, he wasn't able to help her very well. He had her on the bed in the second bedroom of his place with the injured leg elevated and he kept trying to feed her but she was getting sicker and sicker.

A knock on his door pulled him from her side. He was surprised to see that it was Isobel, the neighbor from down the hall, because she was only an acquaintance.

"Hey," Isobel said, looking lonely and hoping for an invite inside.

"Hi Isobel. How are you holding up?" Ben asked her. He kept the door mostly closed. There was some blood in the entry from Anna's leg that he didn't want to explain to Isobel. Besides, Anna was a jealous person who'd get the wrong idea if she knew another woman was at his door looking for company. The blood loss and shock would only have made her more temperamental. Ben was about to give Isobel a gun and tell her to go back to her apartment when Anna stumbled into the living room.

"Who -" Anna mumbled.

Ben rushed to her as she collapsed. Isobel opened the door enough to see the blood on the floor.

"What's wrong with her?" She asked.

"Stay there! Don't come in! I'll be right back." Ben picked Anna up and carried her back to the bedroom. When he returned he gave Isobel a handgun.

"What happened to her, Ben? Is she infected?"

"I don't know yet. She's not well, that's for sure. Stay safe Isobel. Don't come back here."

He closed the door on her.

Anna was dying in front of his eyes. Ben had heard news reports of how bad the hospitals were and even though Northwest was just up the road, it would have been a death sentence for him. If he wasn't injured on the way, there were bound to be hundreds of wounded on the hospital grounds, all seeking similar aid. Casualties there would be high. Ben decided that Anna would fare much better with his one on one attention in the secure environment of Willow Brook.

The topic of people-eating people is never very appetizing and the stress of taking care of Anna had kept Ben unaware of his growling stomach. He had some toast and juice. The television was the only distraction that Ben had from Anna's moaning. That evening it confirmed to him that the infection was contagious. Bite wounds were fatal and the disease could be spread through saliva and other bodily fluids.

"Fuck," he said aloud as a thought occurred to him, *I have to find out if she was bitten.*

THE FOURTH DAY

Isobel hadn't heard a single gunshot all morning long. She'd sadly become used to the *pops* here and there. The silence gave her the nerve to finally take some more glimpses outside.

Her apartment looked out onto a street usually busy with vehicles but now there was only a slow parade of dead people wandering with no determined direction. All they do is shuffle unless provoked and yet that is enough to instill in each of the uninfected the fear that this is actually the end of the world. *They would take my life if I let them,* Isobel reminded herself, *and that makes them very dangerous.*

Pop* *Pop*Pop*Pop* *Pop

Finally someone alive is trying to keep living! Isobel felt a little less alone but she got worried when she realized how close the shots sounded.

BEHIND CLOSED DOORS

In Jeff's defense he hadn't been thinking straight from the excess amounts of cough medicine and the infection spreading through the city. His wife, Sheila, was a controlling woman that he'd grown to despise. With the turn of world events she had become increasingly hard to deal with. Louder and crazier by the day, which made her dog, a standard poodle named Bianca, crazier and louder too.

On the fourth day, Sheila lost it. Jeff had fallen asleep on the couch again and his wife woke him up by screaming and throwing the car keys at his face.

"We need some more FUCKING dog food Jeff. I told you to buy extra when you went shopping. What the FUCK is wrong with you?" Her words echoed in his ears along with the sound of the canned goods she was pulling from the cupboards in her desperate search for canine nutrition. Jeff tried to answer calmly but the dog had started to bark.

"You know what Sheila? NOTHING is wrong with me! The only issue I see with myself at this moment in time is that I am still putting up with YOU and that fucking dog!"

This took Sheila's anger to another level. She looked for the nearest can and chucked it at her husband's head. He ducked and sensing she was out for blood he knew it was time to end this. He was much larger than her in stature and probably stronger but she was always so much stronger emotionally, mentally. He ran straight at her and lunged, his hands connecting with her neck. Jeff squeezed for all he was worth, knowing if she survived the choking she would kill him instead. He was stronger than her and he was proving it; defeating her and ending her cruel words.

He wasn't proud of it, but he did the same to the dog. It wouldn't listen to him and besides, they were out of dog food.

He had dumped the bodies off the deck and sat down to read. Something he'd been unable to do in the noise of his former life; with the presence of his former wife. Gunshots had been fired across the hall while he was finishing a chapter but he was so relaxed for the first time in years, he didn't care at all.

IMAGINATION INFECTED

Rob had a difficult time raising his son on his own. His wife had died four years ago in a car accident and Gabe, then only three, had survived. It was a miracle for sure but one that pained Rob every time he looked at Gabe, watching him grow older without a mother; wondering if he was doing enough on his own.

Now that something bigger was happening, bigger than what to cook for dinner each night, bigger than the pressure of teaching his son how to know right from wrong, bigger than untied shoelaces, it all seemed a bit more manageable.

Unfortunately, now it looked to his seven-year-old like monsters were real. For the last three nights Gabe had been waiting in fear that one of them would come out from under the bed.

The morning presented more terror. Gabe was trailing crumbs around the apartment from his breakfast pop tart as Rob had coffee and eggs. He almost dropped his cup when he heard a gun being fired inside the building. Rob went to the front door and watched through the peephole. He saw Ben, the stocky man that lived to the left down the hall, walk past his door and further down the hall towards Isobel's place. He hadn't stopped at all and he had blood all over him. Rob was pretty sure he saw a gun. Instinct to protect his child kicked in and Rob locked the deadbolt, moved a chair in front of the door and went to check on Gabe.

He returned to the dining area and his heart sank at what he found. Gabe had left his chair and sunken under the table. But he wasn't crying or cowering, he was playing with action figures, making gunshot sounds.

"What are you playing champ?" Rob was curious how the gunshots had inspired his child.

"Zombies and Indians! They use-ta be cowboys but something happened. Then the Indians stole the guns and now they are winning." The boy stopped playing and came out from under the table. He looked up at his dad and the worried look on his face. "We are gonna win if they get in, right? We just need one of the other Indian's guns."

"I don't know if we can trust the other Indians yet. The one with the gun that we heard already has war paint on. Let's finish eating."

The two ate the rest of their now slightly cooled meal. Rob reflected on his child's coping mechanism. He wasn't sure if it was healthy or not and he had no one to ask for advice. What would his wife had said? Would she ban the word 'zombie' or encourage Gabe to play to his heart's content and discourage Rob from micromanaging their child? Rob decided he would just have to let Gabe do his own thing.

ANNA

She could hear running coming closer to her door and then, on the other side of it, her neighbor Ben yelling her name.

Isobel opened the door before thinking and she looked upon a blood-covered and wide-eyed Ben. He'd shot someone and he still held the gun, dangling in his right hand. He pushed past Isobel, which was a bit relieving to her, and went straight to her bathroom.

Had dangerous people gotten in the building? She didn't have answers yet so she closed and locked the door and went to the bathroom after him. Ben was avoiding looking in the mirror as he frantically washed the blood from his arms and face. Isobel stood in the doorway scrutinizing every inch of his skin that was visible looking for bites. *Clean.*

"Anna kept coming at me. I couldn't kill her." He mumbled with his head in his hands as he sat on the couch in Isobel's living room. Isobel sat across from Ben in an armchair with the borrowed handgun set close to her on the coffee table, between her and him. She couldn't bring herself to look at Ben because he had a bit of crazy in his eyes and his dead girlfriend's blood on his shirt. She kept her eyes directed somewhere between the floor and the gun.

"What happened to her Ben? It was a bite, wasn't it?" Isobel had to know. Ben took a deep breath and on the exhalation started to explain what happened to his girlfriend.

"I put her in th- . . . I put Anna in the bath because she said she was cold. She was crying the whole time. She was so frightened after being attacked that she hadn't stopped crying since it happened. She was in a lot of pain so I thought a soak might help her relax. When she was naked in the water the blood washed away I saw her leg. There was a big chunk missing from her calf.

"I had heard on the news that bites made people die but it didn't look like a bite, not from a person, there was too much skin and muscle missing. An animal would more likely have taken that much tissue.

"I should have taken her to the hospital but they kept saying to stay inside and she was uncomfortable when she moved. Then her body started going numb. I couldn't reach anyone to send an ambulance anyway! I left her in the tub and went to the kitchen. I . . . I made coffee.

"When I went in to check on her she had already died and come back. She must have gotten out of the tub first, because it was drained, and then died on the bathroom floor. But like I said, she was back up again and she started coming at me. Her breasts and hair were hanging down and dripping water everywhere. She looked really pissed off and she grabbed me and tried to go for my arm.

"I knew it was the infection when she started to try to bite me. I love her but I didn't want to catch it. I had to protect myself. My gun was on the side table by the door so I picked it up, closed my eyes and pulled the trigger. She released her grip but quickly got hold of me again. When I opened my eyes I saw that I had hit near her heart but it didn't make a difference to her! I just kept shooting and she kept coming.

"I shot until she fell. It was when I shot her in the head that sh . . ." He stopped there and started crying again.

Ben and Isobel went to take care of Anna's body. They put her in the bathtub and covered her bullet-riddled nakedness with large black garbage bags taped to the edges of the tub. Isobel felt like a criminal with a weak stomach or without conviction, as she kept stopping to puke in the toilet while they were disposing of Anna. They closed and sealed the bathroom door and apartment door with tape as well. Ben had made a mess of the place in his bout with Anna. It had become uninhabitable.

Ben moved in with Isobel. He crashed on the couch. As he was recounting his story earlier, Isobel kept waiting for the cops to show up. Someone must have called 911. There was a dead body down the hall! But no one ever came and Isobel remembered that she herself had never picked up the phone to call 911 for others in peril during the last three days. The sirens stopped yesterday anyway and Ben had told her that it was pointless to call. He either got a busy tone or a pre-recorded and repetitive message that told him to keep the line clear for emergencies. *This was a fucking emergency!* Isobel had helped to dispose of a body! On the fourth day a single corpse didn't qualify as an emergency anymore.

Ben had brought over a lot of food as well as some extra bedding and several bulk packages of water. Isobel had never had roommates and didn't want them either but it was much safer and less lonely with another person around. Ben also brought more skill with a weapon and he had dealt with one of the infected. Before today, Isobel had never seen a dead body that close before or touched one.

One had definitely never touched her and she planned to keep it that way.

FUCK IT LIST

When Tom Vaughn moved into Willow Brook he considered himself lucky to land in 306. A corner apartment with an extra window in the bedroom, no one living above him to stomp around, and a next door neighbor that was young, hot, and instantly added to his "to do" list. He'd benefited from the first two strokes of luck but not yet the third. The world was ending and Vaughn was determined to add her to his "done" list. So he drank a little bourbon for support and walked next door.

He tried the doorknob first and found it locked. "Figures," he mumbled. "She's probably locked up tight herself. I'll change that." He grudgingly knocked, a bit louder and more threatening than he meant to due to the bourbon making his hands heavy.

Molly Mathay opened her door and stood face-to-chest with her huge next-door neighbor. "Hi Tom, um, what's up?"

"Hey . . ." Vaughn couldn't remember her name, he wasn't even sure that he knew it to begin with. "Can I come in?"

Molly was suspicious. Tom had never come over before and he was a creep, a military-obsessed, angry creep that today smelled like some kind of alcohol. "No, I'm kind of in the middle of something." She closed the door a little and it made her feel better.

"I think we can both agree that things being how they are, one could get lonely and want to more actively seek comfort in others."

Was Tom blushing? Had he changed his ways in the face of death? Molly was caught off guard by his sensitive choice of words.

"So, you wanna fuck?"

"You bastard! No! I don't want to fuck! Not you anyway! Leave me alone!" Molly slammed the door and locked the dead bolt. She was disturbed and pissed off that she hadn't looked through the peephole before opening the door to Tom, the dick on two legs. She could have avoided the whole situation.

On the other side of the door, Tom had already convinced himself that Molly would show up to his apartment later, begging for him to get inside of her.

On her side, she was shaking and already heading to the kitchen to deal with the emotions in a plate or two of food.

THE FIFTH DAY

Both Isobel and Ben slept well on the fourth night. They woke up to a gentle collective moan coming from outside but the walls of the building were thick enough that it was slightly muted.

"It's like a twisted sleep noise machine," Isobel laughed.

"I think they call this setting 'Undeadscape'," Ben played along, smiling.

"You're getting that one confused with 'Hospital Ward' or maybe 'Complaining'."

"A bit darker than the usual Ocean Waves, Mountain Stream or Woodland Birds for sure."

The smile left his face as he remembered killing Anna.

They decided over a breakfast of cold cereal and bananas that they needed small projects to keep occupied. Being stuck inside especially in dreary Seattle will wear on everyone eventually, even those who hadn't had the unfortunate opportunity to kill a loved one yet.

The most urgent tasks were to find out if they were alone in the building and then to fortify the place to ensure their survival.

The plan for the day:

1. Gather important documents from the main office (floor plans, tenant lists, etc . . .)
2. Go door-to-door, starting on the third floor, and count bodies (living, dead, and undead)
3. Kill any undead

4. Collect all bodies and place in basement
5. Fortify all of the first floor windows and doors
6. Arm tenants
7. Take stock of supplies
8. Wait it out until the end

The end an unknown date and resolution, it still felt important to have it on the list.

"Something we can look forward to." Isobel patted him on the back as she got up to make coffee.

THE MAIN OFFICE

Ben and Isobel set to their first project. The main office is on the first floor and Isobel hadn't been to ground level since Tuesday, four days ago. She was scared to death. Not knowing what they would find, they both brought handguns. As if on cue, the moment they reached the bottom of the stairs they were greeted by a walking corpse. It was badly rotted and barely recognizable as one of the office staff, except for the nametag labeling it as "Susanne" the "Building Manager".

the infection is accompanied by a slight increase in speed of decomposition in human tissue.

Covering their mouths from the awful smell, they both attempted to take aim with their free hands. Ben waved Isobel off and he shot the office lady. With a loud *pop* his bullet took a chunk of the decaying head with it to a nearby wall, the one with the mailboxes. Seeing a piece of head blown off put Isobel into a temporary shock. Her legs were weak and she had to rest against the wall or she would collapse completely. She coped in difficult situations by thinking practically. *They are going to have to replace those keyholes, maybe even the entire set of mailboxes. I don't see any easy way of cleaning the brains out,* she focused on the mailman's probable confusion during repairs. *Where would he leave the mail if the boxes were under maintenance?* This was all of course under the assumption that the mail would be delivered again someday. But, unknown to Isobel, the mailman looked quite similar to the way the office lady looked now, somewhere beyond the walls of Willow Brook; forever wandering the streets, but no longer delivering mail.

Ben was whispering and somehow yelling at the same time for Isobel to focus on finding the keys to the office. Given a new, less bloody item to fixate on, Isobel found the office keys quickly. They were attached to a belt loop of Susanne's khaki pants but the door, which was directly across from the stairwell, was already unlocked and ever so slightly ajar.

Ben stealthily locked the front door of the office that opened to the street and closed the blinds. The only desk in the room was heavy but they were able to move it against the door to hopefully deny any further entry. With the key to the file cabinets, courtesy of Susanne, they could find the information they needed but, there were rotted bits of flesh on some of the drawer handles, also courtesy of Susanne. Ben wiped the handles clean with an unused napkin from a fly-covered, half-eaten teriyaki takeout meal on the desk. The poor woman was interrupted by death in the middle of her lunch.

They now had floor plans, a current tenant list, and a city map in hand. Before going door-to-door, they returned to the second floor and Isobel's apartment to scan the tenant list and label the floor plans to help guide and prepare them. They wrote the last names and number of occupants on each apartment and checked their guns.

"It isn't going to be fun discovering how inaccurate these numbers have become," Ben said somberly.

MEET THE NEIGHBORS

It took Ben and Isobel all day and part of the evening to secure Willow Brook. The third floor was where they started their door-to-door head count.

3RD FLOOR

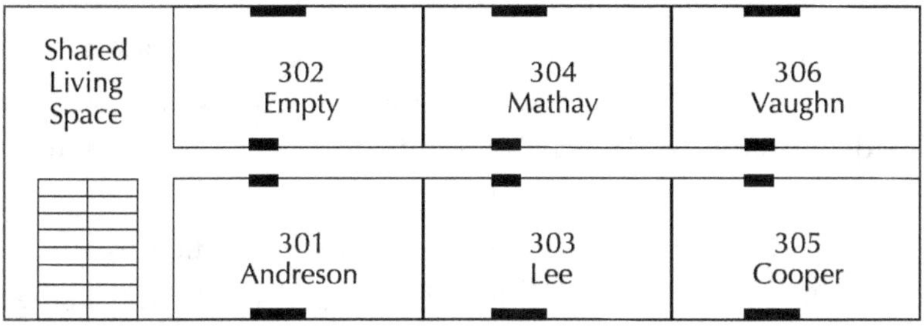

The hallway was slightly smoky when they reached the top of the stairs. 302 was empty, as the tenant list had said. In apartment 301 they expected to find 2 people but it was also empty except for some moving boxes and packing supplies.

There was no answer when they knocked on 303's door. Ben unlocked it with the master keys taken from Susanne and found that no one was home. He locked it back up to give Mr. Lee a chance to come back. If he didn't show up within a day or two, they decided they would come back up and take his food and anything else useful.

304's tenant was the cause of the smoke. The door was open and a heavy fog came from the apartment. Music played loudly and no one responded to Isobel or Ben as they called out from the door jam. They entered with guns drawn on high alert and, in the kitchen, gave Molly Mathay quite a scare.

"I thought you were one of them!" She was screaming with a dirty spatula raised in one hand, the other hand resting on her heart. Isobel and Ben lowered the guns and Isobel ran forward and hugged Molly. She was so overjoyed to see another survivor, especially another woman.

"Maybe you shouldn't leave your door open with only a spatula to defend yourself," Ben suggested, laughing a hearty laugh that made Isobel smile. The sight of the fully loaded spatula truly was so funny that even Molly started laughing.

"I burned something and had to air out the smoke but I didn't want to open the window and let the dead smell in. Maybe you shouldn't come in without knocking," Molly reprimanded her visitors.

"We did knock, and yell," Isobel said as she pointed to the stereo system that was pumping out a foreign band, "but you can't hear anything when it's turned up to 11."

Molly jogged over to the radio and turned it down. "Sorry about that. I don't like *hearing* them outside either. So, what's up?"

"We are checking out who is left in the building and making sure that it's secure."

"Glad somebody is doing something nice for others, unlike the asshole in 306. He came over yesterday and asked me if I wanted to screw him, just because the world was ending! I've had my door locked and closed because of him, until the burnt food anyway."

"We were about to check in with him. Hopefully he doesn't greet us with the same proposition," Ben joked. Isobel thought it was nice to see him smile some more.

Molly laughed too but her face turned grim. "Be careful around him. And if you guys need me for anything," she offered, "you know where to find me; just follow the smoke." She walked them to her door and watched as they walked to 306.

Tom Vaughn greeted Ben and Isobel with a hunting rifle. Even before knowing he had asked Molly for sex, Isobel never liked the guy. He double-parked, complained to the office about trivial things, and left cigarette butts smoldering everywhere he went. He was an all-around dick so she wasn't surprised to have the gun in her face. Ben felt the same as Isobel, except for the surprised part. He never expected to have a gun in his face. They tried to explain to Tom what they were doing but he didn't care.

"I have enough supplies to keep me alive in here for months. I don't see the point in being friendly. If they get in and you run up here and they follow you, I'll shoot all of you, alive or undead. Have fun in your little club." He finished his impolite declination by slamming his apartment door in their faces.

Ben looked at Isobel and she nodded in silent agreement.

"We won't come back to him unless we absolutely have to," Ben declared.

That left one more apartment on the third floor for the pair to check. The Coopers, a young, very pregnant and very determined couple, were set on getting to a hospital in case their baby decided to arrive.

"We aren't risking a home birth without a trained midwife! We've been up for days discussing it. There isn't another option. She could die here!" Austin was standing in front of Jill. *A woman can always convince another woman. I can't let them talk alone,* Austin thought as he kept an eye on Isobel.

"Jill, do you agree with him?" Isobel pressed on.

"I do; he's my husband. I'm scared to go outside but you have to sacrifice for your child. You'll feel the same way when you have a baby."

She kept her eyes down as she replied, staying focused on the task of getting everything she would need into two bags, a duffle bag and suitcase, with the awkward movements her large belly caused. Austin had stopped paying attention to Isobel and Ben and was attempting to make phone calls, each as unsuccessful as its predecessor.

"You won't get through. We're too far into this," Ben tried once more to get through to Austin. "The hospital is one of the worst places to go, haven't you been listening to what the news is telling us!" But Ben was as unsuccessful at convincing him to stop as Austin was at making the calls connect.

"We are adults and until today you haven't shown any interest in us or our lives so I'm not quite sure why we would trust the life of our child to you now."

With that said, Austin forced Ben and Isobel out of the apartment. Just before the door closed, Austin had one more thing to add.

"You'd better let us leave before you board up the front door! We won't be held prisoner."

The door closed and Isobel wanted to cry. "Have they looked outside lately? Their car is parked across the street. That's impossible."

"That is their mistake to make, I guess," Ben said as they returned to the stairwell to check the second floor.

2ND FLOOR

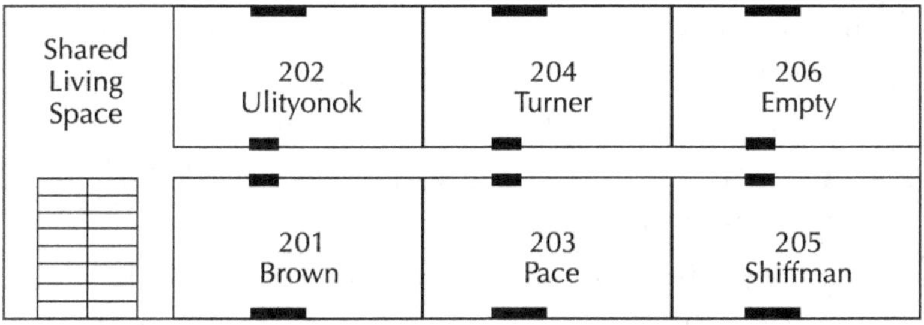

Ben and Isobel knew that Angela Turner of 204 was dead. While eating breakfast that morning they watched her corpse walk by the building. She must have been bitten while jogging on one of the first days because she was wearing spandex and tennis shoes; splatters of her own blood covering the workout gear.

206 was empty and smelled of fresh paint. Rob Pace was supposedly living in 203 with his son but no one answered when Ben knocked. Isobel waited a moment and then knocked herself. This time the door opened.

"I'm glad to see you are alive," Rob commented with relief in his voice. "I saw Ben here walk by the other day covered in blood with a gun in his hand, he went to your place so I was sure you were a goner. I can see now that I misinterpreted the scene."

"His girlfriend was infected and he had to . . . *help* her. He came to my place because he was in shock and didn't know what to do. We're friends." Isobel informed him.

"If you are friends then you can come in and meet my son." He opened the door all the way and allowed them to enter. The apartment was messy, Isobel noticed, *guys really don't do well without women, do they,* she mused. Once she was further inside she noted that the place was quite tidy but a scattering of the child's toys was making it look less so.

Just like Molly, they had music turned up to drown out the noise from outside. Rob talked to Ben while Isobel and Gabe played with toys.

"I'm concerned about the first floor. With all the windows and sliders in the apartments they are bound to get in," Rob worried, "it's only a matter of time. If we can find someone to volunteer to watch Gabe, I'd be happy to help you guys reinforce everything."

"Have you met Molly from the third floor before? She's really easy to get along with. We could ask her to hang out with Gabe," Ben suggested.

"She's great!" Isobel added in.

"I *have* met her actually; we've gone out for drinks once before. I'm sure she wouldn't mind at all. Gabe has met her too which will help him feel at ease without me around for a few hours."

Isobel went upstairs to ask Molly if her earlier offer to help still stood. Her heart leapt. She was happy to spend more time with the Pace family. She stopped cleaning her dishes and followed Isobel downstairs to assume her role as "the babysitter". To which Gabe responded that he "wasn't a baby".

Molly agreed. "You've got it all wrong guys! I'm not a babysitter . . . I don't play with babies." She sat down immediately; legs crossed Indian-style and started to build Legos with Gabe, who was smiling ear-to-ear at Molly, a pretty girl he remembered as liking his dad, who was nice, and who knew how to build with the multi-colored bricks.

Now a group of three, Ben, Isobel and Rob checked the last apartment on the second floor.

(UN)CHARISMATICALLY COLD BLOODED

Jeff had found no joy in killing Sheila and the dog, not in the acts themselves. His satisfaction and content came from the silence that fell across the apartment when the deed was done. He'd been able to enjoy one wonderfully lonely day before the silence was broken once again.

Ben was regretting rapping his knuckles on the Browns door. He knew they had problems and he had heard fighting from their apartment yesterday, while he had been making coffee for his injured Anna across the hall.

"I hope the dog is tied up," Ben said. "I hate that thing." Last year he had the chance to meet the dog and its owners when they moved here from New York.

"I hate it too. It attacked me the other day," Isobel said.

"It attacked me downstairs about a year ago when I was checking the mail. That dog is psychotic."

"I don't hear any barking," Rob observed.

"Strange. It never stops barking, I swear to God."

Ben knocked again and Jeff, Sheila's husband, slowly opened the door.

"Oh, hi guys. I hope I haven't been making too much noise. Come in!" he said happily; his eyes a subtle mix of fear and exhilaration.

Ben had never seen Jeff like that, all chipper and smiley. The contents of the kitchen cupboards had been thoroughly emptied onto the countertops and it looked, just as it had sounded, as though Jeff was alone.

"What happened in here Jeff?" Rob asked as he picked up a dented can of string beans.

"Sheila was looking for some dog food. She did this. I was sick and she wasn't handling this well, and she just lost it. But I took care of it and things are fine now." Jeff strummed his fingers on the countertop impatiently.

"Did she leave?" Ben asked as he turned to look down the hallway.

"Kind of. She is . . .I . . . they are dead. I . . . strangled them. I couldn't handle the bitching or the barking anymore. But don't worry, I'm not dangerous. I won't hurt anyone else. I've been putting up with her shit for years. You all know that, don't you?" The words spilled from his mouth. He held his hands up in surrender.

"The dog too then, Jeff? What have you done?" Isobel was trying very hard to figure that out.

"I'm sorry. I know it wasn't the right thing to do. This plague outside has got my thinking messed up but I'm ok now." Now that the truth was out the look in his eyes changed from fear and exhilaration to desperation.

Isobel had a bit of a moral dilemma. She'd taken Ben in even though he'd shot his girlfriend, but she was a zombie! Jeff? He was a killer plain and simple, and one without a pang of regret. Isobel and the others couldn't stand Sheila either but they didn't want her dead. *I've seen people eating people, touched a dead body, seen brains blown out, and heard a murder confession in under five days time,* Isobel thought, *the world truly has been turned inside out.* Because of this shift, everyone had to change their way of thinking. Jeff did what he felt he had to do to survive this nightmare. What could they do but believe that? What would they have done if the situation was their own? With living people becoming a scarcity, they had to try to find the good in those left, in one another. Hope their hardest that there was a speck of it to find and cling to.

There was no more work to be done in 201 except help Jeff clean up the mess by repacking his cupboards. As the group put his life back in order, they concocted a story about Sheila's whereabouts that sounded plausible. If the truth came out the other residents might not be as understanding as Ben, Rob and Isobel had been. Still the three of them felt wrong inside for the cover-up.

Before going down one more flight of stairs to the first floor, they armed themselves the best they could. Ben and Isobel had their handguns. Rob had a machete from Ben, who'd used it while hiking during the summertime. And it was decided that Jeff would not be given anything sharp or loaded. He was trusted with a baseball bat from Rob's apartment, a purchase Rob had made for Gabe but he'd yet to use it. Isobel grabbed a few pairs of rubber gloves from Angela Turner's apartment and an old blue tarp that Ben had used for camping. She put Jeff in the lead so they could keep their eyes on him.

1ST FLOOR

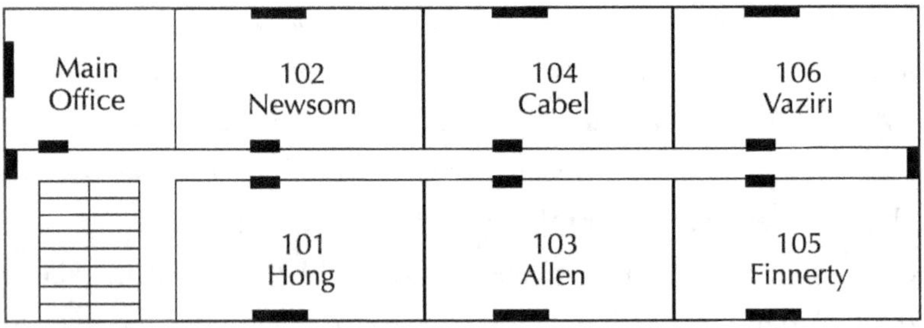

The second floor residents moved slowly down the stairs, listening as hard as they could for any of the undead. Once at the bottom, they went silently to work. Rob and Jeff kept a look out near the front door as Ben and Isobel picked up the body of the office manager. Ben let Isobel lift the feet end of Susanne's body since he'd made a mess of the head end earlier. Isobel kept her eyes closed as they placed it in the center of the unfolded tarp that they had laid on the hallway floor.

They left the tarp in front of the main office door, to wait for more bodies, as they started the frightening task of going door-to-door on the first floor. The windows of

Willow Brook were old and, with enough pressure, easy to break through. Isobel had no idea what they might find.

UNCERTAINTY

The Cabels were hunkered down. They hadn't left their apartment in days. Edward had taken some of Moira's heavier hand-stitched quilts and nailed them over the windows and sliding glass door to keep the light and the life from drawing the dead towards the apartment. Moira was the friendlier of the two and had always tried to be polite with others in the building. Edward was 86 this year and she, 84. They were the oldest people living at Willow Brook and the younger generations needed some guidance, she thought. But since the dead were walking around she had felt it best to withdraw; keeping the door locked and only the company of her husband. It pained her though and she often looked through the peephole for signs of life.

For the first time, she saw movement. "Something's going on in the hallway. A few of the residents are out there. Edward, come over here!" She snapped at her husband whose nose was in a book.

"Alright, alright. Let me finish the chapter." He grumbled without looking up.

"Come right now! They have guns!"

Edward jumped up as quickly as his 86-year-old body allowed. He had never been a gun enthusiast but, the times had changed and a loaded weapon was something he had been dreaming about.

"Don't open the door yet Moira. Let's see what happens." Edward moved to the peephole but was disappointed. "You can't see anything! There's no one there."

"They were there a second ago. They looked like they were planning something."

Edward remembered the gun. "You are sure they were people from the building?"

"Absolutely. That girl from the second floor and the man with the little boy were there."

"They brought the boy down?" Edward was astonished. Who in their right mind would bring a child anywhere that you had to take a gun to visit?

"No, I was just telling you who the man was."

"Oh. And they were alive?"

"Yes."

"I'm opening the door a crack. Just to see what's going on." Edward grabbed the doorknob and Moira's hand followed to stop him.

"Be quiet and don't let them know we are here."

"I know! Now, let go."

Moira moved her hand from his to her side, where she started to nervously twist the pale lavender fabric of her cardigan. Edward opened the door and peered down the hall just long enough to see two men near the front door and the girl and the father that Moira had seen. He closed the door.

"They are going into that Asian boy's place."

GATE TO HELL

The sliding glass door was halfway open but the glass was still intact. *Why would anyone open that door?* Rob was hoping they'd find Ryan so he could ask him that very question. The apartment was torn apart and two bodies lay on the living room floor. They were unmoving and both had the handles of kitchen knives protruding from their heads, one from the chin, and the other from an eye socket, both blades completely sunken in.

"Oh my god. Who are these people?" Isobel gasped. The wounds were more disgusting than bullets and bite marks. "Neither one of them is Ryan."

"Look at the bite wounds. These people were infected." Rob had knelt down and was wiggling the handle of one of the knives.

Isobel hit him on the shoulder. "Stop that! It's gross! Get up and help me."

He hopped over the bodies to close and lock the sliding glass door. His shoes pushed up blood from the carpet. The hanging blinds had been torn off their track in the chaos of the event so the dead outside could see Isobel and Rob.

They checked the remaining rooms and didn't find anything or anyone else until they reached the bedroom. Ryan stumbled out from behind the door, grabbed Isobel and went directly for her shoulder. *A corpse is touching me!* Her mind was screaming. And then she was screaming like the SUV driver days ago, shrill and without end. She couldn't believe that it was happening. Ryan's hands were ice cold, his teeth were biting air and he smelled of urine and feces. Isobel was so close to him that she could see the flecks of dried blood surrounding several wounds on his arms and face. Before he had knifed the strangers in the living room and stopped them for good, they had succeeded in passing the infection to him.

"Don't let him bite you!" Rob yelled as he pushed Ryan off of Isobel and raised the machete high in the air. He swung down and the machete hit Ryan's arm with a *thwack*. Rob pulled up again and this time managed to lodge the blade in Ryan's shoulder, which enabled him to hold Ryan at a distance.

"Finish him, Isobel! Shoot him!" Rob ducked his head and she barely regained composure to put a bullet just below Ryan's left eye.

Ryan had been a decent guy. He'd helped Isobel move in to Willow Brook three years ago. Now, thanks to her, his body lay on the floor in a dirty heap of ruined life. She burst into tears and Rob embraced her tightly.

"It's ok, it's alright. You had to do it."

"I know. I just wish I didn't have to."

SNACK TIME

"Did you hear that?" Gabe yelled, looking at the floor. He and Molly had built a castle and were about to attack it with an army when a scream erupted and a gunshot popped somewhere below them.

"It'll be fine. Don't worry, ok?" Molly smiled at him. "Hey, maybe we should take a break and eat something."

"I'm not hungry," Gabe said.

"Oh, well, do you have anything you can share with me?" Molly asked happily.

"Do you like crackers?" Gabe jumped up and ran to the kitchen. "I can give you three."

Molly laughed. "Only three? I'm hungrier than that! Bring me the box."

Gabe complied and carried the entire box to the living room.

SPOOKED

Isobel's screaming and the gunshot had gotten the attention of Ben and Jeff, who'd come running in to help. Several of the undead outside the complex had noticed too. The corpses turned towards the noise and it became evident, with thirty of them approaching, that the group would have to reinforce the sliding glass door. They moved the entertainment center and the couch and managed to block the visual connection but the damage had already been done. The flesh eaters knew there was life in the building. Rob, Isobel, Ben, and Jeff stood there for a moment behind their miniature blockade, quiet and stunned.

"We need to move quickly now. If they get in we'll have to shoot them and that will only draw more," Rob broke the silence and they knew that he was right. Keep on task or die. So Isobel distributed the gloves with shaking hands and they moved the three bodies to the tarp. They had only checked one apartment and already the blue plastic was looking full. Isobel turned back to apartment 101 and locked the door forever.

When she turned to face the others she saw faces peeking out of apartments 102 and 104; drawn out by the sound of gunshots and screaming.

"Markus? Edward and Moira?" she had remembered their names from the tenant list. She approached Edward and

Moira's door as Markus came quickly out after hearing his name. "We live here. It's ok. Are you alright in there?" Isobel tried to sound as friendly as possible, though her heart rate was still elevated and her breathing ragged from the altercation with Ryan Hong. She also still had the gun in her shaking hands. She handed it off to Rob.

The Cabels came out slowly, their eyes darting back and forth from the tarp of bodies to the weapons still in others' hands. Long life can give one insight and, therefore, make the aged more cautious; a good quality for survival. After a second and third scan of the group, the elderly couple determined them to be friends and invited everyone into their darkened apartment for a moment of peace.

"So they got Ryan, huh? That's a shame." Markus was excited with all the people around him but saddened at the loss of his neighbor across the hall; he'd had a bit of a crush on him.

Rob nodded his head solemnly. "But you'll be happy to know that he didn't go without a fight. He took two of them out before he died." An image of the feet of the dead on the tarp, one set bare and cut open, the other in scuffed men's dress shoes, gum stuck to the bottom of one, crossed Rob's mind and he shuttered.

"Good for him!" Markus smiled and threw a fist in the air. "By the way I'm Markus, nice to meet you." He extended his hand.

Ben politely shook his hand. "We know who everyone is," Ben waved the tenant list, "but I guess we should hang on to our civility and introduce ourselves anyway."

As the group exchanged pleasantries Isobel was admiring the handiwork of the old couple. Even though the sun was shining brightly outside, the apartment's only source of light came from lamps and candles due to blankets blocking and covering the windows and door. The result was effective. There wasn't one bang or bump against the glass on their side of the building. They were invisible to the dead.

"Do you know about anyone else on the first floor?" Jeff, who had been very quiet until now, asked. "Any information would be helpful."

"Well . . . the Allen family across the hall in 103 went out of town two days before everything started. They asked us to watch the cat. But the cat didn't come back after the first day; probably got spooked."

"What about the two apartments at the end of the hall?" Ben asked.

Moira looked worried. Edward explained. "We heard a gunshot from Juan's place on the second day. I don't know what that means for him but, he never came and asked for any help after that."

"And the girl in the wheelchair, well, we hardly ever see her anyway so I assumed she was fine on her own. She has a lot of pride over her being so independent too. I didn't want to bother her," Moira added.

"Let's check the Allen's apartment for supplies then, get it barricaded, and see what's up with Juan and Katie," Isobel said.

"Here," Rob nudged her, "you probably want this." Seeing that she'd regained composure, he gave her back the gun she'd relinquished.

The Allen's curtains were all drawn, the apartment closed up tight since they were out of town. It took only moments for the group to move the non-perishables from the cupboards and into a laundry basket that Moira had provided.

ALL KINDS

When things get difficult there are several types of people. To be more specific, three types:

1. Those that will do anything to keep surviving
2. Those who have an equal want to live but don't have the guts that the fighters do
3. Those that would prefer to submit and simply fade to black

Ben and Tom Vaughn were in the first category. Isobel was in the second with many of the other residents. The renters of apartments 105 and 106 were squarely in the third.

SUICIDES

The gunshot that the Cabels heard on the second day was Juan Vaziri saying farewell to the newly fucked up world. They found his body in the hallway just outside the second bedroom. Like his security deposit, there was no way that Juan was coming back because most of his head was further down the hall, ruining several walls and doors. Moira said a prayer for Juan while the others went to work in the apartment.

Ben, Jeff and Markus blocked the windows and doors. No one touched his body because it was too messy to move to the tarp. Isobel and Rob took any food and first aid but also a few warm blankets, a radio, batteries and three flashlights. The supplies were piled onto a blanket to lug upstairs. There was time to grab more but the scene was gruesome and depressing and no one wanted to stay in 106 longer than necessary.

Before leaving, Edward took the gun from Juan's hand. "Thank you, young man," he said quietly. His heart felt heavy and sad for Juan but he was very grateful that his death had enabled Edward to acquire a gun.

Katie Finnerty, a college student living alone in 105, went less messily. She had emptied a bottle of pills and a bottle of alcohol to end her life. Because her brain was relatively undamaged from her chosen method she came back, only it wasn't a problem for her uninvited guests because Katie was crippled from the waist down and confined to a wheelchair.

the infection does not cure ailments nor does it increase or return strength or mobility to damaged limbs.

"How'd she end up in a wheelchair?" Isobel asked as she watched the younger girl drag her undead self around the dirty kitchen floor.

"I'm not quite sure but I think it was a car accident in high school," Markus replied, he was looking at pictures of

Katie's childhood that were stuck to the fridge. "She didn't have the wheelchair in all these photos."

"We need to get her out of the kitchen so we can search the cupboards," Ben pointed out. "Maybe we can move her into the living room?"

"She'll bite us if we try to touch her." Isobel shivered.

"There is no way I am putting a finger on her," Markus added.

"She wants to bite us anyway so why don't we taunt her in that direction? It will be slow going but I'm sure it will be worth it. She shops for large amounts of food at a time to minimize the number of trips so we'll find some quality stuff in here."

Rob volunteered to coax Katie out of the kitchen. She really wasn't a threat, except to their ankles and the closer Rob stood to her, he found, the faster she moved. The promise of living flesh kept her going.

Finally clear of the kitchen area, Rob and Ben trapped her in a makeshift pen made out of the coffee table, a recliner, and the entertainment center. She spent the rest of the visit holding her body up with one hand while clawing the air with the other. How desperately she wanted to consume them.

"Shouldn't we shoot her?" Moira was looking at Katie with concern while the others unloaded the kitchen cabinets. Edward raised the handgun he had acquired from Juan.

"No," Ben placed a hand on the gun to stop him, "that will attract more and I don't think we should kill anything unless our lives depend on it. We need to stay human as long as possible."

Moira nodded in agreement but Edward wasn't ready to lower the gun.

"So we're just going to leave her here to starve? I don't see how that is more human."

"Edward, leave her be. You might need those bullets for someone else." Moira had stepped in front of the gun to show her husband how serious she was. He dropped the gun to point at the floor and hugged his wife.

Ben and Rob dragged the tarp of bodies to the basement while the others followed. They placed the corpses in an empty storage unit in a far corner. The tenants had a moment of silence in front of the tidy stack of dead before closing the door.

"Farewell to all of you. Ryan, Susanne, and you two strangers, whoever you are, rest in peace," Moira said softly.

"Look!" Markus pointed out a half-window that was placed high on the wall of the basement. It gave them a view of the front lawn. Their eyes were level with the directionless feet of the dead. Everyone gathered at the small pane of glass and watched for a few minutes until it became too much.

Isobel felt it routine to mark #4 off the list of tasks. Collect all bodies and place in basement. Check.

The group went back up to the first floor hallway but, the work wasn't done.

"Markus, Edward, Moira, you should grab everything you want and move it upstairs. We can help carry any larger items. Leave your things in the common area at the top of the stairs for now. We can sort out living arrangements later," Ben directed.

"I don't want anything but some clothes, my tea and books, a place to lie down, and my reading chair," Edward replied.

"Jeff and I can help with the chair and your bed," Rob offered.

"How nice of you both," Moira smiled and led the way back into their apartment.

"I can keep watch while you help Markus, Ben," Isobel suggested.

"If you are ok with that, away we go!" Ben cheered half-heartedly.

While everyone else was gone, Isobel found a few precious moments to herself. She sat down on the carpet about halfway down the hall and waited for everyone to return. The handgun was starting to feel heavy in her hand but she couldn't trust the world enough to set it down, even for a second. She needed a sense of security and sleep, both desperately.

LAST SECOND THOUGHTS

"Maybe we should stay, Austin." Jill had her bags packed and stacked next to their front door but she was standing in the nursery. The smell of fresh paint, pale lavender, had finally faded from the air just two days prior. It felt like a room now instead of an idea.

Austin had come into the room. He had his jacket on and the car keys in his hand. "Don't start with that again . . . *please*. There is no way that baby is coming out of you anywhere but in a hospital."

Jill slowly sat down in the rocking chair and placed a hand on her belly. "Too bad the baby doesn't know about the world. If she knew, she could wait for a bit. Stay safe inside of me."

"You are being weird. Can you focus? The neighbors are going to lock us in here if we don't hurry." He extended a hand to his wife. "We should go downstairs."

"Are you sure about this?"

"We can't risk a home birth without help. I've been waiting for nine months to meet our first child. I'm not going to let what is going on outside take this opportunity from me."

REALLY SECURED-ACCESS

The moving of the Cabels and Markus only took twenty minutes. Ben and Rob brought hammers and nails down for everyone to share. The decision was made to board up the doors on the first floor with cabinets, more doors, and furniture from the other apartments. There were just too many windows to worry about within each unit. It was noisy work and it attracted a lot of unwanted attention from the dead outside.

"Phew. I didn't think it would take that long," Ben said as he wiped the sweat from his forehead some forty-five minutes after they started.

There was one door left, the front entrance, and then the complex would be sealed from the crypt that was the world. The Coopers were standing by, waiting for the perfect moment to make a run for the car. Most of the dead had left the front entrance area for the sides of the building but a few stragglers remained.

"Are you ready?" Austin asked his wife as he grabbed her hand and pushed open the front door.

She didn't answer; she only followed him with her eyes closed tight. She couldn't stand to look at what they were running into. But the cold air of the evening hit her body like a brick and her eyes shot open. An involuntary scream emitted from her mouth.

"Shhh!" Austin shot back as he squeezed her hand.

The other tenants watched as the couple finished crossing the lawn in front of the building.

"I think they are going to make it!" Isobel cautiously hoped.

"Look! The zombies are moving toward them. Austin better pick up the pace." Rob was standing next to Isobel at the windowed front door.

FRONT ROW SEAT

They finally reached the car and dumped the bags near the trunk. Austin took Jill to the passenger side door and, despite his shaky hand, had it quickly unlocked and open for his wife. Jill slowly lowered herself into the seat and closed and locked the door. She watched nervously as her husband returned to the bags at the back of the vehicle.

The dead were headed towards the car. Austin was able to get the luggage in the trunk and get around the car to the driver's side door. His adrenaline had kicked in and his hands were shaking more than before. The keys weren't cooperating in his hand.

"Come on!" Jill yelled. She was trying to lean over and unlock the door for her husband. In that moment she cursed herself for not getting automatic locks. Her belly was too large to allow her to stretch across the center console and driver's seat to the small lock in the door.

Austin leaned down to the window. "I love you, Jill," he said before breaking into a run. He planned on doubling back when the crowd of dead had thinned out.

Isobel was pounding on the thick pane of glass set in the front door. "Austin, keep moving!"

"Where is he going?" Moira asked. She couldn't see well in the darkening evening.

"He ran behind the building across the street," Rob answered.

Jill was looking around frantically; yelling her husband's name. Behind the building Austin ran straight into a horde of no less than fifty of the undead.

"Shit!" he yelled and turned back around. A hand gripped his arm. One set of teeth and then another fell on his jacket. The leather would protect him for a moment but he had to get away so he slid out of his jacket. Free from them he ran back around the building and into another group of corpses.

Jill saw him reemerge from the south side of the building. She resumed yelling his name but it only drew more dead into the path between him and the car. It seemed that with each minute that passed, another two bodies came shuffling into the mix.

Austin had only twenty more feet to cover before reaching the car. He pushed past body after rotting body. The moaning was increasing as the dead grew agitated at the passing meal. They became more determined than ever to get a piece of Austin. He made it to the car door but stopped short when he realized that the keys were back in his jacket pocket behind the office building across the street.

Even if he could make it back, even if he could find the keys in the little daylight left, it would be too late because a set of teeth caught his bare arm. He looked at his wife as his body was pulled to the ground; he looked at her until he disappeared under the dead.

"They got him," Isobel said as she backed away from the window, her stomach reeling from what she had witnessed. Moira embraced her.

Ben moved closer to the door and caught a glimpse of the growing pile of dead, all trying to feed on Austin's body. "He'll be covered in wounds if they don't tear him completely apart," he observed.

Jill was screaming but forced herself to stop and mourn silently with hope that the zombies would slowly lose interest.

"What do we do now?" Markus was sitting on the floor leaning against a wall of the hallway, his head in his hands.

"I'm not going out there," Jeff said as he climbed the stairs to the second floor.

"We won't be able to do anything tonight. It's too dark to send anyone out," Isobel reasoned, but really she didn't want to go out there either. She hoped that someone would volunteer by morning.

"They insisted on leaving," Moira added. "They didn't listen to any of us."

"But she is pregnant. She could have that baby at any moment," Edward said.

"We should board the door for the night and discuss it in the morning. It's been a long day for everyone." Ben picked up a hammer and some nails. Markus grabbed some wood and they set to it.

"I've got to check up on Molly and Gabe. See you guys upstairs." Rob trudged wearily up the stairwell.

Isobel stayed and watched until the last nail was in.

UNREQUITED LOVE

"Hey guys. How'd it go?" Rob asked Molly but Gabe answered.

"She ate *all* the crackers," he said, lifting the empty box upside down to prove the point.

"Sorry. I burned my breakfast and my lunch was small."

"It's fine. You can come eat our crackers anytime you want."

"Dad! No she can't! I like crackers too," Gabe pouted and ran to his bedroom.

"Thanks for watching him. I'd better go comfort him over his cracker loss," Rob smiled.

"Is there anyone alive downstairs?" Molly asked.

"Three people. But Austin died trying to leave and Jill is trapped in their car outside," he said sadly.

"What?"

"I don't want to talk about it anymore right now. We're dealing with it tomorrow."

"Ok. Night," Molly said briskly. She was a little pissed that Rob was unwilling to fill her in completely on the events that had unfolded below. Molly returned to her third floor apartment. She felt sadness for Jill, who had always looked after Molly like a mother; though Jill was more like a sister at only two years her senior.

A knock on her door startled her from her sorrow. She jumped up from her couch and opened the door, hoping to see Rob standing before her.

"Hey baby," Tom Vaughn barely slurred out. He was so completely sloshed that he was leaning on the doorframe for support.

"Tom, I'm not in the mood. I'm *never* in the mood. Austin is dead. Jill is trapped and I'm alone up here with you."

"I've got something that will make you feel better." His hand travelled down to his crouch. "You said it yourself; we got the whole third floor."

"That's not what I meant." Molly had fear building in her chest. The sadness was making her feel small and vulnerable. She knew Tom could see that. She knew he could take advantage of that and she wouldn't be able to fight him off. She was trapped now too.

"Shit I have to crap. I'll be back," Vaughn excused himself back down the hall.

Molly closed her door and ran to pack her things. She found herself praying for Vaughn to be constipated, which was strange and made her laugh a little. She didn't care if she'd have to sleep in the second floor hallway, she was moving no matter what.

NUMB

An hour had passed and the dead people had gone off in search of easier meals than Jill, a sardine in a sealed tin.

She had seen Austin when they were done with him. She couldn't cry anymore, only watch as he rose again, covered in his own blood, to join in the hunt as one of them. She felt nothing; as though she herself had the symptoms of the infection spreading through her limbs.

SECOND FLOOR SLUMBER PARTY

"Edward and Moira, you can move into 206. It's a bit empty but we can all donate some items tomorrow to help supplement what you brought up." Isobel gestured to the door across the hall from hers.

"I've always loved moving into an empty apartment," Moira said happily but Edward looked unhappy. 104 had been his home for many years and it would take a lot to make 206 feel like home to him.

Markus was about to move his things into Angela Turner's apartment when Molly came down from the third floor, a suitcase in her hand.

"Tom is going to do something horrible one of these days and I won't let it happen to me. Do you have any spare room?"

"You can take 204," Markus offered.

"No one's heard from Angela?" Molly frowned. She was overjoyed to have the opportunity to move away from Vaughn but she felt a bit odd taking someone's place that was unaccounted for.

"Ben and I saw her outside, Molly. She hasn't left the neighborhood but she is . . . gone," Isobel assured.

Rob and Gabe were naturally in their own apartment and Ben and Isobel were happy with their arrangement. That left Markus without a place to stay.

"I guess I'll have to ask Jeff if I can room with him."

"Neither of you will have a choice. Ben's place is out of commission," Isobel reminded everyone. "Don't try to go in there."

Everyone was ready to go to sleep but the zombies were relentless. Smashing glass could be heard down on the first floor. The undead battering on the building had increased ten-fold since the hammering and Austin and Jill's botched escape earlier in the evening.

"Let's gather as much crap as we can and throw it in the stairwell. We have to block it in case they get in and figure out how to climb stairs," Ben said. "We can take a lot from my place and then reseal it."

"There's stuff in Angela's place that I could do without," Molly offered after reemerging from her new apartment.

When the stairwell barricade was finished, a few of the residents stood around surveying their work.

"What happens if we need to get out?" Markus asked.

"We have fire escapes from our balconies," Isobel pointed out.

"Ah, we can climb right into the arms of the loving dead," Edward said poetically as he walked toward 206 and to bed.

An hour later, Isobel was standing at her living room window, looking into the pitch-black night.

"Do you think we did the right thing?" she asked, though she wasn't sure if Ben was still awake.

"What do you mean?" Ben asked, from the couch-turned-bed behind her.

"Leaving Jill out there. Do you think she understands why we couldn't come after her?"

"It was a suicide mission to begin with and she didn't look back, not even once, to see if anyone would come for her. Go to sleep Isobel." Ben turned over and pulled his blanket up to his chin.

"What happens if she tries to get back in?"

"She dies trying. Even if the door wasn't boarded up, she doesn't have any keys. Even if she had keys, we filled the stairwell up."

"So that's it? We just move on without her?"

"No. I didn't say that. It's been a long day and I think we'll be better equipped to tackle the problem with some rest."

"See you in the morning then," Isobel sighed and walked to her bedroom.

AN INQUIRY

"Don't you have a wife, Jeff?" Markus asked as they brushed their teeth.

"Yeah . . . I do. She's out of town. I haven't heard from her," Jeff answered quietly.

"I hope you do then. Hey, thanks for letting me stay here. That second bedroom of yours is really nice."

"Kind of crazy how most of us were just names on mailboxes to each other before," Jeff reflected as he stared at the younger man. Warmth emanated off of Markus, an instant likeability that Jeff found refreshing, especially when compared to the cruel relationship he'd recently found his way out of.

"Yeah, we can't ignore each other now," Markus smiled and left the shared bathroom.

LULLABY

Jill watched the lights go out in the building for the night. She was lucky that she kept a fleece blanket in the backseat of the car for emergencies. It was turning out to be a cold evening. She draped the blanket across her belly, closed her eyes and envisioned her warm bed on the third floor. She didn't dare hope though that she'd see it again.

"Go to sleep and good night, go to sleep little baby," she sang aloud to her unborn child, repeating the only line she knew, over and over again until she passed out from exhaustion.

THE SIXTH DAY

THE FIRST MEETING

On the morning of the sixth day, the residents gathered in the common area of the second floor for breakfast and a meeting.

"Everyone looks like crap," Isobel noticed.

"Huh?" Edward asked as he removed earplugs.

"Didn't anyone sleep well?" she asked.

Most didn't answer and those that did confirmed insomnia.

"A pregnant woman had to sleep in a car last night. I couldn't stop thinking about it," Markus grumbled over his coffee cup.

"Yeah, that was tough," Rob said.

"Well, was anyone able to come up with a plan or the courage to go outside for her?" Ben asked.

"Nope," Jeff said. Moira just shook her head.

"Keep thinking on it then. How is everybody?" Isobel changed the subject to something she hoped would be more positive.

Ben stood up like it was an AA Meeting introduction, which made a few of the residents laugh until he started talking. "I miss Anna. I can't stop thinking about her." Ben looked down at his hands, the ones that had gripped the gun that killed her. "This is crazy."

"I'm sorry you had to see her like that in the end," Moira said.

"I'm glad she didn't bite anyone," Ben shook his head, "she wasn't a part of the problem, you know? That is all the comfort I can find in it." He started tearing up and sat down. Moira dragged her chair closer and put a comforting arm around him.

"Like I said yesterday," Markus chimed in, "I'm just happy to see living people. I rented that apartment downstairs because of the view . . . so much for *that*." He laughed but his voice took a quiet and serious tone as Ben's had before him. "Thank you for coming downstairs, any one of us could have easily ended up like Juan or Katie." He stood up, and walked around to Ben, Jeff, Rob and Isobel, shaking their hands in appreciation. Once he was back to his seat, Rob spoke up.

"I was worried about Gabe. This is scarier than single-dad type worries. Molly has been so gracious in watching him and keeping his mind off of the serious stuff. I feel like we can make it through this, now that I can focus on helping."

"Speaking of Molly and Gabe, where are they?" Isobel asked.

"This is a tad too heavy for Gabe so I asked Molly if she'd play a board game with him."

Moira, who was still comforting Ben, turned her attention to Jeff. "Where is your wife Sheila? We haven't seen her since this started."

"Don't you mean we haven't *heard* her?" Edward muttered.

"Edward!" Moira scolded.

Jeff started to explain. "It's fine Moira. Sh . . ." But he stopped mid-sentence, his face a stark white.

"She went out of town with the dog to visit her parents the day this started, didn't she Jeff? We haven't heard from her or seen her yet. Jeff is a bit distressed about it," Ben completed Jeff's sentence.

"Well rightfully so! I bet she is just fine though. She's a tough lady. Anyway," Moira moved on, "we like the new place. It certainly is easier to sleep without worrying about those assholes crashing through the windows."

"Moira! Keep your mouth clean. God might still be listening," Edward seized his opportunity to scold her back; using his cane to gesture towards the sky.

"I don't know that He is listening anymore. Though if He is, maybe He can finally hear us now that the televangelists have shut up," Rob said.

"Nah, the moaning of the dead is even louder," Ben's tears had dried and he let out a little chuckle at his joke.

"No more heavy topics like religion and politics. They are a quick way to breed disagreements. Who hasn't checked in?" Isobel asked, looking around the gathering.

"I didn't really," Jeff said. "It's nice to have Markus with me. We're getting along well. It feels like college."

"Agreed," Markus smiled.

"So what about Jill? Should we risk our own lives to save someone who completely ignored our pleas to stay inside? Should we let her stay there to starve or attempt an escape on her own?" Isobel repeated her worries of the previous night aloud.

"If we are going to save her we should make a decision before tonight. She could go into labor any time now. If it happens out there it will be much harder to rescue her and the baby. She will be exhausted and unable to move quickly. The baby will need to be carried and it might make noise. The issues will multiply." Ben had considered so much more than she.

"So, tonight or never?" Edward surveyed the group. "It sounds reasonable." Everyone responded in favor of the timeline.

Moira closed the meeting with appreciation. "Thank you, everyone. It's a shame the world had to end for us to meet you all. Let us pray to the Lord that we have some time to know each other, if He can forgive me for my dirty mouth."

the infection has the talent, found with many fatal diseases, of simultaneously destroying lives and bringing people closer together.

After the meeting the group left to their own apartments to brainstorm any possible rescue options. It was quiet that morning. The sun was shining for some unknown reason. The heat of it made the stench ten times more unbearable. The corpses in the street paid no attention to the rays beating down on their decaying, dripping skin.

NOISE COMPLAINT

The Cabels could hear movement upstairs.

"What could be making all of that noise?" Moira asked as she looked worriedly at the ceiling.

"That Tom Vaughn lives up there. Gruff guy if you ask me. He doesn't hold doors." Edward furrowed his brow.

"One person can be that noisy?"

"Maybe someone else could go upstairs and see what's going on. I'm too old to climb more stairs." Edward rubbed his knees. He was sore from moving house the night before.

When Edward didn't move to find a volunteer, Moira stood up and walked across the hall to Isobel and Ben.

"It's kind of you to be worried about Vaughn, Moira. But he wouldn't do you the same favor," Ben said.

"Oh I'm not worried about him. I'm worried about what could happen if he brought someone else into the building. He could expose us all. Who knows what type of people he might be friends with too? I'm not eager to meet them."

"Ha. I'm fairly certain he doesn't have any friends," Isobel scoffed at the idea.

"We'll go up there after lunch if it makes you feel better," Ben assured her.

"Just ask him to keep it down," Moira requested.

After eating, Ben led the way upstairs to the third floor.

"You know, he's got more guns than I can count. He could have killed us all and had the whole building to himself."

"Can we have a bit of hope then since he hasn't?" Isobel said cheerily.

"I just think we shouldn't give him a reason to change that. Proceed carefully."

"Proceeding carefully," Isobel said as she knocked lightly on Tom Vaughn's door. Ben had his hand on his gun but he moved it when he saw the look on Isobel's face.

No answer. Isobel knocked once more and waited.

She tried the knob and it was locked. Ben pointed to her jacket pocket.

"Use the keys from the office," he said.

"I thought you didn't want trouble." Isobel smiled as she unlocked the door and opened it as slowly and quietly as she could. Whether a living or undead Tom Vaughn greeted them, she decided, she would be equally terrified.

"Tom?" Isobel whispered. No reply. It seemed as though he wasn't home.

"Where is he?" Ben asked.

Vaughn's apartment was messy; at least it *looked* like a mess. On closer inspection it was incredibly well stocked. He had at least 15 guns and their respective ammunition, boxes of canned goods stacked in one corner, almost to the ceiling, and a lot of survival gear. Isobel was stunned.

"It looks like a fucking bomb shelter in here."

"Yeah, kind of like he knew something was going to happen; like he'd been preparing for this for a long time."

TOM VAUGHN'S 1ST ASSIGNMENT

Tom had had a successful run. He'd managed to gather a lot more food for himself and also spend a few minutes in the sporting goods store down the main road. He was clutching a new machete as he climbed the fire escape to his apartment. He threw his duffel bag into the window and entered after it. Sweat was running down his face. As he wiped it off he noticed he wasn't alone.

"What the fuck are you doing here? How'd you get in?" He still had the machete in his hand, his knuckles white from the tight grip he had on it.

Isobel was looking at the machete as she answered. "We have keys from the office. We heard a lot of movement a little bit ago and wanted to check on things, you know? Make sure you were all right."

"How sweet of you both, really. But if you didn't look around, I'm doing just fine."

"What was all the noise about?"

"Just trying to organize my loot."

"So you really have been leaving the building?" Ben asked.

"It's a free country man. I'll leave when I want."

Isobel had anger rising in her. She was so pissed off it made her forgot for a moment that Tom Vaughn was holding a machete in a room full of loaded guns.

"You could have exposed us to the infection! Not only that, you are bringing attention to our hideout. The dead will follow you back and destroy the building trying to come after you! How could you be such an idiot?"

Vaughn didn't know what to say. He'd never been reprimanded so sternly by a woman, especially while he was holding a weapon. He stared her down while he thought of his reply.

"I didn't bring the infection. I've brought medical supplies and food. Besides, staying cooped up just pisses me off more. I feel better now that I've had some fresh . . . well, outside air. I wouldn't call it fresh; it smells like something died out there." He let out a huge laugh.

"The Sergeant has a sense of humor. Who would have guessed it?" Ben said under his breath.

"Hey, I was thinking about using one of the other apartments up here to store some of this stuff in. My place is getting kind of cramped."

"Everyone has moved to the second floor so that would be fine if yo-"

"I wasn't asking for your fucking permission," he scoffed. "Who died and made you Building Manager? I was going to ask if you guys could help by moving a few boxes."

"Could you spare a few guns in exchange for the help? We don't have much downstairs in the way of weaponry."

"Sure. But don't give them to the women. No offense Isobel, is it? You all get too emotional."

Isobel ignored the comment and she and Ben moved some boxes into 302; making small talk with Vaughn as they did.

"What's with the fat girl in the car? Isn't she from across the hall?" he asked.

"She isn't fat Tom, she's pregnant. She tried to leave with her husband. He didn't make it and neither did the car keys. She is stuck out there and we are trying to decide if we can pull off a rescue."

"Huh. Every time I ran by she was talking to herself. I thought she was crazy so I left her alone, you know? Maybe she'd been bitten or something."

"She is fine. We watched her get in the car. They didn't have a chance to bite her. They were after her husband."

"Do you think she wants back in? I can get her if you guys want."

"Really? Tom that would be great!" Isobel couldn't believe what she was hearing. Tom wasn't known for selfless acts. She dropped the box she was carrying and embraced him quickly to show her appreciation. He pushed her away.

"Hey, just because I'm going to get the fat girl doesn't mean I want to join the girl scouts. I'm not interested in making friends. I could use a little excitement, is all."

Isobel picked the box back up. Everything Tom did was about him, always. He didn't care for Jill or for anyone in the building unless it benefited him in some way.

"There isn't a way in through the first floor. We boarded everything and blocked the stairwell," Ben got back to business.

"She'll have to climb the fire escape like I do. If she doesn't make it, well, she wouldn't have made it in the car either," Vaughn shrugged.

"When are you going out for her?" Isobel asked.

"Before dinner, before the sun goes down."

"Thanks. We'll tell the others," Ben said.

"Hey," Vaughn said before they returned to the second floor, "you can come back and visit if you want. I hate to admit it but, it was nice to see your ugly faces."

"You don't mind?" Ben asked.

"Don't bring anyone else and never, *ever*, let yourselves in again!" Tom stipulated.

RUN, FAT GIRL

Ben and Isobel carried a handgun and two shotguns, plus ammo for everything, to Isobel's apartment. They went door-to-door on the second floor to tell the others about Tom's offer to rescue Jill. Isobel's apartment afforded the best view of the street and the Cooper's car so everyone gathered there in eager anticipation for the event. Isobel went out onto her small balcony to get a better view and to keep an eye out for Tom. They only had to wait a half hour before he came running around the building. His skills were impressive, using the trees to stay out of view, moving quickly and silently until he was at the passenger side door of the car.

To Tom Vaughn, the lady looked like she was asleep, something he didn't have time for. He pounded on the window, startling her from rest. Tom pointed at the door lock. Jill only looked up at him in confusion. She couldn't figure out how she knew him or if she really did.

Come on Jill, Isobel thought from her balcony, *think straight. Unlock the door.* Isobel willed for Jill to hear her silent plea. *Unlock it!* The dead started moving toward the car. Tom saw this and pointed determinedly at the lock once again. Jill saw the zombies coming back and shook her head. Near paralyzed by fear, she just sat there shaking her head *no*.

"Hey! This way, come over here!" Isobel started yelling in an attempt to distract the zombies; buy Tom some precious seconds to alter his plan. They turned towards the building for a moment but again focused their attention on Tom and Jill. Tom wasn't going to die for this woman. He took out a crowbar and started smashing it against the window. Jill cowered in the front seat, shielding her body with the blanket she'd slept under. He hit the window until it broke.

Tom reached into the hole he'd created, unlocked the door, yanked it open and grabbed Jill's wrist violently to drag her out of the car.

"Snap out of it you bitch!" Tom was closer to death now than he had ever been, weighed down by an unborn child and its mother's fear. Some of the zombies were nearing grabbing distance.

The baby kicked in Jill's belly, bringing her into the moment and awakening Jill's instinct to survive. She started running, but just as suddenly as it came it left her and she stopped. She was staring at something in the distance. Tom followed her gaze and found it resting on the partially eaten body that was walking straight for her.

"Do you know him or something?" Vaughn couldn't tell who it was, or who it used to be. "That one got pretty mangled, huh?"

"Austin!" she wailed.

"Your guy? Holy shit." Tom wasn't sentimental or sympathetic. He was on a mission to rescue her and stay alive, both he didn't plan on failing. He yanked her hard, away from Austin's walking corpse and they disappeared behind the building.

Isobel's heart was racing as she stepped in from the balcony. The room was silent. No one said anything. Ben and

Isobel contemplated going upstairs. Ten minutes passed, it felt like an hour. And then, a gentle knock at her door. Markus jumped up to answer.

"No, I'll get it," Isobel said, remembering that Tom wasn't interested in the other residents. Isobel stepped out into the hallway and there he was, just Tom.

"Oh my god, did she make it?" Isobel asked, wringing her hands from the anxiety as she looked from one end of the hall to the other; Jill nowhere in sight.

"Calm down. She made it just fine. She had to climb slowly, her belly made it hard to reach the rungs of the fire ladder. But she made it and now she's upstairs in her apartment."

"With the baby and all those emotions she is carrying, she shouldn't be alone. I'll ask Molly if she'll take a roommate."

"Whatever. I'm going back to my place." Tom left as though he hadn't just saved a life; two lives. He didn't wait for a thank you and he didn't want one. Isobel went back inside to the group to deliver the good news. The group broke up and Molly and Isobel went upstairs to see Jill.

IN GOOD HANDS

"I don't mind having her as a roommate. It isn't my apartment anyway. I think it will be great for her to spend some time with Gabe too," Molly decided as they walked the last few feet towards 305. "She has her first baby coming and she needs to focus on that . . . instead of Austin."

Jill's apartment door was wide open. They found her passed out in the master bedroom, luckily on the bed. She was breathing softly, a men's blue dress shirt, darkened in areas by her tears, was pressed to her nose.

"I'll stay here and wait for her to wake up," Molly offered.

"She's in good hands with you, Molly. Thank you." Even though Molly was young, twenty-two Isobel thought, she was smart, kind and she wouldn't leave Jill's side.

"Well, it will be good for me too. More than you know," Molly smiled gently.

On her way out, Isobel closed Jill's door and glanced at Vaughn's across the hall. She considered thanking him but alone she didn't feel as brave.

MOLLY MATHAY, CARETAKER

Evening. The rescue earlier brought attention to the building again. The pounding was the loudest it had ever been. Ben had been trying to trick his mind into all sorts of alternative sources of the noise. Construction, a loud horror movie, etc . . . but it only worked for a few minutes. He resorted to wearing earplugs, like some of the others, while he read a novel he'd borrowed from Edward. The story made him smile and it felt good to do so. Isobel had left to check on Jill again before going to bed for the night.

The door to 305 was closed so she knocked and it took only a second for Molly to open it. Her eyes were watery and red, as though she'd been crying. Isobel followed her into the living room where Jill was sobbing heavily. Tissues were strewn across the couch, the coffee table and the floor. The men's dress shirt from earlier had followed Jill into the living room. She had it draped over her belly. It felt wrong to Isobel to be intruding on such a personal moment.

"Sorry for the mess," Jill acknowledged her without looking up.

"You don't need to apologize. I'm really happy you made it back. Can I sit?" Isobel asked as she gestured to the couch.

"Yeah, um . . . yeah," Jill said, pushing a bunch of used tissues from the cushions to clear a spot, adding them to a pile on the floor.

"Have you had a chance to eat?" Isobel asked. She saw a bowl and plate on the side table.

"Molly heated up some soup and toast."

A film had formed on the top of the soup as it cooled and the slice of bread was only missing its crust. She had barely touched the meal. Molly felt hungry still and planned on eating the leftovers later.

"Did Molly tell you about moving to the second floor? We think it would be good . . . for when the baby comes." Isobel asked.

"Yeah she did. I'd rather not stay up here. Even though Tom saved my life, it doesn't make up for the years he's been a complete asshole. When he came out to the car to get me I didn't want to get out because he's been indecent to me in the past. Austin and I almost moved out of this complex because Vaughn tried to force himself on me in the stairwell last year. No one knows about it because Austin thought it would only cause more trouble for us, and Vaughn would just claim he was drunk anyway. Now he might think somewhere in his messed up head that I owe him. I can't sleep with him across the hall. Besides, this apartment is full of Austin." Jill looked around and started crying again and Molly came quickly to her side, putting a hand on her shoulder.

"There is plenty of room Jill. We can bring down stuff for the baby too. We can decorate Angela's place just how you want it," Molly said happily, trying to move Jill's thoughts away from her dead husband.

"It's getting late. Can I help you two bring anything downstairs for the night?" Isobel asked.

"There's some stuff ready to go in the bedroom. Toiletries and clothes."

Molly was alone with Isobel in the bedroom. "I don't know how you convinced Tom to get her but thank you. She would have died out there," she said as she grabbed a blanket.

"Don't thank me," Isobel threw her hands up in the air, "it was Tom's idea. He thought it would be fun."

"Fun, huh?" Molly huffed. "That guy is a dick."

"Yeah. The definition of the word."

When Isobel returned to her apartment she found that Ben had fallen asleep on the couch, his bookmark fallen to the floor. She picked it up and eased it into place where his thumb was still tucked in the pages. She set the book next to his handgun on the coffee table.

Outside, the front passenger door of Jill and Austin's car was still open and the dome light was on, lighting up a bit of the dark night; a tiny hope that hadn't quite flickered out.

MACABRE PARADE

The next day the sun was gone and replaced with clouds and the promise of rain. In 201, Markus was looking out the window and it made Jeff very nervous. Sheila could be in the area still. He felt close to Markus and strangely wanted Markus to feel the same about him. He didn't want to lose his trust.

"Looks like it might rain, huh?" he asked Markus, attempting to engage him in conversation and divert him from staring at the faces of the dead below.

"Hopefully it'll wash some of the stink away." Markus laughed and turned toward Jeff. "What do you want to do today?"

"Get to know each other better," Jeff said.

"Like twenty questions or something?" Markus asked.

"Sure."

"I guess I'll start by asking the one question I am sure everyone in the building wants the answer to. Why in the hell did you marry a woman like Sheila?"

The question made the brown hair on Jeff's arms rise in prickly goose bumps. He wasn't angry about the question. He had often wondered the very same thing. "Long story short, our parents are friends and they pressured me into accepting. She proposed and I obeyed my folks. Let's stay off the topic of Sheila though." Jeff didn't want to lie more about Sheila's whereabouts if he could help it.

"You're right. Sorry. Ask me a question."

"How long have you known that you were gay?"

"All my life."

"And have you ever been with a woman?"

"Hey, it's my turn to ask! Have you ever been with a man?" Markus smiled.

Jeff could feel his face get hot and only part of him hoped that Markus didn't notice.

Isobel ate breakfast, cold cereal, on a stool she had brought onto the balcony. She had decided to spend the morning watching the dead.

"I might as well see what you are up to." She knew she was talking to herself.

One of them was stalking a cat. From what Isobel had seen so far the plague didn't affect animals but they still seemed to be desirable as nourishment for the zombies; second choice on the menu when human was fresh out. The fumbling hands of the corpse caught the cat but Isobel wasn't sure how it happened. The cat looked pretty confused too. Angela Turner, her former second-floor neighbor, was using the sidewalk today, though unintentionally. The sun from the day before had done something terrible to her exposed skin. It was sliding off of her in small patches. Isobel knew from watching crime shows that there was a special word for that stage of decomposition but she couldn't remember it. Angela's arms were spotted, the white of her skin and the fading crimson of her decaying muscle were of strong contrast to each other.

Isobel wished that Angela would go somewhere else in town. She hated recognizing the faces of the dead. It reminded her that it could happen to anyone. Austin had wandered away, which was probably for the best.

"Do you want to play with me?" Gabe asked Jill. She and Molly had gone over to visit with Rob and his son. Molly and Rob were in the kitchen talking with one another. She was left on the couch; the child sitting on the floor by the sliding door, playing with action figures.

"Hmm?" Jill looked toward the boy. She had been daydreaming again or mourning, she wasn't sure which. Her due date was only two days away and with each passing hour she was thinking more of her dead husband and less of anything else.

"I saaaaiid, do *you* want to play with *me*?" Gabe certainly did not like repeating himself. He was used to a lot of attention from whatever adult was around him. Jill wasn't interested or interesting at all. "Don't ya have a baby in there?" Gabe pointed to her belly.

"Uh huh." Jill barely said it loud enough for Gabe to hear but she nodded her head at the same time.

"Maybe the baby will play with me!"

"Do you like girls?"

"No! Tell her to stay in there." Gabe turned away in disgust.

Jill sighed. "I already tried."

"Are you guys having fun?" Molly had joined them in the living room. She brought with her some goldfish crackers and fruit snacks for Gabe. He took them happily but shook his head no and went back to playing alone with his toys.

"What's up with him?" Molly asked Jill.

Jill shrugged and excused herself to the bathroom.

URGES

Later in the day, Molly could feel the pressure building; the stress that drove her to make bad, unhealthy decisions and think slightly evil thoughts. Jill was napping in the second bedroom. Molly stood in the doorway watching her breathe slowly. *Dumb bitch,* she thought. *I wouldn't have run outside with a baby inside me.* Molly caught herself there. She needed to leave the apartment before this continued. She knew just where to go and just what to do.

She slowly opened her apartment door and checked the hallway for anyone. It was empty, which was common for that time of day. She walked briskly to the stairwell that led to the third floor and the common area there, where they stored all of the food.

Standing on the top step she was filled with elation. Stacks of canned and dried goods stood before her. Food made her happy and happiness was all she wanted to feel right now. Molly grabbed six cans of pears, some beef jerky, baked beans, granola bars, and chips and stole away to her old apartment. She had food there too that she knew she could rely on if the group's stockpile ran low.

Once inside, she sat on the kitchen floor and gorged. It felt so good to be full and to make choices without anyone else giving their opinion. Jill would wake up soon and wonder where Molly went. Molly didn't care. She wanted only to take care of herself.

She sat for ten minutes and then she grabbed a large garbage bag, vomited out all she'd consumed and then threw the knotted bag in her old bathtub. She cleaned up and left to return downstairs but she ran into Tom Vaughn in the hall.

"You're back. I thought I scared you away." Vaughn tried to touch her hair but she moved to avoid his hand.

"I'm not back; I was just leaving." Molly kept walking but Vaughn caught her arm and pushed her against the wall.

"What were you doing in there?" Vaughn questioned her, his face only an inch from hers.

Molly turned her head away to try to get some breathing room. "I felt sick. I wanted to be alone."

"Hmm. You don't look sick. In fact, you look really *healthy* to me." Vaughn reached a hand under her shirt. Molly gasped and Vaughn put his other hand over her mouth to stifle the noise.

"Molly?" a woman's voice called from the stairwell.

Vaughn groaned unhappily and released Molly from his grip. He disappeared back to his apartment before the source of the voice, Isobel, arrived at the top step.

"There you are. I went to check on you and Jill but no one answered the door." Isobel looked Molly over. "Are you ok?"

"Yeah. I'm fine. Let's go back downstairs." Molly smoothed out her shirt and followed Isobel. She didn't want her savior to see her body trembling.

Vaughn was fuming. He got what he wanted, especially in this new world. He was so close to having her and he knew if they hadn't been interrupted he would be enjoying her right now.

He needed a prostitute; someone he could pay to let him do anything he wanted. He picked up his phone and tried in vain to reach any of the old numbers he'd been able to rely on in his times of need. He thought of running to Aurora Avenue, a popular place for street walkers, but thought better of it. They'd all be dead; wearing high heels or hooker boots was a quick way to end up a meal for the undead.

He did the only other thing he could do, turn on a dirty movie and take care of himself.

"Jill's baby will be coming soon. I think I want to volunteer to help," Moira suddenly said after a long silence; she had been concentrating on her knitting project, a hat and booties for the expected newborn.

"You bore three. I think that means you have the most experience," Edward said between drags on his pipe.

"We'll have to get some supplies together. And I'll need some help during the labor." Moira set her knitting project aside and grabbed a pen and paper to start planning.

THE SECOND MEETING

Moira had made a hasty list and asked the residents to gather before dinner, with Jill, to plan the home birth.

"Hi everyone," Moira started. "Welcome Jill to our group, or back to it, I suppose."

There were nods in the circle. Isobel waved. Jill smiled warmly but with a hint of sadness.

"Thank you for trying to warn us. Austin and I should have listened in the first place and stayed inside." Jill's voice grew weak as she spoke the last sentence, "He would still be here if we had."

"Looking to the future," Moira said brightly, "Jill's baby is due in two days and I would like to act as midwife, if that is alright with you, Jill?

Jill nodded in acceptance. "This is my first child. Half the people in this room must know more than I do about children, you most of all, Moira."

"We'll need some extra sets of hands; someone to assist me, someone to care for Jill, someone to document the birth, maybe another."

"I want Molly to be there for sure," said Jill. Molly smiled. She figured she'd be included since they were sharing an apartment.

Rob raised a hand to offer his help. "I was there when my wife gave birth to Gabe. I went to those labor classes and know the breathing techniques. I can help if you don't mind Jill."

"That would be great, Rob, thanks," Jill said as Moira wrote Rob's name onto a clipboard she'd brought to the meeting.

"I can come," Isobel volunteered. "I'll do whatever you need me to do."

"Thank you Isobel. I think that should do it," Moira smiled as she went over her list a final time.

"Now that we have that sorted out, how are things going with everyone?" Ben asked.

No one had much to say. Markus smiled. Jeff shrugged. Edward asked Ben if he liked the novel. It seemed like getting Jill out of danger had helped everyone to calm down a bit. Leaving her out there must have weighed heavily on their heads. Still, the world was not right yet and many couldn't help but have a sense of foreboding.

"Things might not always be smooth like today. We need to stay prepared and alert. If there is an end to this, we have a very real chance of making it in this building," Ben reminded everyone. "If we are smart about our food consumption and the barricade holds, It's possible that our lives could return to normal."

Molly's heart started pounding in her chest. She wasn't smart about her food consumption. *Did Ben know?* She wondered as she scanned his face but he didn't look her way. Markus, who was seated next to Ben, was looking straight at her though.

"One day at a time." Moira shook her head a bit and took a drink of water to swallow the medicine in her hand.

DIY BIRTH

Everyone at Willow Brook settled in during the next couple of days. The pounding died down; the undead having realized they'd have to work extra hard for the meal inside the building. It was late in the evening when Jill's fatherless child decided to come into the world.

"Her water broke!" Molly was running down the hallway knocking on doors and yelling. "The baby is coming!"

Moira gathered the home birthing kit that she had created. It was an impressive spread that reflected her creativity and resourcefulness during the end times. She brought it to 204 and put it all on the couch.

The kit included:

- Petroleum jelly
- Gloves for sanitation
- Iodine for sanitation
- Towels of assorted shapes and colors for cleanup
- Sterile gauze pads for cleanup
- Turkey baster to clear the baby's nose and mouth
- A chip bag clip for clamping the umbilical cord
- Sanitized scissors for cutting the cord
- A Black and Decker tape measure to measure the baby
- A small shallow pan of warm water to clean the baby
- Blankets and a hat to wrap the baby
- A hastily made birth certificate

- A photograph of Austin, so the baby would see her father

The group looked prepared but they didn't feel it. A firm mattress had been moved to the living room and on it laid Jill in a thin nightgown. She was breathing rapidly and sweating. Isobel had come to lend an extra hand. Rob was there to help with breathing technique and to give Jill a hand to squeeze the hell out of. He felt slightly ashamed to watch and wondered how Jill really felt to be surrounded by mere acquaintances for this momentous occasion.

"Where's Austin? He said he'd be here!" Jill screamed.

"She's delirious, don't mind her," Moira said with kindness in her voice. "How long ago did you say her water broke, Molly?" Moira asked as she examined Jill.

"I think it happened this morning but she didn't tell me; like she was unwilling to accept that it was happening without Austin here. I ran to get you when I noticed her having serious contractions," Molly whispered.

"She's been in labor for hours. She's fully dilated. This baby is ready to come out. We're going to push now, ok Jill?" Moira asked between her legs.

Jill looked around the room for her husband's face and when she didn't see it she shook her head. "No, not yet. Can't we wait a little longer?"

"Come on Jill," Molly coaxed her gently, "the baby has to come out now." Molly wiped the sweat from Jill's brow and tucked her hair behind her ears. "You can do this."

"Ok. Ok. I'm gonna push," Jill replied.

"Here we go," Isobel said, looking to Moira.

It took an hour of pushing and Jill nearly fainted twice from the pain. They had no painkillers to give her that would do any good.

Around eleven that night baby Annabella Cooper finally emerged. Jill had survived but needed some stitches and a lot of cleanup, which Moira tended to. Rob still held Jill's hand.

Isobel and Molly cleaned off the baby. It was emotional for both of the women who had only seen death recently; new life brought a shaky hope. They laughed together when they saw that Moira's baby booties fit perfectly but that the hat was slightly too large for the infant's head. Wrapped in a blanket and crying, the baby was brought to Jill.

"Our little girl. She's so perfect. Austin would love her so much." Jill touched the baby's nose and looked into her eyes. "Daddy would love you so much."

Isobel wrote on the birth certificate, little more than a piece of printer paper with some ruler lines on it, the date and time of Annabella's birth.

AFTERBIRTH

Moira stayed in 204 for a few hours to make sure that everything was fine with both mother and baby. Occasionally Jill would cry out for her husband but then Molly would be at her side to comfort her. The undead outside were pounding furiously on the walls of the building. Jill's screaming and potentially the smell of the birth and life of the baby had encouraged them.

Ben and Isobel checked the stairwell barricade. They stared at it for nearly fifteen minutes, moving home décor into various positions for the tightest and most unmovable fit. Satisfied and spooked after hearing a window shatter in downstairs, they left the stairwell and went to bed.

THE PHOTOGRAPH ISN'T ENOUGH

"How is the little baby today?" Isobel asked Molly as they crossed paths in hallway a few days later. The child was in Molly's arms and Jill wasn't around.

"Annabella is great. She's a quiet baby so far. Jill isn't so good though."

"I noticed. What's up? Is it post-partum depression?" Isobel knew it was common and likely, given the circumstances the child was born into.

"It's more than that. Jill won't stop looking out the window. She's trying to find Austin in the crowd. Every time she thinks she sees him, she runs over, grabs the baby, takes it out on the deck and yells for him. It hasn't been him yet, thank God."

"Wow. She's in major denial."

"I think she's gone off the deep end. She keeps telling me that she wants Austin and the baby to meet."

"Nothing's going to change him back," Isobel sighed.

"Tell that to her. She's convinced otherwise. I've been trying to take Annabella out of the apartment and away from Jill as often as I can."

FULL ACCESS

Rob went out onto his balcony and looked down at the windows and sliding glass doors of the apartments below. All the glass had been shattered and every so often he could see a zombie enter or exit the building through the newly created doors, its feet crunching on the shards without caution or care.

"Hey . . ." Vaughn paused as he checked the dog's collar, "Cheddar." He greeted the golden retriever that stood in front of him, its tail excitedly wagging, a front paw extended to be shaken formally. The dog lived in a now abandoned house a ways down the road from Willow Brook that Vaughn had just broken into. Vaughn wasn't too keen on animals but the dog followed him everywhere he went within the house with what looked like a smile on its furry face. He couldn't help but warm to Cheddar. The only thing he didn't like about the dog was that it wouldn't stop putting its paw up for a handshake. Every time Vaughn stopped, there the paw was in his face. Vaughn took only a few supplies from the house and, before leaving, he gave the dog some fresh water and ripped open a big bag of dog food left by the absent owners.

"Don't eat it all before I come back," he said as he pet the dog's head. Cheddar put his muzzle in the kibble and started to fill his starving belly. Even as he ate, the dog lifted a paw for Vaughn to grasp.

"It was nice to meet you, Cheddar," Vaughn said, laughing, as he gave in and gently shook the paw one last time that day.

Isobel's dreams were filled with strange things that night. A baby walked to the barricaded stairwell with its mother and pointed its tiny little finger at the wall of furniture, silently asking for it to be torn down. The mother, blinded by love removed every item from the baby's path. The undead flooded the building, crawling up the stairs to break down the apartment doors. Then, Isobel was at the grocery store because Willow Brook was empty of food but, no matter how hard she tried, she couldn't read the shopping list in her hand. In another part of the dream Markus shot Vaughn. Upon waking she couldn't remember why.

ONE FOR YOU AND TWO FOR ME

Her dream was somewhat of a premonition. The next morning she went upstairs before breakfast to grab some food. She was shocked at what she saw, or rather, what she *didn't* see.

The group kept all of their food stored in the third floor common area. It made keeping stock a lot easier. The only problem with this plan, it turned out, was everything. It wasn't locked up, no control of it beyond verbal instructions given to each resident on how much they could consume in a day. But, as Isobel looked at the small pile of food left, they'd put too much trust in one another. Someone in the group had obviously been eating more than their ration or hiding extra away for themselves.

Isobel began to panic a little inside. *What will we do if we run out of food?* She worried. She grabbed a breakfast bar and went back to her apartment.

"Is that all you're going to eat for breakfast?" Ben asked.

"It's almost all there is. Someone's been taking too much food. Who would do that?"

"That's a tough question. And I don't even know how to start looking for the answer. Just when you think you know the people around you."

"I figure with the number of mouths we're feeding, we'll be screwed in a week and a half if we don't stop whoever is doing it and find some more food."

Ben and Isobel sat quietly for the rest of the morning; pondering who could have jeopardized the group. At lunch, Isobel chastised the group as a whole for the incident, hoping to put pressure on the individual who was responsible. After lunch Ben went to visit with Edward and Moira, leaving Isobel alone. A knock came on her door.

Thank God, Isobel thought, *someone is going to confess.* Isobel opened the door and let Markus in.

"Thank yo-" she started to say but he cut her off.

"It's Molly," Markus said with confident excitement in his voice.

Isobel's mind couldn't wrap itself around the name *Molly.* She was sure that Markus was here to apologize. She hadn't even considered Molly as a possible culprit.

"She is bulimic. You know, binge and purge," he whispered, even though they were alone. He walked around the apartment touching things, waiting for a response.

"Molly? She takes care of everyone else. How could she abuse her body like that? How could she not think of the impact on the group?" The questions came spilling out of Isobel. "This isn't regular life. We can't just drive down the street to the store!"

"Calm down, Isobel. When you have a mental disease you don't make rational decisions," Markus said.

"How do you know she is bulimic?" Isobel asked.

"About three months ago I bumped into her downstairs. She dropped some mail and I helped her pick it up. There was a brochure for some kind of therapy retreat. I handed it back but I saw the name of the center on it. I ran upstairs and searched the Internet. Kind of snoopy of me but I couldn't help myself. It was a body image clinic that specializes in eating disorder treatment. You don't get a brochure from a place like that unless you request it."

"I should check her old apartment on the third floor. That is the only place she would have privacy. Ben is with the Cabels, do you want to come with me?"

"Field trip!" Markus exclaimed. "I love a good scandal!"

LITTER BUG

Molly was frantic. She had run upstairs as fast as she could after lunch to try to hide the evidence of her bad decisions. Her old apartment was a mess. Empty food containers were scattered everywhere and it smelled like vomit. She was able to fill one garbage bag with trash and toss it over the railing of her balcony before her secret was exposed to all.

Isobel didn't knock and that made Markus even more excited. She used her set of keys to let them in. The smell hit her nose and she cringed. Markus felt proud as he surveyed the proof of Molly's betrayal. Piles of empty cans and plastic bags, a can opener, used paper towels, all littered the floor.

"I knew it!" Markus blurted out.

Molly's heart nearly stopped when she came out of the bathroom, a bag of vomit in her hand, sweat building from her brow, to stand face to face with Isobel and Markus.

"What . . . I . . . why are you in here?" Molly stuttered and yelled. She dropped the bag of vomit on the carpeted hall. Markus watched the plastic bag fall and said a small prayer that it wouldn't burst open onto his pants. It hit the ground with a soft splat and the plastic held. Molly didn't give them time to answer. She pushed through them and ran out of the apartment.

"Oooh. Someone's in *trouble*," Markus said to Isobel.

Rob and Gabe were in the hallway when Molly came running by.

"Dad, she looks sad."

"Yeah she does. I wonder what happened upstairs." Thinking it might have something to do with Vaughn, Rob followed after her. "Stay here champ."

Rob found the door to 204 open a hair and he let himself in. Jill and Molly sat together on the couch, Jill's hands rubbing Molly's back as she cried loudly.

"Hi Annabella," Rob said as he walked over to a bassinet in the corner of the living room. The baby was asleep despite the noise of Molly's entry and emotion. "Is everything alright, Molly?"

"I was getting better you know? I was in therapy and I was making . . . progress. Things were looking up for once in a long time." She kept her head down and it looked like she was talking to herself more than to anyone in the room.

"What are you talking about?" Rob asked. He truly was stumped.

"I have an eating disorder, Rob. It's my fault we are screwed on food. I tried to stop but I've been so stressed about the baby and everything that I went a little crazy last night."

"How much did you eat?" Rob thought maybe she could consume twice her portions at best.

"I don't know but I was up there for three hours."

Markus and Isobel had taken their time coming downstairs after Molly. They knew she couldn't go anywhere, none of them could. The two of them walked into 204, Gabe followed behind, looking for his dad.

Molly saw Markus and her eyes drilled into him. *How long did you know?* She knew it was his fault she'd been found out. "Why did you do this to me?"

"Whoa, whoa. I didn't *do* anything," Markus pointed at himself dramatically.

"You told Isobel and now almost everyone knows."

"I'm not a tattle-tail. I'm a do-gooder. Some of that food you wasted was for me! I'm just trying to survive."

"Ok guys. Calm down. Molly, we were bound to find out. Markus, you could maybe have given Molly an opportunity to tell the group on her own." Rob tried to be a neutral force in the argument.

"She was upstairs cleaning up anything that tied her to the problem. I don't think she planned on admitting anything!" Markus yelled, pointing at Molly as he buried her deeper.

"What do you want me to do, Markus? It's an obsession," she said, exasperated, "and I'm sorry."

"I accept your apology Molly. As for everyone else, that is up to them," Isobel said.

Markus left without saying anymore. He didn't like feeling his mortality. It would be awhile before he could forgive Molly for her wrong.

THE THIRD MEETING

Dinner the same day brought yet another meeting of the group.

"Thanks everyone for meeting like this all the time," Isobel said.

"It's not like we have other plans," Edward said lightheartedly and everyone laughed at his apocalyptic humor.

"On a serious note though, I called *this* meeting so that Molly could talk to everyone all at once. Molly?" Isobel looked to her expectantly.

"I don't think I can do anything but come out and say that it's my fault that we don't have enough food to last us through the month. I am bulimic. I'm sorry. Really I am. I've been through therapy, before this, and I just have to work hard to put everything I learned there back into practice. The circumstances are a little bit . . . different this time though."

"You messed up the rationing, Molly," Rob, who'd had a little bit more time to think about Molly's decisions, reprimanded her.

"I didn't mean to hurt anyone. I love you all like family now, especially Gabe and Annabella. This problem is just bigger than me."

"I want to believe that you can control it but I think we should put the food supply in an apartment up there and lock it up; create a controlled system to divvy it out," Ben suggested. "So this doesn't happen again."

"I agree with, Ben." Markus said.

Moira grabbed Molly's hand and squeezed it. "I'm sorry Molly, but I agree with Ben too."

"It's fine Moira. I brought this on myself. Everyone has a right to be angry with me."

At that moment Gabe poked his head around the corner. He'd been listening to the whole meeting. "I'm not mad at you Molly." Rob waved his hand at Gabe to join the group and Gabe ran to sit on Rob's lap.

"No matter where we store it or how we lock it up, the problem right now is that we don't have enough." Jeff reminded the group.

"I have a plan for that," Isobel said. "We all know that Vaughn goes out regularly and is skilled at . . . well, staying alive out there. I'm going to talk with him about taking some of us out to bring back food."

"How will we decide who is going?" Edward motioned with his cane around the circle of residents. The room became silent. No one wanted to think about going outside.

Isobel broke it, knowing a decision had to be made. "Well, you and Moira, though very agile and healthy for your age, won't be able to fight, run, or haul as much food as the rest of us so you don't have to worry about it. Jill just had a baby and isn't very . . . stable. She will stay here too."

Molly was terrified to be alone with Vaughn inside the walls of the building. She didn't want to be stuck with him *and* the undead but she knew they would expect her to go.

"I'll go," Molly volunteered, hoping that someone would speak out against it, "even if you weren't going to say my name."

"I *was* actually going to suggest you. We need to be responsible for our actions so this is how you will repay the group, by replacing the rations you consumed. Ben, if you feel up to it, I'd like you to go with Vaughn and Molly. You have the most familiarity with firearms and you are the strongest of the men."

"Hey!" Markus called out. "I'm strong too."

A few residents laughed but Molly didn't find his comment funny. It was his fault that she'd have to leave the building; have to spend time with someone who'd tried to molest her.

"Ok, Markus, you can go," Isobel countered with a smile.

Markus turned white and shook his head.

"Don't worry Markus, I'll go. I'll come upstairs to talk to Vaughn with you too, Isobel," Ben offered.

"Perfect."

Markus, Jeff and Rob moved what was left of the food into an empty apartment upstairs. Isobel locked the apartment and waited for Ben to meet her at Vaughn's door. She wanted to plan that day so that it could get done before the food situation at Willow Brook became desperate.

TOM VAUGHN'S 2ND ASSIGNMENT

Only one knock and Vaughn stood in his open doorway, smelling like half of a stolen bottle of Wild Turkey whiskey. Isobel could tell that they'd interrupted a personal male moment because a porn DVD flickered on the television in the living room behind him and his pants were unzipped.

"Should we come back later Tom?" Isobel asked as politely as she possibly could. He was mean when he was sober; she wasn't about to tick off the drunk and blue-balled Tom that was *barely* standing in front of her.

"Nah! Now's perfect, come in!" He made a big, sweeping motion with his arm to gesture Ben and Isobel inside 306. She walked in, and after a nervous glance down the hall in the other direction, Ben followed her.

Vaughn stumbled to the living room and began knocking stolen goods onto the floor to clear the couch off for his visitors. He didn't apologize for the mess, turn off the smut or zip up his pants. But, like a good host, he offered them each a beer. Ben tried to get straight to the topic of the visit but Tom didn't want to talk business just yet.

"The skies have been clear lately; been kind of nice to see the blue," Vaughn said with a hint of melancholy in his voice as he looked toward his sliding glass door and beyond. The self-professed loner was lonely so Isobel and Ben stayed for a while. They talked about random things - Mt. Rainier, the proper way to clean a rifle, how many women they'd been with, which for Isobel was none. Ben and Isobel relaxed when they finally saw some humanity in Vaughn.

The slider was open to the porch. It felt strange to Ben sitting around, surrounded by guns and drinking beer; getting drunk while dead people walked around on the street below.

"Relaxation and safety like this will be hard to come by, as we get deeper in this disaster," Isobel said, feeling the lightness of sobriety leave her. Three beers later, the sun replaced by the moon, their faces lit only by the same flickering porn, which must have been set to loop, they finally started to talk about the next day.

"We need your help again, Tom. Molly has an eating disorder and she ate all of our food." Isobel said drunkenly.

"Not all of it, *a lot* of it." Ben corrected her.

Isobel ignored him and continued. "We were thinking about going out tomorrow, with your help, to look for more. As a punishment, Molly has to go."

"So just me and her, eh? The fat bitch was a hassle but I wouldn't mind spending some alone time with Molly. I'm in."

"No. No, Ben is going too. We need more than what two people could bring back."

"Oh. That's too bad."

Ben spoke up, wanting to assert his usefulness. "I'm pretty good with my handgun."

"That's good I guess," Vaughn smiled, "We should go around noon. The dead aren't very active midday. Not sure why but that's what I've noticed; shouldn't have to get too violent."

"Where're you going to get the food from?" Isobel asked. She remembered how messed up the grocery store had been before things had gotten really bad. It was probably destroyed now.

Tom's answer was frightening. "I've been out there every day since this has started, traveling as many as twenty blocks in any direction. I haven't once seen anyone else alive. We can raid the houses."

"There has to be someone out there. We can't be the only survivors. That's impossible." Ben walked unsteadily to the dark windows of the apartment. He scanned back and forth, his eyes searching for hints of light that could mean life beyond the walls of Willow Brook. He found none.

"A lot of impossible sure is happening these days. From what I can tell, no one is home, anywhere." Vaughn said grimly.

A THIEVES MARKET

After Ben ate a small breakfast of oatmeal and a juice box, he went to Molly's apartment so they could walk upstairs together.

"You look worried, Molly. You ok?" Ben patted her back lightly. She turned and scowled at him.

"You aren't? We're about to entrust our lives to a disgusting man who thinks more with the southern region of his body than the northern, probably drank whiskey for breakfast and is waiting for any excuse to pull a trigger," Molly spoke quickly and took in a deep breath when she was finished.

"I can see you've really slept on it."

"I didn't get any sleep," Molly said wearily.

"It's a figure of speech," Ben explained.

"I know!" Molly said, exasperated. Ben decided it would be best to stop talking to her for the moment. He could see the dark circles under her eyes and the exhaustion in them.

Vaughn's door was propped open and he was wide awake, running around his apartment getting ready. It looked like a war room.

"You should take this machete. It will compliment your handgun well and save your life in a pinch if one of them gets too close," Vaughn said to Ben as he divvied up some weapons between the three of them.

"Molly, you can have this wooden bat." She accepted the sports implement from him but begrudgingly. *Why can't I have a gun?* She wondered but didn't ask.

"I will take this assault rifle." Vaughn held it up for them to admire, a grin spread across his bristly face.

"Come here." He waved them over to his low coffee table; on it were worn satellite image printouts lay side by side creating a birds-eye-view of twenty of the blocks that were south of Willow Brook. Ben and Molly examined the map. It had marks all over it but no key with which they could decipher them.

"We'll go this way." Vaughn said as he took a black marker and drew a line to mark their path. Molly counted the cross streets, the neighborhoods, the houses that he passed and speculated in her head how many potential zombies that represented. She guessed hundreds but feared thousands, remembering to account for "visitors" from out of the area. Molly shook herself out of the obsessive mathematical daydream she'd fallen into to see that Vaughn's marker line had ended at a cul-de-sac of fifteen tightly-packed houses some ten blocks south of their current location.

"That far huh?" Ben was surveying the map with more general interest and less terror-fueled math than Molly. He nodded his head as if to say that he agreed with the route and accepted the challenge of it.

"Don't want to attract a crowd of zombies next door now do we? If they gather around us here, we have several blocks to lose them."

Vaughn circled seven houses.

"These are empty and haven't been overly looted yet." He drew a large "X" on four of the remaining houses.

"We won't be going into these ones unless absolutely necessary."

"Why not?" Molly asked, not sure if she actually wanted the answer.

"The air is bad. Decomposing bodies can be a real health hazard."

Molly felt chills crawl her body. "Yuck," was all she could muster in response.

He left the remaining four houses unmarked. "I haven't scouted these ones yet. Who knows what's in them. We can find out today if you want, assuming we don't draw too much attention from the zombies in the area."

"How are we going to carry the food?" Molly asked.

"We'll all be wearing backpacks and they are going to be heavy so get ready for that." Vaughn pointed to three large bags that looked more like oversized duffle bags with straps than backpacks.

"Like hiking!" Ben said cheerfully. He'd once been a prolific hiker of the Cascade Mountains, something he missed about the dying world, the ability to escape for a weekend.

"Only, minus mountain streams and plus zombies," Molly said dryly, quickly killing any happiness and enthusiasm Ben had for the comparison. "Besides, that won't be enough food."

"I've got some collapsible, stacking storage bins and a handcart to roll them back on. It will slow us down but it's our only choice. Vehicles make too much noise."

They kneeled around the map a few minutes longer, each preparing in their own way for the journey that lay ahead.

"Well I'm ready," Ben said standing up.

Molly followed his ascent from the floor and then bent down to check that her running shoes were tightly tied. "I'm ready too."

"Quick! To the fire escape!" Vaughn exclaimed as though the building was on fire. He laughed but neither Ben nor Molly thought that there was anything funny about it.

BEAT TO RE-DEATH

Ben was actually quite nervous about going outside but he tried his best to hide it because he knew that Molly was much worse off. She was shaking as they climbed down the fire escape. The ground at the bottom was clear of any undead because everyone who stayed behind was making as much noise as humanly possible on the opposite site of the building to draw them away from the scavenging team.

Vaughn led with determination and confidence. Molly, who was in between Vaughn and Ben, could see zombies in the distance; little moving shapes littering the landscape but much too far away to notice her. That didn't keep her from clutching the baseball bat so tightly in her hands that Ben could see the white of her knuckles. He followed behind her, his handgun loosely in his right hand. The machete, wrapped in its army green sheath, hung from his belt and gently hit his leg as he walked.

"Just keep low, be quick, and stay quiet!" Vaughn said in what Molly considered a loud voice. He had the handcart and the plastic bins folded and strapped to his back, under his backpack, but he still managed to stay low and move quickly. *Two out of three,* Molly thought.

They used abandoned cars and the thick trunks of trees to conceal themselves. Molly knew it was the best strategy but she couldn't help but feel it also helped the zombies to sneak up on them and trap them.

"Get down!" Vaughn whispered as he threw an arm behind him to motion the demand. They'd only made it two blocks from Willow Brook before being spotted by a group of the undead that were hanging around a bus stop.

There were three of the ghouls. "One for each of us," Ben said as he holstered his handgun and withdrew the machete from its guard.

They lumbered forward, toward the gathering party.

Molly was staring at one of the two women in the group who was missing both of her arms. The left arm stopped near the elbow. The right arm was ripped completely out of the socket at the shoulder. "How did that happen to you?" Molly asked as though she was addressing the dead woman directly.

Vaughn had moved away from Ben and Molly, sticking close to the front end of a parked sedan, waiting for the right moment to attack.

The second woman's face had been eaten away. Molly could see bite marks elsewhere on her body but no other major injuries. This woman scared Molly more than the armless one because she was making chewing motions with her mouth and opening and closing her hands into fists.

"I think that one likes you, Molly. Molly?" Ben had lost sight of her. He found her on the ground on the curb side of the same sedan Vaughn was using for cover. Her legs had given out and she was too terrified to look anymore.

"It's alright Molly. Vaughn will take care of them."

And Vaughn did. He went for the third zombie, the man, first. Using the butt end of his rifle he destroyed the man's skull. He did the same to the ladies, never turning the opposite end of his gun toward them. Panting, he returned to the curb and took a short rest near some bushes. Molly looked beyond him and into the front of a brick building that had been a dentist's office before the fall. The full glass front door was gone, broken into thousands of pieces. Bloody handprints, smeared and obscured, were a terrific contrast to the smooth laminated white of the front desk. She looked away.

"I want to go back," she said through stifled tears.

"They won't let you back in without food." Ben reasoned.

"They don't know what it's like out here!" she yelled. "You have blood on you, Vaughn!" Her eyes travelled all over his body searching for more.

"Keep your voice down!" Vaughn yelled back at her as he wiped some blood from his arm. "It's a tad bit hard to beat three zombies to re-death and come out clean. Besides, the blood can't infect you unless it gets inside through a wound or down your throat. So don't get hurt, watch what gets in your eyes, and fight with your mouth closed."

Molly's face grew paler but she had no choice except to stand up and move on. They made it eight more blocks without event, save for Molly finally vomiting on the sidewalk. Watching Vaughn beat the trio of zombies to what he had called "re-death" had caught up with her system. She was disgusted.

"Feels good to vomit for the right reason, huh Molly?" Vaughn said without looking back at her.

Ben, who had stopped to hold back her hair, fumed at his remark. "Vaughn, that was fucking uncalled for. Give her a break."

Vaughn shrugged his shoulders. "I was just saying."

"Don't say anymore about it. Let's get this over with and get back home where it's safe."

"Thanks Ben," Molly said once she'd spit the last bits from her mouth and taken a swig of water.

"It's like he gets paid to be an asshole. I don't get it," Ben cracked, trying to make Molly smile a little. They both laughed and caught up to Vaughn who had continued on without them.

Arriving at the entrance to the cul-de-sac they stood hidden from view behind a large sign, on it the name of the abandoned neighborhood, Alpine Fields. They reviewed the map printout.

"Alright, here is where this gets interesting. I've given the houses nicknames so we can quickly identify them if we need to make decisions on the fly." Vaughn paused. He looked as though he was waiting for applause or congratulations for his great idea. None was offered.

"Well, let's hear them," Molly urged him to finish the meeting. She couldn't help but feel that her feet, and the feet of her companions, were visible between the posts of the sign.

"The names will make more sense when we get in there. They are Pink Horse, Gnome City, Dead Lawn, The Boat House, UPS, The Forest and Cupola." He pointed to the rooftops of each house on the satellite map as he called its name.

"Those names are very creative, Vaughn. Now can we go? I feel like a sitting duck here." Molly knew that starting with flattery and following with reason would go much further with Vaughn than almost any other conversational formula other than an offer of sex.

"Sure thing. Pink Horse is first."

He skipped playfully into the cul-de-sac and Ben and Molly followed with much less zest.

PINK HORSE

"Creepy," Molly said, eyeing a bright pink My Little Pony horse that stood atop the mailbox. Vaughn may have put the toy there to mark the house or it might have been left by the child who had owned it. Either way it hurt for Molly to look at it. She was pretty sure it was a happy childhood that had ended. They walked past the large dining room window of the house; its curtains were open. The flowers on the table inside were dead; never to be replaced with a fresher bouquet. The front door was unlocked.

"Creepier!" Molly shivered.

"Don't worry," Vaughn said as he touched her back, "I left it unlocked last time I was here and zombies break windows, they don't turn doorknobs honey."

Molly moved away from his hand. "Don't touch me unless I ask you to."

"So there's hop-," Vaughn started.

"It will *never* happen."

Inside, they secured the house by checking every room and closing all the windows and doors. After Molly closed the heavy drapes of the dining room she took the vase off the table and threw it, and the dead flowers, away.

The hallway walls were lined with family pictures. In one of the images an immortalized little girl, owner of the pony and all the toys in the pink bedroom upstairs, stared back at Ben. He felt on the verge of breaking down right there in the middle of the unfamiliar hallway. He and Anna had talked about marrying and having a child, hopefully a little girl, someday. Without Anna those plans were only dreams now, or sad memories.

Once the house was clear and secured, they gathered in the kitchen pantry. Ben felt pure elation, a world away from the sorrow he'd just held on to. The pantry was fully stocked with plenty of canned and dry goods for the taking. Molly and Vaughn carefully sorted through the items and loaded everything they could into Ben's backpack. This might be easy after all, he hoped, as he hauled the sack full of loot back onto his back.

"On to the next place then," Vaughn said, satisfied with what they'd taken. They left Pink Horse and were moving on to Dead Lawn when Ben stopped.

"Look over there!" he whispered and pointed to the entry to the housing development. A corpse was moving towards them but hadn't seen or otherwise sensed their presence.

"Wait for it to turn away and then move as fast as you can to the next house," Vaughn told them. The corpse, as though he heard Vaughn's suggestion and thought it a good one, turned away and exited the development. "Go!" Vaughn said just above a whisper.

DEAD LAWN

Dead Lawn was just that. Dead. The owners hadn't taken care of it or the home either. The house had been built, like the others in the neighborhood, within the last ten years. But it was in such a state of disrepair that it had aged twice as many years, looking like it would fall over in less than ten more. The dead grass crunched under Molly's feet as she made her way to the front door.

"We can't go in that way. It's locked," Vaughn said. "We have to go in on the side." He showed them to a window into the garage that hinged at its top. It opened inward with a push of his hands.

They took turns climbing into the window and onto a convenient stack of boxes inside. The garage was dark and packed with junk and shadows. Across the garage Molly could make out the door that led into the house because it was cracked open slightly and some light was peeking through. She focused on the tall crack of light as she moved towards it, bumping into a bicycle and what felt like a plastic Christmas tree. Ben or Vaughn, she couldn't tell who, stepped on a squeaky toy and swore into the darkness. Molly watched in fear as a shadow moved past the crack of light. Something was on the other side of the door. She stifled a gasp and lifted her bat.

"Put it down, it's a dog. A very *friendly* dog I might add," Vaughn said, his voice booming in the darkness and quiet of the garage. Molly lowered the bat and pushed the door open. A large, dirty dog stood before her, tail wagging ecstatically.

"Cute!" Molly ran and embraced Cheddar, allowing him to lick her face and to thrust his paw towards her. "I love dogs!" she exclaimed as she silently read his name off his collar's tag.

"Good, *you* can shake that paw then." Vaughn had a strange hint of relief in his voice.

"He knows tricks?" she asked, looking around for a treat or something to give the dog.

"I wouldn't call that a trick. It's more of an annoyance. It gets old fast."

"I'll play with you all you want, Cheddar. Vaughn just doesn't like anything cute or friendly. Don't take it personally." She talked to the dog's face as though it could understand her but really she was enjoying an opportunity to put Vaughn down in a playful manner.

"I like plenty of cute things especially if they are willing to get friendly with me," Vaughn said with a wink as he stared down at her.

"Don't touch me with your eyes either, Vaughn." Molly looked at her shirt to make sure he couldn't see down it.

"You're too young to be a prude."

"And you're old and alone. How is that working for you?" She looked directly and defiantly into his eyes.

Ben wasn't around. He had left them to check the house. Vaughn wanted to smack Molly for the insult, watch her body fall across the floor but she toppled over without his help. Cheddar had pushed his paw full force into Molly's shoulder, making her lose her balance. She hit the floor with a thud and burst out laughing. Vaughn laughed too, dissipating the tension of the moment.

"I told you," Vaughn said. "He'll do that all day long."

Molly reached out to Cheddar, jokingly asking for his help to lift her off the floor. He extended his paw again and Molly took it as she returned to a more upright position. Molly and Vaughn walked further into the house and Ben rejoined them in the kitchen.

"That dog hasn't gone to the bathroom inside at all," Ben noted.

"He uses a doggie door to let himself out back." Vaughn pointed to a flexible rectangle set low in a door at the end of the galley kitchen.

"It looks like he's a self-sufficient pup," Molly said as she stepped over the huge bag of kibble that lay ripped open on the kitchen floor. Crumbs sprinkled the outer edge of the mess like an asteroid belt.

"I put that there for him you know. And the water bowl too. I'm not a total asshole."

Molly said nothing in response. Ben had already begun looking through cabinets for rations and chose to ignore the comment. Three of the lower cabinets in the kitchen were filled with cans of vegetables and fruit. It was Molly's turn to load up her backpack. Ben also managed to fit a few more cans into his own bag, having to sacrifice some baked beans to make sure the zipper could still close.

Vaughn switched out the water in the dog bowl. Molly gave the dog a rawhide bone she'd found in a cabinet and pet his head. She bent down and shook his paw delicately. "It was so nice to meet you Cheddar. Thanks for the people food."

They climbed back out the window of the garage.

"Is that dog the reason you don't use the front door?" Ben asked Vaughn.

Vaughn nodded. "The world is a dangerous place. He'd meet all sorts of people and end up shaking the wrong one's hand."

FAMILY REUNION

With Molly gone on an unwanted adventure, no one was focused on watching Jill and the baby. Concern in her had dropped three days prior, when she'd stopped looking for Austin. He hadn't shown up and Jill was defeated and decidedly saner. No one could be sure why Austin picked that day, that moment, to shamble back into view and back into Jill's life. From around the corner by the convenience store his torn and rotting body slowly made its way towards its old home.

"Come on baby. Let's go see if Molly is back yet." Jill said as she picked up her child and walked outside to the balcony. "Do you see her anywhere? There's a lot of people down there but not the one we are looking for." Jill's eyes scanned the crowd of undead, searching for quick movements or changes in direction that would signal the group's return. Her eyes fell on a head covered in patchy red hair and her heart leapt.

"It's daddy! Annabella look! Do you see him?" Jill hurried back inside to grab the backpack-like baby carrier. She placed Annabella in it and strapped it tightly to her back. She walked back to the balcony and leaned over the edge. "Austin! Honey, it's me! Look who I have here!" She yelled as she pushed the fire escape ladder into position for her descent.

"Did you hear that?" Edward asked Moira as they sat at home in 206. Edward had been reading an old newspaper that had been printed just before the world fell apart. It was filled with stories that didn't matter anymore, issues that had been resolved overnight, and photos of people that were most assuredly dead or undead now. Still, he found it interesting.

"Maybe Molly and the others are back!" Moira exclaimed happily as she put her crossword puzzle down and grabbed a sweater. Edward followed his wife out to the balcony. They were speechless for a minute as they watched Jill continue her climb down the neighboring balcony's fire ladder.

"Jill!" Moira whispered. She didn't want to draw more attention from the undead gathering below. Jill paid her no mind and instead began yelling to her deceased husband once more.

"Austin, come here! Annabella won't stop talking about how much she wants to meet you."

"What is she saying? That baby can't talk," Edward said, confused.

"She's crazy. Stark raving mad and it's going to get them killed. Go get Isobel," Moira said with a slight gesture toward the apartment behind them and hallway beyond. Edward did as his wife told him and returned with Isobel a moment later.

They gathered on the balcony and called to Jill urgently. She was moving slowly down the ladder but she had finally made it to the bottom rung and let go, dropping to the ground and nearly falling backward onto her child. Austin had arrived on the small lawn that surrounded the building.

Jill ran through the corpses that had gathered around her, driven by love and devotion to her idea of family. She continued calling his name and he moved toward her but she was mistaken in thinking that it was his name, or any sort of recognition, that was drawing him. Just as eagerly, dozens more of the undead and unknown were coming nearer, as though they might all happen to be named Austin. The real Austin was three feet away when Jill took off the carrier, set it upright on the ground, and pulled the baby gently out of it.

"No!" Isobel yelled. "Jill, stop it! He's going to kill you!"

At this comment Jill finally acknowledged Edward, Moira and Isobel. She turned to them and smiled but said nothing. They watched, terrified of the reunion below. What should be a thing of beauty and happiness, a family reunited, turned nauseating as Jill presented the newborn child to Austin.

"It's our baby, Annabella," Jill said through a half sob, half maniacal laugh. The baby, its arms and legs wiggling around, cooed and spit up. Its healthy pink flesh contrasting wildly against the grays and blacks of Austin's rotting hands as they took the baby. There was no fatherly love or care in his grasp.

"We can't watch this. We can't," Moira said to the others. Isobel and Edward followed her back into 206. Outside, Austin lifted his child and brought it to his lips, not to kiss, but to devour. The oversize knit cap, now speckled with blood, fell from Annabella's head to the ground. Her blood fell onto Jill's face and into Jill's mouth; she was still laughing insanely. Soon the blood mixed with her own, as Austin and the other zombies devoured her too.

the infection appears to cancel all previous emotional connections and attachments.

OLD HABITS

THE BOAT HOUSE

The Boat House was full of what Ben thought of as "fancy food". He couldn't believe the delicious things he found like sardines, caviar and oysters, all the wine (of which they only took one bottle), crackers, tuna and cheese that hadn't been covered in mold yet. He felt greedy in the Boat House and he found ways to stuff more into his backpack and the pockets of his cargo pants. He also took a few books from the library including Walden by Thoreau and The Road by Cormack McCarthy. It didn't make a dent in the collection. The previous residents must have owned around four hundred books. Ben didn't think it made much sense why the owners of the house chose this area or this neighborhood to reside. Their tastes and income level were above those around them. But the spoils in his pockets made him happy they had settled there.

Molly was uncomfortable in the Boat House. The stuffy décor, the unused formal living room, and the expensive china, it all reminded her of her parents. They were a well-off and selfish couple with no time or money for her, even when she was very young. They lived across Lake Washington in Bellevue, an affluent city. She wondered briefly if they might be alive but she knew they couldn't cook for themselves and they would die if the water stopped running.

Molly, Ben and Vaughn spent only a short time in the house as most of what they found lacked any nutrition.

Vaughn led them back outside to the boat that was parked in the driveway.

"There are more valuable supplies in there. Molly, I want you to climb up and grab the first aid kid, the flare gun, and all the food you can find. Ben and I will stay down here and keep guard." Molly hesitantly did as Vaughn asked. He stared at her ass as she climbed the side of the boat.

Inside and alone for a minute, Molly sat down and did nothing. It was a lovely feeling to be alone. No mother and child to watch, no others to answer to. She felt tired from the long walk and lack of food in her stomach. Mostly she felt drained from putting up with Vaughn's company. She dug around in the cabinets of the boat and found a huge stash of food.

"They think a tiny girl like me can move around this much and not eat a thing?" she said to the darkness of the inside of the boat. She looked at the cans of food and carefully selected three to eat. They all had pop-top lids, which made it quick for her. Three cans turned into five, which turned into eight. Finally she had to stop herself because she knew Ben and Vaughn would grow suspicious of the time it was taking her. She found a flashlight and the first aid kit and flare gun that Vaughn asked for. She loaded some food into a sack she found on the floor and climbed back into the daylight.

"Sorry it took so long. There had to be like, fifty cabinets to look through." She smiled and hoped she didn't have any food stuck in her teeth.

UPS

The yard of UPS was pleasantly manicured and a wind chime played a calming song with the help of a gentle breeze that was swirling around the cul-de-sac. Vaughn walked by the abandoned UPS truck at the house's curb and made a muttered alteration to an old postal service motto:

"Come rain, snow, sleet, shine, or zombie Armageddon . . ." He chuckled to himself.

"Don't you think we should look inside here?" Ben said as he slapped the side of the giant brown vehicle.

"Haven't you seen the movie *Castaway*? No one ever mails useful stuff," Molly said.

"We can take a peek I guess and a break more importantly. Climb in everyone." Vaughn walked back to the rear door of the truck and opened it. Molly feared that the missing deliveryman would be inside but the back was half full with undelivered packages and space for them to sit.

Inside, they closed the door and rested their feet. Molly didn't have any more room for food but she politely accepted a small can of fruit. Ben opened a bottle of water and took out one of his novels to browse. Vaughn produced a can of beer from somewhere and started opening packages with a pocketknife, stopping every so often to drink.

"We could use these!" Vaughn exclaimed after sorting through nearly fifteen useless mail items. Ben looked up from his novel to see what had excited Tom so much.

"Walkie-talkies? We don't go anywhere and they make too much noise." Ben was disappointed that it wasn't something better.

"Come on. Didn't you want some as a kid? These were supposed to be for someone named Brian on his 10th birthday, according to the card." Vaughn chucked the card to the opposite corner, turned both the walkies on and tossed one to Ben. "Happy Birthday Brian!" Vaughn yelled happily into the walkie mic and it came out loudly in the speaker of Ben's.

Thump.

The three of them jumped. Something had hit the side of the UPS vehicle. Ben held a finger up to his lips. "Shhh," he said. He clicked off the walkie-talkie. Vaughn did the same. The back of the vehicle was windowless making it difficult to determine what or who was on the other side of the thin brown metal. Vaughn pointed to the cab of the truck and made his way slowly forward until he had a view of the side mirrors. A single zombie was hanging out by the truck, drawn by the noise from inside their rest area.

"I'm going to make some noise on the back right corner of the truck and you guys can exit through the driver's side door. Run straight to the house, the door is unlocked," Vaughn directed them.

Molly climbed to the cab first and waited until she saw the zombie disappear behind the corner of the truck in its pursuit of the source of the noise.

"Go!" Ben whispered from behind her but she sat frozen.

"How can I run outside when one of those things is so close? We should stay put."

"This place is hardly safe. Go or I'll climb over you," Ben said seriously.

"We could drive this thing away and just go back home." Molly had placed her hands on the wheel.

"There aren't any keys Molly." He pointed to the empty ignition.

Molly looked to see that Ben was right. It made her want to cry. She felt sick and wanted to vomit. The weight of the food in her body was really what was bothering her. There would be a bathroom inside the house if she could just get out of the truck. Ben gave her no more time but instead of climbing over her he pushed her out of the door. She tripped when she hit the pavement of the driveway and scraped her knee. Ben was right behind her to pick her up and hustle her to the door.

The door was unlocked, as Vaughn had promised. Ben opened it and they flew inside. He slammed the door closed; not thinking of what trouble the noise could bring them. Molly collapsed in the living room. The carpet she fell on was bright white and it smelled wonderful like it had just been cleaned. The smell of her body, how dirty she had become in the days that had passed since the trouble had started, wafted up to her nose. It made her cringe. Her scraped knee bled lightly onto the pristine expanse of white beneath her.

Ben, in auto mode, cautiously took a look around. Anyone or anything could be in this house if the door was left unlocked. Vaughn had said that the zombies didn't turn doorknobs but Ben could think of several worse things that could. A long, straight hall ran in front of him to the back of the house and the back door; it was open.

"I'm gonna . . . barrrragghhh." Molly vomited on the immaculate floor. "Where the fuck is Vaughn?"

Her chin was covered with her undigested meal and her heart, racing. She was done with politeness. Ben turned back to the front of the house and dared to look through the curtains of the living room window.

"I don't see him anywhere. The door of the truck is open like we left it," Ben said.

"Someone's making noise in the kitchen. Do you hear it?" Molly said quickly, worried that she would barf again.

"Maybe he came in the back. I'll go check it out. Wipe off your face." Ben pointed to some decorative pillows on the couch behind her. Molly picked what she thought was the ugliest one and cleaned her face off on it. She put the pillow on top of the mess she'd made. Before Ben could make it down the hall he saw that someone was coming toward him from the back of the house.

A man, thirty-something and nude except for one dirty sock hanging halfway off his left foot, came stumbling down the wood-floored hall. Ben saw a single bite mark on the man's left shoulder but no other trauma.

"It's not Vaughn, Molly. We have company."

"Who is it?" Molly asked as she stood up. The man emerged from behind the wall and Molly screamed. He whipped his head toward her and jumped over the loveseat between them. She put her bat at his neck but didn't have the strength to hold him away from her. "Help me! Ben!" Stepping backward, she lost her footing on the pillow she'd left on the floor. Ben couldn't shoot the dead man without hitting Molly. He had to wait for the right moment. As she lost her balance, Ben got one clean shot in the man's head.

Molly broke down where she landed. "Is there blood on me, anywhere? Do you think it got in my mouth?" Her face was covered in tears but miraculously, no blood.

"Calm down Molly, you are fine. This carpet is really done for though," Ben joked.

More noise came from the back of the house. Ben aimed his gun and walked partway down the hall.

"Get that shit out of my face," Vaughn said, his mouth stuffed with food.

"Where have you been? You left us on our own and Molly was almost bitten. Are you eating? How long have you been in the kitchen?"

"Whoa there. One question at a time," was all Vaughn said in reply.

"Ok. Have you been in the kitchen this entire time?"

"Yes."

"And why didn't you come help us?"

"Field test. I wanted to see if you learned anything."

Vaughn walked up to the corpse and kicked it with his booted foot to make sure it was dead.

"Nice shot, Ben. You passed."

"Passed what?" Molly asked, unsure of what Vaughn was talking about.

"Nothing, Molly," Ben said. "Vaughn, have you searched the kitchen? Anything good?"

"A few things. I've already put them in my pack."

"Let's go then," Ben suggested.

"Hold on. I want to look at his movie collection."

By movie collection Vaughn meant porn. The owner of the house was single and an avid collector like Vaughn. He dug through a pile in a box near the television, selected a few titles, and led the way out the front door. The driveway was clear of any undead. Molly could see the lifeless body of the zombie they had run from lying on the cement near the UPS truck, his skull broken in.

GNOME CITY

The world was full of all kinds of people.

"Be careful in this house." That was all Vaughn had to say about Gnome City, named so due to what Molly counted to be no less than fifty garden gnomes hiding in the overgrown front yard. He could have said a lot more but he knew that they would have to see to believe.

Molly didn't want to vomit for a third time but the inside of the house could easily qualify as an inducer. A hoarder lived there; a woman from what Molly could tell based on the collections. Dust covered dolls and photographs lined shelves on the walls and peeked out of stacked boxes. The air was thick with the stench of old cigarettes and cat urine and the small bits of wall that were visible, once white, were a dingy yellow color.

"How many cats are in here?" Ben asked with amazement and disgust in his voice. He'd stepped over or around five just inside the crowded entryway.

"I think the question is 'how many fleas are in here?'" Vaughn said.

Ben bent down and tucked his pants into his socks. Molly wasn't going to do the same until she actually saw a cat covered in hopping fleas. Her body started to itch so she tucked her pants into her socks. The cats meowed incessantly at their feet and as they jumped from pile to pile.

"They must be hungry," Molly said sadly.

"I don't think there's any cat food in here. We could let them outside," Ben suggested.

"They'll die. The zombies can catch them and it is starting to get cold out there," Molly said.

"They will have a better chance of finding food if they are free and the heat doesn't work in here anyway."

"How about we give them the option and let them decide for their little cat selves?" Vaughn interjected. "After we do what we came in here to do. Follow me into the kitchen."

They slowly made their way in but both Ben and Molly looked confused as to why the kitchen was any more promising than the rest of the house. Mold grew on plates of abandoned food stacked on the dining table. Old magazines and junk mail dated three years ago littered the floor. Cat feces covered everything. Even though they'd already been breathing the vile air, the state of the kitchen encouraged the donning of their dust masks.

"Why'd we come in here? This place is disgusting." Molly tried her best to enunciate through the thick mask. "You should have put an X on this house."

"Look in the pantry," Vaughn explained, pointing to a wooden door set in one of the walls, "this lady collected food too."

Ben walked to the door but from the outside it looked like a closet not a pantry. He opened it after much negotiating with the piles of garbage on the floor that blocked its outward swing.

"Wow! The plastic bins are going to be full!" he yelled through his own mask. A room ten feet deep and eight feet high and full of shelves was revealed to him. The shelves were chock full of canned and dried food. He set to grabbing all he set his eyes upon but Vaughn grabbed his shoulder.

"We can't take most of it. You've got to take the time to read the expiration dates. Some of the cans date back to the nineties. If you can't find a date or if the can is damaged leave it, or it might kill you or someone else."

"Was she hoarding for Y2K?" Molly joked as she found a can with an expiration date of just after the non-event.

"Or a zombie apocalypse?" Ben added.

"I'm guessing something religious. You should see her bedroom." Vaughn said.

"Where is she?" Molly asked.

Vaughn led them to the woman's bedroom. The walls were tinged with the same dirty yellow from tobacco smoke but they were covered with pictures of Jesus. Molly even spotted a black Jesus and a female version of the savior. In the middle of the room was a bed with a cat-covered corpse on it.

"Oh my god, if she had all that food why didn't she survive?" Molly asked.

"She starved to death in her bedroom, clutching some meaningless piece of newspaper and sitting in her own filth. I found her sitting there and she didn't even get up to try and bite me. The most pitiful thing I've ever seen. She wasn't even good at being a zombie. I shot her just in case she might decide to get up." Vaughn explained.

"It seems like such a waste that she kept all that food only to starve a room away." Molly reflected on the woman's obsessive life.

"No waste. *We're* going to eat it. She helped us!" Ben side brightly.

"Thank you hoarding cat lady," Vaughn said as he bowed to the dead woman.

They returned to the kitchen and went to the task of carefully sorting the food into an edible and un-edible pile. They packed the plastic bins full and stacked them neatly on the hand truck. As they left Gnome City they left the front door open for the cats. Some followed them as they walked to the center of the cul-de-sac; others stayed behind, pulling deeper into the hoarded house, preferring the chaos of home to that of the outside world.

"We'll have to come back," Vaughn said as he looked at the sky. "We don't have enough daylight or any more room to carry back food from the other two houses. But we did well."

NO BLOOD ON OUR HANDS

"Pack it all up. She doesn't need to be here when this happens and it has to happen," Isobel said as she stood in the living room of Molly and Jill's place with Edward and Moira. She was trying to sound strong and say all she needed to before she started to cry. "Pick up anything that belonged to the Coopers."

"We can take it back upstairs to their apartment," Edward said. "No point in throwing it out when there is already a place for storing it."

"It's such a sad thing. They were on the verge of being a family and now they are just boxes of stuff. I hope that isn't our fate," Moira said solemnly. She was taking the time to fold the baby clothes individually as though another child might use them someday.

"A mother's love knows no bounds. That baby only lived days! Has it even been a week since she was born?" Edward's mind worked at processing the loss as his body worked at breaking down the crib.

"I don't think we should talk about it. We just need to clean up what is left and think about how we are going to tell Molly."

An hour later, the scavenging party returned. Rob hastily hoisted their loot up to Isobel's apartment on the second floor with a rope as the group climbed the fire ladder. Molly ascended first.

"Isobel you don't know how happy I am to see you!" Molly exclaimed as she embraced Isobel in a tight hug. Isobel started to cry from the loving contact of another. Molly pulled away to look at Isobel's face.

"What's wrong? Hey, don't cry. We made it back safe and we got a lot of food. Everything's going to be ok. I even found some baby stuff for Annabella." Molly dug around in her backpack and produced a doll from an interior pocket. Isobel took the doll from her. Edward cleared his throat. They had wanted to wait to tell Molly. They wanted to give her a little bit of time to relax from the trip she'd just had.

"Why is everyone so quiet? Where are they? Where are Jill and the baby?" Molly's voice escalated to a panicked yell. She ran out of Isobel's apartment and down the hall to 204. Isobel followed her out and found her standing in the doorway taking in the emptiness of the apartment.

"She did it, didn't she?" Molly asked quietly, though she didn't need an answer to know that it was true.

Isobel nodded anyway and they stood silently next to one another for a while. Molly didn't want to know the details, didn't need to know them. She could envision without aid the terrible event.

"Thank you for cleaning up her stuff. I don't think I could have done that."

"Sure," Isobel said. She gave Molly a quick hug, returned the doll to her, and went back to her own apartment to sort food with Ben.

"Edward told me what happened. Do you think Molly will be ok?" Ben said as he wiped off cans and sorted them by fruit, vegetable or protein.

"Who knows? We'll all miss them but we can't burden ourselves with this. The blame lies with them. They wanted out and that got Austin killed," Isobel said.

"And Jill couldn't live without him and that got her and the baby killed," Ben finished the summary of the Coopers' final days. "You're right. They weren't our responsibility. People will do what they want when it comes down to it."

"Plus, that's two less mouths to feed," Vaughn said as he and Rob came in from the balcony, finally finished with hauling up the bins.

BEST BEFORE . . .

They were well stocked once more. Molly, Ben and Vaughn had procured more cans and boxes of non-perishables than they thought. Isobel stared at the food, neatly sorted and stacked. They brought back albacore tuna, soups, granola bars, sardines, corn, beans, and peas, rice and beans, fruit cups, nuts, powdered milk, and oatmeal, chili, smoked salmon, crackers and more. She dreamed of meals to come.

"Ben, I want your help to devise a rationing system," Isobel said quietly. "I don't think we should involve the others in the decision making process. Let's just figure it out and make sure everyone abides by it."

"Don't you think we're going to piss a few people off?"

"The only person I care about pissing off, other than you, is Vaughn and he has his own food," She replied.

Isobel thought about how much each can held and how many people that meant it could feed.

"Large cans of vegetables and fruit will be divided between 2-3 people. When we have the right ingredients we can make a large pot of a stew or soup and share it with the whole group."

"And no second serving until everyone has eaten," Ben suggested.

"Right. Also, we should make a sign out sheet for when people don't eat with the group. They can mark off what they took and what meal they took it for."

"I don't think anyone will like doing that. It's one step short of having meal tickets," Ben said, thinking deeply. "We could just give food out in two day increments and have one or two meals a week that are group meals."

"Maybe a few more group meals would be better to conserve the propane for the camp stoves."

"Oh shit!" Ben said, a light going off in his head.

"What?" Isobel asked.

"We spent all this time stacking the food and we didn't organize the new stuff by expiration date."

"It's late. We can do it tomorrow," she sighed.

SANITATION

Markus and Jeff, both normally clean and well groomed, had started to notice that the other was looking particularly bear like. It wasn't the hair that was the problem for two men living together in abnormal conditions, it was the body odor.

"You smell like death," Markus told Jeff as they drank reconstituted powdered milk mixed with chocolate breakfast shake powder.

Jeff lifted his arm and sniffed. "It's the scent of the wild; the essence of man. I'm returning to my roots."

"Well it's making me sick. Can you evolve a little and go take a shower on the roof?" Markus asked over his glass.

"Hey now, I just have to take this moment to mention that you also smell like death, and *look* a little like it too. Care to join me?" Jeff shot back.

"I'll heat up some water," Markus said through an overly pouted lip. He knew he smelled disgusting. He could feel the thick layer of muck on his skin.

Fifteen minutes later, a bucket of warm water in tow, the two men climbed the stairs to the roof.

"This is going to feel great!" Jeff said as he tossed a bar of soap into the air and caught it as it fell. He saw a flick of movement near the camp shower and he tensed. "You don't think one of those things could get up here, do you?"

"Don't be silly. We barely made it up the last flight of stairs."

"I just saw . . . " Jeff stopped as his eyes rested on the source of the movement.

"Hey!" Molly yelled. She was completely naked and soapy and barely hidden behind the curtain they'd poorly rigged for privacy.

"Sorry about that! We didn't know anyone was up here!" Markus yelled back as he covered Jeff's eyes playfully.

"We'll wait over here," Jeff pointed back towards the door to the stairs. "Take your time."

Markus and Jeff sat down on the cool rooftop and watched as their bucket of warm water lost heat to the fall air. Not five minutes passed before the door squeaked open.

"Oh, hi guys!" Rob said happily. He and Gabe had emerged from the roof access door with towels, shampoo, and their own bucket of steaming water.

"Doesn't anyone use baby wipes for a bath anymore?" Jeff asked concerned about the line that was forming for the camp shower.

"I'm not a baby!" Gabe yelled and then quickly went to hide behind his father.

"We know that Gabe," Rob consoled his son. "Hey, I think Thursday might be the official shower day."

"Is it Thursday?" Jeff asked as he looked at his watch. The battery had died a week before and he'd been meaning to ask Vaughn to find him a replacement.

"I don't know. It just feels like a Thursday. So, who prompted the shower excursion?" Rob asked the two of them.

"Markus reeks," Jeff said, laughing.

Markus sneered at him. "He who smelt it dealt it. What about you guys? You look clean enough."

"I found Gabe in our bathroom covered head to toe in hand sanitizer. He had the right idea but that gel didn't do much. He was so dirty I think all it did was move the dirt around."

"He does look a shade or two darker, now that you mention it," Jeff said.

"It's my Indian tan," Gabe said proudly.

"Love it while it lasts. You are going to be pale as a ghost after you are clean," Rob teased.

"Jeff, Markus, you guys are up," Molly said as she walked quickly past the group of men, a towel wrapped tightly around her head and one around her body. She hadn't shaved her legs in a long time and she didn't want them to make jokes about it. She was able to make it back into the stairwell without a sideways glance at her unsightly lower limbs.

"Gabe, let's go wait inside. It's cold out here," Rob said shivering.

"I'll carry the bucket!" Gabe yelled.

"It's heavier than you. I've got it." Rob opened the door for his son, lifted the bucket and followed him into the building.

"I love hot water," Jeff said. As he showered he was reminded of his wife. "You know, Sheila would always cut my showers short. I got seven minutes exactly. She had a schedule for everything."

"You can spend as much time as you want in there," Markus said. He meant that, especially because he could see Jeff's nakedness through a rip in the plastic curtain. *What would happen if I jumped in there right now?* He wondered. The urge was strong but he didn't want to force himself on Jeff.

"Can you believe this?" Jeff asked as he stepped out of the shower, flashing his flaccid penis at Markus.

"What? Mine's that small too when it's soft," Markus commented.

"Not my cock! Look at all this hair!" Jeff pointed to his pubic hair which, unmanaged, had blossomed into a jungle.

"Oh. Yeah. That is kind of crazy," Markus laughed.

"It looks like your beard," Jeff played.

"Did you just compare my finely coifed facial fuzz to your deathtrap Amazon pubic poof? Are there monkeys living in there?"

Jeff rushed at him and embraced him. He pressed his body against him; his lips into Markus's in a passionate kiss. He had wanted this to happen. He had lain awake at night hoping for this closeness.

"I want this too," Markus said as though reading Jeff's thoughts. "But let me shower first."

FINDERS KEEPERS

Vaughn was happy to be outside without anyone else to look out for. He had no particular reason to be out there so he was just puttering from house to house, finding more of the same thing. He had a good memory for how he'd left a house, when he'd left it. Whether the door was locked, the blinds open or closed, cupboards full or empty. Today he noticed that someone had drawn the curtains of a house just two blocks from Willow Brook.

"Exciting!" he said to himself as he slowly opened the front door to find out who it was.

The first floor was empty but there were muddy shoe prints in the entry and leading up the light carpet of the stairwell to the second floor. He walked carefully, unsure of where any creaking floorboards might lie. The last thing he wanted to do was alert the person to his presence. He came to a closed door; the only closed one in the hallway. He wasn't expecting to see what he saw after opening the door. A young girl, a teen, was asleep on the bed; her belongings lay in a pile next to it.

He watched her for a while. No one was around and that instantly aroused him. She was here for the taking but he had a better plan. He had to fight hard to keep himself from touching her as he found a piece of paper to write a note that would change both of their lives.

HAYDEN

She woke up just after noon. The room she was staying in was unfamiliar but even more so now for there was a smell to it that hadn't been there when she'd fallen asleep; cigarettes and leather. It smelled like a man.

She jumped out of the bed and backed into the far corner from the door, tripping over her bag as she moved. A piece of paper slid gently to the floor. Someone had been here but, judging by the note, had already left. She relaxed a little as she read:

I found you here and I didn't want to disturb you. You looked like you could use the sleep. There's a whole group of survivors living just up the road, there is even another kid but he is a lot younger than you. We have food and secure shelter. There isn't an easy way in though; you'll have to get their attention. They will be more likely to let you stay if you don't mention this note. I live on the third floor if you want to say hi when you get here. The place is called Willow Brook.

-Tom

She smiled. Her luck hadn't been this good and though she wasn't looking forward to going back outside she knew it was the only hope she had of survival.

LOVE IN THE DEAD AIR

Rob watched Molly and Gabe as they played together. Things felt great now that no one was worrying about the baby or the food. Everything was in its place and life, or a semblance of it, could go on inside Willow Brook.

"Molly, I'm going to visit Isobel and Ben for a sec, do you two need anything?" Rob asked in a voice he hoped didn't sound condescending.

Molly looked up and smiled. "I think we have everything we need."

Rob found Isobel and Ben eating a late breakfast in their apartment. "Am I interrupting?"

"Not at all. Do you want some coffee?" Ben asked.

"That would be great," Rob said as he sat down on the couch that doubled as Ben's bed.

"We even have some little creamer cups that haven't gone bad. I don't know where Molly found them but you should thank her," Isobel said, standing up to prepare him a cup since Ben hadn't moved.

"I'll remember to do that."

"So what's on your mind that you've decided to stop by?" Isobel asked as she set his coffee down on the table in front of him.

"Well, instead of gathering every time something goes wrong I thought I would stop by when things were calm for a change; just as a neighbor and not a co-survivor."

"Don't get too comfortable. You never know what's going to happen," Ben said.

"Of *that* you are right. But, I really think things will settle down," Rob sighed and sipped his coffee, "or maybe I mean that I don't see what could go wrong next."

"The dead are walking so anything is possible. Things we can't even begin to prepare ourselves for could be in the works for us right now," Isobel said ominously, but laughed.

"You might not be prepared for this but, I've been hearing some . . . ahem . . . strange noises from the Brown-Newsom residence next door."

"Really? Are you sure?" Ben asked.

"Yep. Last night and this morning. I don't like to gossip but I think Jeff and Markus have really hit it off," Rob made an obscene gesture with his hand.

"Rob!" Isobel yelled.

"Gabe isn't here and I had to make sure you understood what I meant," Rob laughed.

"Jeff has been emotionally and probably physically abused by Sheila for years. It's possible that Jeff has turned to Markus for comfort and affection. I think it's great. Jeff deserves some happiness. We all do," Ben said, looking to Isobel. She didn't look back.

"He definitely has something to be happy about. He is the only one of us getting laid. They got so loud the other night that Gabe heard them and ran scared into my room thinking that zombies had broken into the building."

Isobel smiled. "I don't even want to know what you told him."

"Sometimes men love men. That is all I had to say. Now this morning he has a gay Lego couple running a restaurant. He's pretty open-minded."

"Yeah, he's a good kid. Pretty resilient in all of this too it seems," Ben said.

"He's playing tough for me. I do the same for him. We are tricking one another. Looks like we fooled you too."

TEEN SPIRIT

Gabe was playing near the window and watching the rain start when he saw a girl run by. She looked different than the monsters to him. She was faster and looked scared.

"Molly, there's someone out there," Gabe said without turning away from the window.

"I know, Gabe, there are a lot of people out there."

"She's different," Gabe clarified.

Molly pulled herself off of the floor where she'd been sitting surrounded by toys and went to the window. Gabe was right. A teenage girl was running back and forth in the street in front of Willow Brook, screaming. Her brown hair was greasy and stringy, her clothes and face smudged with dirt, her adolescent form worryingly thin. She was running around so much that she looked on the verge of fainting.

"How does she know we are here?" Molly asked aloud. "Come on Gabe. Let's go to Isobel's and tell the others."

Gabe smiled and followed Molly happily. He liked being included in the adult stuff sometimes.

"Can you hear me? Let me in!" Hayden yelled but she wasn't seeing any movement in the building. She was growing weak from the exertion but she couldn't stop; the dead would get her. She saw the convenience store on the corner. She ran around the backside of it and managed to climb up to the roof. She was trying to make herself more visible. Her throat hurt from yelling but she still couldn't see anyone responding to her pleas. *Maybe I have the wrong building?* She thought to herself. She pulled the note back out and reread it.

"Help me!" she yelled. She wanted to yell for Tom, the man who had left the note but she could tell from what he wrote that it wouldn't be a good idea. A massive crowd of the dead milled around at the foot of the store. They had smashed in the entire glass front of it; tabloids and candy bars littered the entry. She listened to the crunching of the wrappers and the horrible sounds of the dead as she sat in the rain, shivering and waiting for a response.

Isobel, Ben and Rob went to the windows of 205 at Molly and Gabe's request. They could all see the girl, perched on the edge of the roof, soaked to her bones by the falling rain. The hands of the dead reaching into the air trying to grip her ankles or anything else they might get a hold of. Occasionally she would yell something and wave her arms.

"How does she know we are here?" Isobel asked.

"That's what I was wondering," Molly said.

"We can find that out later. What we need to decide is whether or not we can help her," Rob said.

"We have room since, well, since Jill and the baby, you know . . ." Ben couldn't finish his sentence, but he didn't need to.

"Does she look like she could have been bitten? We can't let her in if she is going to expose us," Molly said.

"I can't tell from here. I think it's a risk we'll have to take. We can quarantine her or something, right?" Isobel looked to the group for some sort of agreement. Everyone nodded but Isobel was unsure of the next step. "How are we going to do this then?"

"I'm going to ask Vaughn if he has a megaphone. We need her to stop yelling. She'll be lucky to get off that roof with all the dead that she's brought here," Ben said.

OUR OWN LITTLE WORLD

Markus and Jeff had spent the last day in bed together. They could hear the yelling from outside but they didn't want to move.

"Isobel will take care of it, whatever it is. She always does," Markus said.

Jeff lay next to him, feeling happy and safe. He held a fear in him that Markus wouldn't stay with him if he knew what happened to Sheila.

"Do you ever think about leaving?" he asked.

"Sure. All the time. It isn't that bad here but I miss my friends and I wonder if they have survived. What about you?"

"I think we should leave together. We could start a life together; make our own rules."

"Sounds nice," Markus said as he turned to face Jeff and threw an arm over him.

ACCORDING TO PLAN

Vaughn had been watching the goings on from the Coopers' old apartment. He could see the girl clearly through a set of binoculars he'd brought over from his apartment. The rainwater had washed the dirt from her face and wetted down her dirty hair, giving the illusion that she had just taken a shower. It had also made her thin shirt almost disappear as it stuck to her skin. Vaughn couldn't believe she'd taken his advice from the note. He was about to unzip his pants and enjoy the view when he heard someone knocking on his door across the hall.

He looked out the peephole of the Coopers' door. "I'm over here," he said as he opened the door to Ben.

Ben came into Jill and Austin's old apartment slowly. "What are you doing here?" he asked, unable to hide the suspicion in his voice.

"I was outside earlier and I heard that girl over there so I came over here to see what was going on. That's all," Vaughn said as he lifted the binoculars to prove his story true.

"Oh. Ok. We could use those and a megaphone if you happen to have one. I'm going to get her."

"Do you think that's a good idea?" Vaughn asked, trying to hide that he thought it was a fantastic one.

"We've already decided it's the right thing to do. Will you help or not?" Ben asked in a rushed way.

"Sure," Vaughn took off the binoculars and handed them to Ben who followed him to his apartment for the megaphone. Vaughn could barely hide his smile.

SHELTER

Hayden was really starting to feel the chill in her bones. She had a sweater in her bag but it wouldn't do her any good. She and the bag were soaking wet. She hadn't taken her eyes off of the building and she thought she'd seen people gathering at one of the windows on the second floor. The sliding glass door of that same apartment opened and someone came out onto the balcony, raising something large up to their face. Hayden jumped up and started to wave her arms. She moved as much as her fatigued and cold body allowed, splashing in the puddles that had grown on the convenience store roof.

"Save your energy. We see you," a woman's voice reached her easily with the amplification of a megaphone. The zombies below turned and started toward the apartment building. "We are sending a man named Ben down to get you. I need you to do what I say and do it quickly. Wave your left arm if you can do that for me."

The woman's voice was stern but there was kindness in it. Hayden did as she was asked and waved her left arm.

"Don't make any noise. We have to draw them away from you and the only way that will work is if you keep absolutely quiet. Wave your arm again if you understand."

Again Hayden did as she was asked.

"Pick up your stuff and get ready to climb back down. I'm going to keep talking in this thing to keep them distracted," Isobel explained.

Hayden picked up her rain-soaked bag; put her hair in the one rubber band she had and waited for the cue to descend the ladder. Ben climbed down a fire escape on the other side of the building and ran in a large circle behind the office building across the street.

"Climb down to the street when the last of the dead have reached the intersection. Then run behind the office building over there," Isobel pointed with the megaphone to the building that Ben had run behind. "Ben will meet you on the other side. Stay close to him and do what he says."

The last of the zombies, a little boy with a hole in his chest, reached the intersection on their track toward Isobel's voice. Hayden climbed down from her temporary refuge on the rooftop and made her way behind the office building to safety.

LET IT ALL OUT

"Come on you beasts, the freshest meat's in here! I've never felt more desired in my life and I haven't showered in weeks. Aren't you sick of eating the homeless cats covered in fleas? Don't you want to bite into something with a bit less hair?" Isobel screamed into the megaphone. It felt great to yell at them and see them react from a safe distance. Isobel was revving up to say some more when Moira appeared out of nowhere and grabbed the megaphone from her. She had a few things to say to them too.

"Or would you like some aged meat better? You have ruined my retirement you mindless ghouls! Devoured the whole of my knitting circle and slaughtered the pharmacist. You make me want to kill and that . . . frightens . . . me . . ." Moira broke into a heavy sob. Edward, as though that sob was a summoning bell, had arrived to carry her off in a loving hug back to their apartment and a cup of tea.

Isobel raised the megaphone up to her mouth once more and was about to begin another tirade when Ben opened her apartment door. Behind him the teenager stood, wet and shaking but smiling from ear to ear.

"She looks a little crazy," Rob whispered to Isobel.

"She's just in shock," Isobel whispered back. "Molly, can you take her in the bathroom and help her get cleaned up?"

"Um . . . ok," Molly thought too that the girl looked a little psychotic with the grin she was wearing and she wasn't sure why she had to be the one to tend to her.

"I'll get some extra towels and some dry clothes for her," Isobel said as she went into her bedroom.

Rob and Ben sat down and waited anxiously. It was exhilarating to meet someone new when you'd seen the same faces for weeks.

CRASH COURSE

"So what's your name?" Molly asked as she hastily undressed the tense girl. She tossed the dirty and dripping wet clothes into the sink.

"My name is Hayden," She said quietly, embarrassed to be near nude in front of a stranger.

"Well Hayden, since we are alone right now, let me tell you a few things about life here," Molly felt compelled to influence the girl since she figured the others would make her share her apartment again.

"It can't be worse than out there," she said.

"True. But still, you should know a thing or two. First, they are Nazis about the food and it is controlled and rationed. Don't eat more than your share. I learned that the hard way. Second, no one is in charge but there are a couple of people who act like they are."

Molly picked up a bottle of shampoo and started to scrub a week's worth of dirt out of Hayden's hair.

"Who?" Hayden asked. She wanted to suggest Tom, so she could find out more about him, but she knew it wasn't a good idea

"Isobel, the one on the megaphone, is nice enough but she kind of runs the show with Ben, the guy who brought you in."

"They seem like good people to me," Hayden said.

"Just don't be surprised if they try to tell you how to act," Molly warned as she finished shampooing Hayden's hair and rinsed it with bottled water.

"Ok, anything else I should know?" Hayden asked as she dried her hair with a towel.

"Use these baby wipes and disinfectant soap to wipe off the rest of your body," Molly showed her what she meant. "It's our version of a shower when we can't use the camp shower on the roof. We brush our teeth with bottled water."

"But the water and electricity still work. Why don't you use them?"

"They aren't reliable and we could lose them at any time. Also, we aren't quite sure about the quality of the water. We don't want to get sick. So, we decided to switch to the backup system. We'd have to eventually anyway," Molly said.

"I drink the water all the time and I'm not sick, but whatever. Anybody else I should know about?" Hayden pushed for more information, hoping the note writer Tom would come up in the conversation.

"Everyone is pretty harmless but there is a guy on the third floor that you should watch out for. His name is Tom Vaughn, but he goes by Vaughn."

Hayden's heart beat a little bit faster at the mention of his name. She thought it strange that he would sign the note 'Tom' instead of 'Vaughn' if what Molly said was true. "What's so bad about him?" Hayden asked innocently.

"Everything," Molly answered. A knock came on the bathroom door. Isobel opened it and brought in another towel for Hayden's body as well as some clean clothes.

"Did you check her for injuries?" Isobel asked politely, avoiding any reference to bite wounds.

"I didn't see any. She's clean and free of infection."

"And her name is?" Isobel asked Molly.

"My name is Hayden," Hayden responded, annoyed by Isobel talking as though she wasn't there.

"Well, Hayden, if you could get dressed and come meet the others I think that would be great."

"Yes, ma'am," Hayden responded.

Molly could hear a hint of sarcasm in Hayden's voice and it made her smile.

Fifteen minutes had passed since Molly and Hayden had entered the bathroom. When they emerged, Rob, Ben, and the other residents who had come to meet her, could not believe what they saw. A beautiful teen, although slightly emaciated, stood before them. All that time without a proper diet had almost killed her.

"I didn't find any wounds. No bites, no cuts and she scrubbed her skin with disinfectant soap. I think she is healthy," Molly updated everyone.

"Hi," Hayden said shyly.

All the residents started to ask her questions at the same time.

"Don't overwhelm her," Isobel stopped the barrage of questions. "Hayden, how old are you and where did you come from?"

"I'm sixteen and I lived in Maple Leaf."

"What happened to your family?" Ben asked.

"My parents died on the second day so I've been alone ever since. I tried to make it to the houses of friends and I did but most of them were dead before I got there," She started to cry and Molly put an arm around her. "I spent nights in abandoned houses. I decided to try one more friend; he and his dad were still alive but my friend got attacked and was dying. I left there two days ago. I haven't had much luck since then with food because the dead are everywhere. I've had to keep running."

"How did you know we were here?" Rob asked.

Hayden hesitated. She couldn't tell them about waking up and smelling Tom, finding his note. "I saw candles burning in your building last night so I knew you were alive in here," She gestured around the room. "It looks like you have it pretty good."

"Don't be deceived. We've had our share of tragedy," Molly said solemnly.

"I'm sorry," Hayden said.

"We all are; and sorry for your losses as well," Isobel said. "We'd like to invite you to stay if it would suit you."

"I'd love that. Thank you all. You saved my life."

"Where will she stay?" Molly asked.

Isobel smiled at Molly, volunteering her recently vacated second bedroom.

"I'll show you to our apartment then. Come on," Molly said to Hayden.

APPEARANCES

Vaughn was waiting upstairs. He had cleaned up his apartment, washed up, and had just one beer to relax. He sat on his couch and looked at a tabloid magazine he had picked up. The group had taken the girl in as he knew they would, now all he had to do was give her everything she wanted so he could get the one thing he needed.

"Play it cool," He told himself.

FIRST IMPRESSIONS

Hayden was settled in to her new place on Molly's couch but very eager to meet Tom, who had been kind enough to leave her peacefully sleeping and to offer her this refuge. She couldn't find a moment of rest from all the residents. She went from loneliness and desperation to an overload of attention. She finally had to ask for some time alone.

"I was thinking about taking a walk upstairs to check out the rationing system," she lied. It had now been three hours since she'd climbed the fire ladder. She was clean, dry and well fed. It was time to meet Tom.

"Can I go with her dad?" Gabe asked Rob pleadingly.

"I'd rather go alone. I'm feeling a little overwhelmed."

"Are there any boy kids out there?" Gabe asked her as she walked away from him.

"I didn't see any. I'm sorry. I can play a game with you sometime if you want," she offered.

"It's not the same," he said unhappily.

Hayden felt nervous. Her heart was beating as she envisioned a handsome twenty-something greeting her at his doorway. She reached the top of the stairwell and stopped. The hallway here looked exactly the same as the one below. Six doors to six different apartments spread at perfect interval down the hall.

"Which one?" She asked herself aloud.

"Hey, I'm down here," a strong voice said from the end of the hall. "You made it."

"Tom?"

"Yeah. But I prefer Vaughn."

A MINOR ISSUE

Molly awoke to the sound of things falling off the bathroom counter. The apartment was dark, which was frightening to her, but she knew it could only be one person.

"Hayden?" Molly asked as she pulled her blanket tightly around her and walked slowly across her bedroom.

"Wha? I wasss jus brussing mah teef," she slurred loudly and fell onto the floor of the bathroom with a thud. Molly shone a flashlight down on the girl. Hayden had toothpaste all over her face and she had her bra in her hand. The entire bathroom smelled of whiskey.

"Where did you get alcohol?" Molly asked, sounding more motherly than she intended. She knew there wasn't any in her apartment.

"T- um . . . Vaughn. We hat a parrrrrtty an we drank and ffffucked. It wasss niccce," Hayden tried to stand up again but was unsuccessful.

"Oh no," she said; the only clear words out of her mouth. She puked on Molly's feet and the area rug near the sink.

"Fuck," Molly said as she reached in the dark for a towel. "Did you say you guys had sex?"

"Hmmm?" Hayden asked before she passed out on the floor.

Molly had no choice but to clean the girl up. She cursed to herself the entire time especially as she carried, half-dragged, Hayden to the bed in the second bedroom.

THE MORNING AFTER

Molly woke up early and went to see Isobel before even eating. She didn't think Isobel would be awake yet but she planned on waking her if that was the case. She knocked twice on the door of 205 and Ben answered, looking confused.

"What's going on?" he asked as he rubbed the sleep from his eyes.

"I need to talk to Isobel about something. Let me in." Molly pushed the door open, walked passed a still groggy Ben, and went all the way down the apartment's interior hall to Isobel's bedroom door.

"Isobel, wake up! We have to talk!" Molly yelled through the thin wood of the door.

The door opened and Isobel stood in a matching pajama and bathrobe set. She didn't look happy to see Molly.

"Can this wait until after I eat?" Isobel asked through a yawn.

"No. I haven't eaten either. That girl we let in is trouble."

"What? Already? You told me she was free of wounds. She seemed nice and appreciative of our help. What could *possibly* be the problem?" Isobel looked annoyed, like maybe she thought Molly was overreacting.

"She left my apartment last night at some point, I don't know when. That doesn't matter. When she came back she was drunk and holding her bra. She said some incoherent stuff about Vaughn."

"You think he gave her alcohol?" Isobel took Molly more seriously the second she heard the name Vaughn.

"He gave her a lot more than that. She said they had sex."

Isobel was making Molly walk toward the kitchen as they talked. She dragged her slippers along the carpet which made Molly feel that under Isobel's leadership, she was a lazy person.

"She's a minor. That's illegal," Isobel said as she poured a bottle of water into a pot to heat water for coffee.

"That's my point!"

"How did they meet? He never comes downstairs," Isobel wanted as much information as she could gather.

"I'm not sure how she came to meet him."

"Was she upset when she told you?"

"Nope. Happy as a clam. Drunk as a skunk."

"Is she awake yet?" Isobel asked.

"No, no. I think she'll be sleeping a bit late today. She really was a mess last night," Molly said, thinking back to the vomit on her feet.

"Well, what do you think we should do?" Isobel asked with a hint of exasperation as though the conversation was going nowhere.

"If her parents were alive they wouldn't allow it," Molly said assuredly.

"But they aren't alive and one could hardly expect a girl of her age to listen to a group of strangers," Isobel pointed out.

"I'll talk to her myself then," Molly huffed. She had wanted Isobel's strong support but she seemed uninterested in taking up the battle.

"It's up to Hayden to decide how she fits in our family," Ben said from the living room.

"He could have drugged her and raped her!" Molly yelled. She was still reeling from her encounter with Vaughn in the third floor hallway. She knew what he was capable of. She knew the man would do whatever it took to get what he wanted.

CAREFUL CONFRONTATION

Back in her apartment, Molly fixed herself breakfast. She grudgingly saved some for Hayden, whom she'd lost a bit of respect for. She busied herself with an old magazine while she waited for Hayden to rise from the dead.

Hayden awoke and went straight to the bathroom. To Molly it sounded as though she brushed her teeth at least three times. When Hayden came into the living room she was holding her head and walking slowly.

"Uuugh. Is this what a hangover feels like?" Hayden asked as she fell onto the couch.

"Never been drunk before?"

"I have but I've never had a hangover. Tom gave me something strong." Hayden leaned forward and laid her head in her lap, relishing the coolness of her legs.

"Probably some kind of whiskey. It's his best friend."

"Oh, do you know him well?" Hayden asked; interested in learning more about the man she'd given all of herself to.

"No!" Molly scoffed. "I was making a joke about his familiarity with alcohol. Why did you go up there after I warned you about him?"

"Why not? He seems like an ok guy to me."

"You don't know him. He's a creep."

"I thought you said you didn't know him well," Hayden countered with a snide smile.

"I know him enough to know that he'll fuck anything with a girl's name if he gets the opportunity."

"He saved my life. I owe him something in return."

"What the *fuck* do you mean by that?" Molly was confused and pissed that there was something more going on that she was unaware of.

Hayden started to pick up some of her things. She looked for her makeup bag, which she had managed to grab and keep with her the entire time she'd been outside.

"I mean if it wasn't for his kindness in telling me about this place I would still be hiding in a cold room without food or weapons, wondering if each day I woke up was going to be the day that I'd die."

"He brought you here?" Molly was baffled. "Where'd you meet him?"

Instead of answering, Hayden opened the small, zippered pouch that held her cosmetics. From it she pulled the scribbled note from Vaughn and handed it to Molly. She read the short note twice, attempting to find some hidden message between the lines.

"He is up to something. The Vaughn I know would have assaulted you in that room and left you to cry yourself to sleep. The bastard brought you here so he could use you. Don't you see that?"

"Maybe I choose not to see it," Hayden shrugged.

"You've been here *one* day and he's already in your pants. That is hard to ignore."

"I'm not stupid if that's what you think and I don't like him. He says he'll get me anything I want from the outside. We have an agreement."

"What out *there* could possibly be worth a minute with that man?" Molly was still having trouble comprehending what she was hearing from the scrawny teenager.

"Soda, makeup, chocolate, magazines. Other things that you guys don't have and probably wouldn't get if I asked for them."

"Those things aren't necessities, Hayden. If you haven't noticed we are trying to survive here! That doesn't leave a lot of room for the fancy stuff."

"I'm sixteen. My needs are different than yours."

"Just don't come to me when you find out that all that matters to Vaughn are needs of his own."

FRESH AIR

Isobel went upstairs to see Vaughn the next day. She wasn't going to bring up the topic of Hayden, as she knew that Molly wanted her to. She was there to ask Vaughn a favor. The building was starting to feel claustrophobic. As each day came to a close it felt as though the walls too were closing in tighter and tighter. Vaughn answered his door after one knock. *Maybe he thinks I'm Hayden,* Isobel thought. *Horny bastard.*

"Hey, Iz!" Vaughn smiled. Isobel was the one woman in the complex, other than Moira, that Vaughn never thought about screwing. Because of that, it was much easier for him to talk to her normally, without distraction. He wasn't sure why he didn't want to dominate her. She seemed to him to be one of the guys, a dominator herself.

"Hi. Are you going out today?" she asked as she walked into his apartment. It smelled like a perfume Hayden had brought in with her.

"Yes I am but not until a bit later in the day. Wanna come?" He wouldn't mind her company out there. She wasn't going to whine like Molly and it didn't hurt to look at her, like Ben.

"I do. I need to get away for a bit. I need to feel alive."

LONELINESS

The day was crisp and clear. A perfect fall day and its afternoon promised more of that perfection. Isobel hadn't given Ben much time alone. He was happy for that. He was able to keep his head from thoughts of Anna. With Isobel making plans with Vaughn he looked for distraction elsewhere. He picked up his acoustic guitar; something that had been spared any blood or brains in his apartment. Today was the first day he strummed its strings and the gentle hum of them overwhelmed him with emotion. He wasn't good at playing anything. He knew a handful of notes, mostly the more sorrowful sounding ones, all of the minors. He closed his eyes and built an image of Anna on the back of his eyelids. He tried to remember her smiling. She could always hear a wrongly played note but she always encouraged him to try again. His goal had been to learn at least one song and play it all the way through for her. "Something I can dance to," was her request.

He imagined that moment; saw her legs moving to a gentle melody produced by his fingers and hard work. He smiled until a wound appeared on her leg that he couldn't imagine away.

Ben stood up and smashed the guitar down on the coffee table. The wood body cracked and splintered. He brought it down again. The neck split. He wanted to see her and hold her again. He felt that he had two choices:

1. Remove the tape of his apartment and bathroom doors. See Anna. Remind him that she was unreachable, untouchable.
2. Pick up his handgun, pull the trigger and hold her again.

He picked up the gun but it didn't feel right to him so he set it back down and walked out of the apartment door. He would mourn her properly, at her side.

"I liked the strumming but that bit at the end, with all the banging, you need to work on that part," Edward laughed. He had entered the hallway at the same time as Ben. He could see the pain on Ben's face. He put a hand on Ben's shoulder. "Something's bothering you. Do you want to talk?"

Ben nodded his head and broke down again.

"Come in and sit with me for awhile," Edward gestured into 206.

"You know she hated me when we first met? It took me three weeks to convince her I was worth talking to," Edward told Ben between drags from his pipe. Moira was sitting in the living room with them but politely minding a crossword puzzle.

"I can't believe that," Ben looked at Moira and caught the tail end of a smile. "You guys are perfect for each other. Anna and I talked about this all the time, you know, growing old together."

"I know you are missing her," Edward pointed at Ben with the end of his pipe. "You carry it around with you and every day without her, it grows heavier on your soul."

"What would you do if something happened to Moira?" Ben asked. "Sorry Moira." He quickly followed.

"That is an important question," Moira looked up at them. "One I would love to know the answer to. Edward?"

"It would pain me, of course. She is a part of me. But we all have to keep living on as long as we can. Fight for our own survival. That is what the ones we love who have passed on would want, right? You'd want me to keep living, Moira, wouldn't you?"

"I would. Besides, I think you'd sooner live without me than you would that pipe of yours. Best to stay alive until you at least run out of tobacco," Moira laughed.

"Bahhh. Can't get a serious answer out of her, ever!"

Ben stayed for hours, delighting in the company of the Cabels. They were right. The best he could do to mourn Anna's loss was to live.

FORMS OF DECAY

Gabe couldn't stop looking out the window. His toys lay abandoned on the living room carpet, his half-consumed lunch sat on the table. The dead were getting grosser and he was fascinated.

"What is that?" Gabe asked his dad.

"What are you looking at now?" Rob said as he pulled himself up off of their overused couch. He joined his son at the window. The glass was grimy and covered in small handprints. "You're going to start cleaning the window, dude."

"Look at that guy! He is super icky! All his skin is gone," Gabe pointed at a bloody corpse that kept walking into things, trees and such. He'd rubbed his own skin off.

Rob's heart sank at the interest in his son's voice. Gabe had always liked worms and dirt. He was a boy after all. But now it sounded like Gabe was developing morbid fascinations. "Do you want to do something else, sport? Maybe we could go on the roof and toss the football or something?"

"Yeah! Let's go to the roof. I can see more from there!" His son jumped away from the window to grab a jacket.

LEFT OUT

"Don't you have a date with Vaughn or something?" Molly asked Hayden. The teen had been getting in her hair all morning; hanging around the shared apartment and singing loudly to pass time.

"He's going out and he doesn't want me to come," Hayden said with as much pout in her voice as a five year old whining over an unshared toy. "He's taking Isobel. I don't know why he'd want to hang out with her. The way she acts, she's practically a dude."

"That is probably why. There is a point when men get sick of women, you know."

"Vaughn will never get sick of this," Hayden ran her hands down her body.

"Gross. Don't talk like that in front of me. What you do with him, I don't want to hear about."

"Yes, ma'am!" Hayden saluted Molly. "But don't you ever want to be adored?"

"He's too busy with his son," Molly regretted divulging her continued interest in Rob to Hayden as soon as it had come out of her mouth.

"Ooooh, you like that Rob guy? I guess he's ok. He looks like my dad. Do you want me to say something to him? I could."

"No, don't say a damn thing!" Molly's cheeks flushed red from embarrassment and anger. "He's made his decision."

"You have to *look* like you want a man. You look like you want a cave to curl up and die in."

"I'm not going to advertise. I'm not a flirt like you."

"You really do have issues, Molly."

"And you don't? I'm trying really hard not to judge you for your choice in men."

"What did he do to you?" Hayden asked bluntly.

Molly was surprised that the teen was smart enough to catch on to the personal element in Molly's rants regarding Vaughn.

"I'm not going to talk about it, especially with you. Just don't piss him off, ok? You'll get hurt."

THE MALL

Isobel used to enjoy taking walks outside, down the block, to the mall. But she hadn't been out since the first day. On this particular outing Vaughn was going to the mall to look for a new pair of boots and anything else that might strike his fancy. Hayden had given him a list of requests too since he'd forbidden her to accompany him. He and Isobel left two hours before the sun was to go down.

"We are going across the freeway. Less dead up there and it'll give us a good vantage point to scope out the mall."

Vaughn explained as they climbed down the ladder of the fire escape.

Isobel was happy to be outside but fearful of what could happen to her. There was no barricade to hide behind, no second floor safe zone to protect her from the undead. She carried a handgun in a holster and a metal bat. Vaughn had two different guns and several more weapons hidden under his clothes. Isobel, who was unfamiliar with most weapons, couldn't tell what kind they were but, she knew they would do major damage to anything so unlucky to be in front of the firing end. Vaughn was wearing a backpack as he usually did when he went out. Isobel had a backpack too. She might find something she liked and she was planning on getting books for the others.

It was only one block east to the freeway from Willow Brook. They crossed the street in front of the building and made their way through the parking lot of a large office complex. Zombies filled the lot, shuffling between abandoned vehicles, leaving rotting bits of body smeared on windows and doors. Some of them walked noisily which allowed Isobel and Vaughn to keep track of them. Some were amazingly stealth on their feet allowing them to get close without warning.

Isobel was whipping her head back and forth so much she thought she'd end up with a pulled muscle. "We should tie bells to them. Shit. They are like ghosts."

"You need to calm down a bit lady," Vaughn could see her fear. "Why'd you come out here in the first place? Your heart is going to jump out of that chest of yours."

"I told you why," Isobel self-consciously put a hand over her breasts since Vaughn had taken his comment as an opportunity to stare at her there. She was still a woman after all. They made it to a stand of trees on the edge of the lot where they took a moment to catch their breath.

Isobel felt almost invisible to them here and she wanted to stay for a while. "There are so many," she said, "I can't believe how many. It looks like most people didn't fare very well. Everyone is dead."

"Yeah but we aren't. That's what matters. 'Sides, they don't know they are dead," Vaughn pointed out as he motioned her to start moving once again. She followed him over a chain link fence, through a grassy area and up an equally grass-covered embankment that bordered the freeway. She felt winded from the mini obstacle course but found strength to climb over the guardrail and continue on.

"Whoa. Straight out of a horror movie."

Isobel had seen the freeway from Willow Brook before but seeing it up close was another experience altogether. The commuting traffic was still there from the day the plague hit Northgate but the cars weren't moving nor were the people. Many of them had died in the backup; their cars left to idle until the fuel ran out; their bodies still in the cars or nearby, some starved to death, some eaten. Doors were open here and there; leaving Isobel to believe that some tried to make it out of the mess on foot. She looked south down the freeway and saw a few burned out cars and more of the dead. Someone had hung a hand-painted banner from an overpass. Its large red letters read "No Escape".

"It's true," Vaughn said, reading the sign for himself. "This was the last traffic jam of their lives; one they would never see let up."

Isobel shuddered and continued to survey the scene.

"You are thinking too much about it. Try being more of a casual observer," Vaughn suggested.

"Casual?" Isobel pointed up the lanes. "There is a dead cop on the freeway near his wrecked patrol car. A gun is still in his holster. He didn't have time to pull it out! How can I be casual about this when I know for sure now that no one is coming for us?"

"You still thought someone might come? We have to look out for ourselves, Iz. That is how I've always lived anyway. Officer what's-his-name isn't even going to come back from the dead; they ate so much of him. So pay attention only to where your feet are taking you! Stop thinking and start doing."

"Yes drill sergeant," Isobel said mockingly but, she knew he was right. She'd end up like Juan or Katie if she thought too much longer on the state of things. Vaughn had started to hop over hoods of cars making his trip across all eight or more lanes a quick one. Isobel chose to walk between the cars bumpers; trying the whole time not to think about her ankles being grabbed from under the vehicles. She avoided the vans and trucks too because she couldn't see behind them. Vaughn was waiting on the embankment on the other side, a cigarette glowing between his lips.

"There she is." He swept his arm in front of him, a grand gesture for something as mundane as a mall. It was beautiful though, when Isobel made out the nearly empty lot in the evening light. “Everyone fled the city center, or tried to, the day it reached us. That’s why the freeway looks like that; too many people all at once trying to leave.”

“This is going to be easier than I thought,” Isobel smiled. “There are only about ten cars in the entire lot.”

“We can see them better too, if they start coming for us.” Vaughn tossed his cigarette onto a bare patch of freeway pavement and pulled a tattered brochure out of his back pocket. It was a mall map.

“We don’t need that,” Isobel laughed, “I know exactly where the shoe store is. It’s just on the other side.”

He tossed it to a gentle wind that had picked up and laughed too. “I should know where it is, I’ve been wandering around out here for weeks now. Guess I wasn’t paying much attention though. Lead the way.”

Isobel took a deep breath and stepped carefully down the embankment. She liked having someone behind her to keep her safe but she had a horrible feeling that Vaughn would sacrifice her life in order to keep his own if the need arose.

ZOMBIFIED

Rob's favorite part of any day had become the evening, the night. When darkness fell outside he had the opportunity to watch his son return to normal since he could no longer stare at the dead outside. Gabe was happy, fed and playing with his toys again.

"Raaaarrrgh!!! Mooooaaawwwrrgghh!" Gabe roared as he moved Lego figures around on the dining room table.

"This sounds exciting!" Rob moved closer to watch the action his son had created. When he sat down he noticed that his son's arms were covered in red and green marker.

"What's all this from?"

"I made them zombies!" Gabe said happily as he held up two of the little plastic people. He had scribbled their faces with green and spots of red. "The red is where they are hurt. They ate everyone at the pizza shop and the pizza too 'cause they thought it was people."

"We need to find you a friend, Gabe." Rob sighed.

YOU ARE HERE

The Barnes and Noble loomed over them in the dark, its tall columns creating areas darker still, places for dead people to hide. Without parking lamps in the lot or lights on inside, the brick façade and rows of books were eerie. Isobel went through her list of books. Gabe wanted a dragon series and some comic books. Rob wanted some educational books for Gabe since he'd have to be homeschooled in some form. Molly wanted the three Sookie Stackhouse novels she hadn't read yet. Ben "would appreciate an older classic". Edward asked for something on the Civil War. Moira didn't ask for anything but Isobel had seen some yarn and needles when the Cabels were moved to the second floor. She decided to look for a book on both crochet and knitting if possible because she didn't know what type of needles they were. The doors were unlocked so they pulled them open, taking a moment in the airlock to try to look around inside.

"Hey Isobel, where am I gonna find that vampire shit?" Vaughn looked confused. Hayden had asked for the Twilight series to reread. Vaughn probably hadn't finished a book in his whole life.

"Why does she want to read about dead people walking around? She could just look outside all day," Isobel laughed.

"Don't ask me. If she told me I wasn't listening."

"Upstairs. Young Adult section."

Vaughn pushed the second set of doors open and they walked inside. Isobel moved to the left and hopped behind the checkout counter to get something between her and the darker black of the store interior. She scanned slowly with her flashlight across blank journals that would remain forever empty, calendars that counted days that didn't matter, novelty items that weren't worth much when things were normal and now just made her laugh to think that anyone ever cared about mini Zen gardens. Those small patches of combed sand and tiny pebble sit abandoned on countless office desks, with no one left to bring tranquility to. Some horse head bookends caught her eye. *Those are heavy looking. I could kill a zombie with one*, she thought as she gazed at the sturdiness of the equine bust. She snapped out of appraisal mode and verified there were no undead nearby. Moving through the discount book rows, towards the language and travel sections, she kept her handgun in front of her. Still, she could find no sign of . . . life.

A door marked 'Employees Only' was propped open and a rectangle of blackness was just beyond. Isobel started to move towards the threatening void when Vaughn came from her right. He was eating what looked like a rice krispie treat from the café.

"Gross, Vaughn."

"It hasn't gone bad. It's like pure sugar, Isobel. You should eat one too. They're still really tasty." He pushed the partially eaten square of cereal and marshmallow into her face. She pushed it away, a bit pissed off at him for wasting time.

"Have you just been snacking or did you look around too?"

"I checked the magazines, the café, computer books, crafts, and the music section. There isn't anyone down here. Let's check upstairs."

"We can't. We've got to look in there still." She pointed to the open door but didn't have the guts to shine her flashlight in.

"What have you been doing over here? Looking at THIS?" He chuckled loudly as he pulled a plastic-wrapped calendar from a shelf behind him. *Twelve Precious Puppies of 2012* stared at her. It was a strange feeling, seeing something so innocent with a gun in her hand, looking for dead people to re-kill.

"You really know how to lighten the mood," she said with a half-laugh. "But more seriously, I'm not as skilled at 'sweeping an area' as you are, Vaughn." A quick image came to her mind of the dead gathering outside the bookstore, following the smell of Vaughn's cigarette and her fear, the sound of Vaughn's booming laughter. Delaying no longer, she raised her flashlight and gun at the doorway. Ten feet down the hallway a zombie stood facing away from them. Its hair mostly gone and its ears chewed away.

"I don't think it can hear us," Isobel said hopefully but quietly. The corpse started to slowly turn around, the light of the flashlight drawing it toward the doorway.

"What do you bet it can still see with those rotting eyes?" Vaughn said. It had completed the turn towards them and finally saw Isobel and Vaughn, waiting to be eaten. It started jogging. Vaughn dropped the calendar from his sticky fingers, found his handgun and blew the head away. He walked into the hall and started checking doors but they were all locked.

Isobel bent down to look at the body. She saw the name badge on her shirt. "She worked here. How sad. She didn't get to go home to her family."

"How do you know that thing is a girl? It's gooier than the rice krispie snack I ate."

Isobel shot a mean look at Vaughn.

"Sorry. Just an observation."

"*She* has eye shadow on. Or, she did anyway before you shot her. My flashlight hit the shimmery blue of it when she turned around."

"Ok. Well, *she* is redead now so *she* doesn't matter anymore. So can *we* move on?"

Back in the main store Vaughn's gunfire had alerted the small group of undead on the second floor. One had already fallen from the balcony ledge and splattered in a grotesque spread in the middle of the lobby between the escalators. The head had cracked open and the decomposing remains of the brain were soaking into the carpet. Isobel brought a hand up to cover her nose. The smell was unbearable. One arm had come off on impact and rested on the New Releases in Non-Fiction table. Another zombie had come towards the down escalator (which had become stairs in the power outages), stepped and tumbled all the way to the first floor. Body rot covered the sides and steps and the corpse, however mangled, was still moving at the bottom. The middle-aged woman was shuddering, trying to move toward Isobel inch by inch. Vaughn found an unabridged dictionary and brought it down on the corpses head.

Dead (ded) *adj.*
1. No longer living.
2. Having no capacity to live: inanimate.

She was dead.

"Who's next?" Vaughn yelled in a macho, bring-it-on type voice, as he looked upstairs. He tossed the bloody dictionary onto the stomach of the dead woman and started climbing the up escalator.

3. Lacking feeling or sensitivity.

Vaughn was dead.

Isobel vomited and wondered to herself: *What book was she looking for that was worth her life?* Isobel still cared for others; she wasn't dead yet.

She followed Vaughn up the escalator, making sure not to rest her hands on anything. Near the top they turned to face the balcony opposite them. Two zombies shuffled about but had lost the direction of the gunshot, leaving them without a clear destination. Vaughn, liking a challenge, took aim at the one closest but hit it in the neck so it continued to move around. The other zombie started to walk towards the balcony railing. Vaughn shot it in the face and it fell out of view.

They checked the Children's section directly in front of the escalator. It was a wreck, books scattered everywhere, but no surprises, no undead children. Isobel found the dragon series Gabe wanted and put it in her bag while Vaughn kept watch. Once again they split up. Isobel went toward the games and upstairs bathrooms. She found a display of classics on the way and selected two for Ben: *A Tale of Two Cities* and *Frankenstein.*

The men's bathroom was empty except for someone's final shit, left in a bowl. The woman's bathroom was not. Isobel tried to open the door but it only moved an inch before it was pushed shut from the inside.

"Go away!!!!" A man's voice yelled coarsely. Isobel jumped back, frightened by the unexpected noise. He didn't sound well, as in mentally stable. "I don't like you. I don't know you."

"I'm not one of them," Isobel assured him, coming closer to the door again, "if that makes a difference."

"You can't have this place. I found this place."

She could hear his footsteps on the tile floor of the bathroom, pacing back and forth.

"I found it!" he yelled.

"I don't want your hiding place. You can keep it," Isobel laughed to herself thinking what a horrible hiding place a cold, unsecured bathroom was, especially once the water stopped running; especially inside a book store with little food or warmth. He didn't have to convince her and he didn't try. He said nothing else for a few minutes so Isobel tried again.

"Do you need any help?" She wasn't going to invite the man to live with them or even tell him where they came from. He was unstable for sure. But maybe she could bring him a magazine or a rice krispie treat.

"Do you have water?" Upon uttering the last word his throat became drier, more rasp, and completely sane.

Isobel had a bottle, three quarters full, in her backpack. It wouldn't do much for a man that refused to leave a terrible shelter. Perhaps only stave off dehydration by a day. Next to it in the bag, Isobel found an unopened granola bar. She tapped on the door with a knuckle. It opened two inches or so, not wide enough to jam a shoe in, but wide enough for passing the poor meal through. A dirty hand grabbed the bottle and bar and the other hand slammed the door closed again.

Isobel decided not to tell Vaughn about the squatter. That wouldn't end well and if Vaughn had taken this side of the top level, it would have started much differently too. Moving down the hall Isobel stood in front of another door marked *Employees Only*. She hesitated a second and then checked for any give. *Locked! Thank god*, she exclaimed in her head. She wasn't cut out for adventure.

She spent some time browsing the comic section for Gabe. While scanning the titles she found a graphic novel series called *The Walking Dead*. She took a couple volumes, thinking they could learn something. She wondered if the authors and artists where still living. *I bet the authors never thought their comic might be used as reference*, she thought. She heard Vaughn finish off the zombie he'd shot in the neck on the other side of the top level.

With the store clear they grabbed the rest of the books for the other Willow Brook residents. In the cooking section Isobel came across a book called *Life in a Can*. The book was full of recipes using only canned goods. A read she would have never even glanced at before, it had now reached a near-Bible importance to her. She excitedly stashed it in her backpack, looking forward to getting creative with her can opener.

Before going back downstairs Isobel looked towards the hallway. She thought about telling the man that he could come out of the bathroom and be safe in the larger store. Maybe there was something more to eat in the café. But there wasn't any way to help the man and keep the knowledge of his existence away from Vaughn.

"Come on Isobel. Enough books. I want some new shoes."

Isobel's happiness over the books she'd pilfered quickly disappeared as they stood together at the windowed-doors at the front of the bookstore, viewing the expanse of pavement. Estimation was not her forte, but she guessed that there were about fifty undead attending the party that Vaughn's gunshots had invited them to.

"Fantastic."

"What was that?" Vaughn had caught the breathy sarcasm.

"Nothing. Let's go."

"You're in the lead, remember cowgirl?"

"Don't call me that." She leaned her right shoulder into the door, gun ready, and pushed.

ON THE RUN

Isobel wanted to leave the backpack of books behind. The combined weight of them made her slow and awkward as she fought for her life. Vaughn was in his element, moving quick and calculated, shooting only when necessary and hitting everything he pulled the trigger away from. Isobel used all the bullets in the clip and couldn't keep her hand steady to swap the empty one out for reload. She hit three of the corpses she shot at but didn't bring one of them down.

"If I make it back alive, I'm never leaving the building again!" she yelled at Vaughn.

"Speak for yourself. I love it out here!" he called back.

The other side of the mall parking lot was deserted. There were undead scattered across the street near Target and in the lot of the Liquor and Wine store. It looked to Isobel like they had a little bit of time.

The shoe store was locked so Vaughn pulled a crowbar from his bag. He hit the glass of the door five times before he could make a hole for them to climb through. They walked quickly passed the high heels, flip-flops, and Crocs. All anyone wanted or needed was running shoes. No loafers, no sandals. They didn't even go barefoot at Willow Brook unless they were sleeping. Running shoes were laced up before breakfast, as they never knew when the dead could be upon them.

Finally they reached the athletic section and started searching with their flashlights. "I can't find my size! Why can't I ever find my size?" Isobel said, frustrated. It didn't help that she had to keep looking up to keep tabs on the approaching dead. They had started lurching across the distant street, drawn by the noise of Vaughn's crowbar on the glass.

"Pick something that will work Isobel! We have to keep moving!" Vaughn already had a new pair of boots laced up and a handful of extra shoelaces in his hand. He was checking out the rest of the sales floor for any dead that may have been locked in the store.

She found a suitable pair that was only a half size too large for her feet. The dead were halfway across the parking lot of the mall. She wanted to grab a second pair but didn't think she had room in her pack. She sat down in the aisle to put them on but she heard something from the front of the store. One of the zombies had reached the glass front doors. She could read his shirt when she shone her flashlight in its direction. *I'd rather be bowling.*

"I'd rather you were bowling too!" she yelled at him.

Vaughn laughed but gestured for her to hurry up. "They aren't going to give up. They're like marathon runners. Really slow marathon runners."

"He found the hole in the door!" Isobel yelped and tried to focus on tying her shoes.

"They made it here faster than I thought they would," Vaughn commented.

The bunny goes around the tree and into the hole, Isobel thought, *to get the hell out of harm's way.* Bodies filled the front of the store now. There were about twenty rows of shoes between them but the aisles were unobstructed so the dead made their way through the store with ease. Isobel hopped to her feet and collected her bag and weapons.

"We'll have to find another way out. There's got to be an exit in the back," Vaughn said. They ran to the storeroom, pulling shoeboxes off the shelves in a poor attempt to slow the undead. The storeroom was dark and soon after entering it Isobel tripped on something and fell to the floor.

"Shit!" Isobel screamed. Her backpack full of books made it difficult for her to get up. Her flashlight had spun away from her and come to rest against a door. A cool breeze came from the crack at its bottom.

"Vaughn, my flashlight, that's the way out!" Isobel pointed. His flashlight shone on her but he moved it away to expose the door more fully.

"Come on then!" Vaughn yelled. Isobel tried to pull herself to her feet but the bag kept her down and a burning pain rose in her left ankle.

"I twisted it. My ankle, I can't use it," Isobel cried, terrified that this would be the moment when Vaughn would leave her to save himself.

"Are you kidding me?" He said as he ran back to Isobel's side to help her to her feet.

Clumph. The sound of feet collapsing cardboard shoeboxes reached Isobel's ear. *Clumph.* The dead were getting closer.

"I can leave the books. It'll be easier," Isobel said.

"No. You don't ever leave anything behind. If you do that, the trip was pointless. Now hop for all you're worth!" The zombies had made it into the pitch-black storeroom. Vaughn and Isobel crashed forward into the back door. It gave way and let them out into the cool night air.

With Vaughn's help, Isobel was able to make it across the parking lot and up the embankment to the freeway.

"I have to stop!" Isobel yelled as she pulled free from him.

"We have to keep moving. I already said that!"

"It hurts, Vaughn! We have to find somewhere safe to stop for a second."

"Fine," Vaughn didn't want to stop but he didn't want to listen to Isobel's whining any longer. "Look around for a vehicle with tinted windows. We'll be much better hidden."

Isobel found a gray van with windows as dark as the night that surrounded them. She tried all the doors and found the back two to be unlocked. She stood and stared at it.

"Well, open the damn thing. Those dead people are coming. One of them has made it to the hill."

"I'm scared."

"Scared, but you feel alive again, don't you?" He smiled. Without a moment's hesitation Vaughn opened the doors to the empty van. He helped Isobel inside, climbed in himself and closed and locked the doors behind him. Three or four minutes passed before the dead reached the freeway. Vaughn imagined them trying to climb over the guardrail. Isobel held her ankle and rested her head against her knees. She needed to cry but she wouldn't allow Vaughn to see her *that* weak.

They spent the night in the van. Vaughn fell asleep quickly and slept deeply, leaving Isobel to analyze every bump in the night. Her ankle was throbbing and her body shivered in the cold. She was reminded of Jill and her night outside.

"Going outside is never a good idea," she said to herself to drive the lesson home.

MISSING AND MISSED

It was midnight and Isobel and Vaughn had not returned to Willow Brook. Ben paced the apartment that he shared with Isobel. He knew she was tough but even tough people made mistakes and ended up dead. Ben went to ask everyone if they'd heard anything. The Cabels were already asleep. Rob was reading to Gabe and hadn't heard a thing. Molly didn't care. Hayden was just mad that she didn't have her books yet. Jeff and Markus weren't taking him seriously.

"Maybe they ran off together. I always thought they'd make a good power couple," Markus laughed.

"Please don't joke. I don't care what happened to Vaughn but I'm worried about Isobel," Ben said seriously. "Even a gunshot would mean something to me."

"There had been shots earlier but that was some time ago. Other than those ones, the night has been quiet," Jeff said.

Ben finally made himself lay down on the couch. He lay awake staring at the sliding glass door that led to the balcony. He willed Isobel's form to appear there, tired and battle-worn but alive and uninfected. She didn't show up.

Ben had spent so much mental energy on his love for Anna that he hadn't realized that he was starting to care for Isobel as well.

BRACE YOURSELF

Isobel woke as the sun was coming up. The inside of the van warmed quickly as the rays shone through the untinted windows of the cab and onto the dark upholstery of the seats. She had forgotten about her ankle as she tried to climb into the driver's seat for a better view.

"Ahh!" she yelled from the pain. No one responded and she realized that she was alone. Vaughn was not in sight.

"That motherfucker!" Isobel looked out the front window and north up the crowded freeway. No movement anywhere. Fearing he had gone back to Willow Brook without her, she would have to stabilize her ankle to make it back without his help. She said a silent *thank you* as she looked around. The van she chose to crawl into was full of computer repair materials. She could make something work. After ten minutes of sorting through the items in the back she had two large pieces of hard plastic from a computer tower and a handful of USB cables. Isobel was proud of her brace. Just as she was wrapping the cords tightly around her lower leg the back doors of the van opened.

"Good morning cripple!" Vaughn said happily. He had an armful of first aid supplies, including an ace bandage and an ankle brace. "I wasn't sure what would help so I grabbed anything related to ankles. What the hell is that?" he asked, looking at the technical parts strapped to her leg. Isobel laughed so hard she started to cry. Vaughn climbed in and closed the doors.

"You look like a cyborg," Vaughn laughed wildly at her.

"Fuck you, Vaughn. I thought you had abandoned me here to die!"

"I considered it," Vaughn said. Isobel stopped laughing and worked at untying the cords.

Vaughn let her pick her own brace and put it on. He opened the doors again and helped her down.

"Let's *hop* to it," Vaughn laughed.

"You are a horrible person," she replied. He helped her along and they made it back to Willow Brook without further event.

(BELOW THE) SURFACE WOUNDS

Ben surprised Isobel with a kiss when she made it to the top of the fire escape and back into her apartment.

"I'm so happy you are ok. I was worried sick," he admitted.

"I'm fine. I just hurt my ankle. We had to stop," she said as she dropped her backpack on the floor and fell onto a chair in the living room, completely ignoring his display of affection. "First, and last time, I'm going out there."

"Did you see any other survivors?" Ben asked.

"No," Isobel lied. Vaughn was still in her apartment, drinking a bottle of water and hanging around for no apparent reason. She didn't want to bring up the bookstore bum.

"What did you get? Besides a sprained ankle?" Ben asked.

"Shoes and books," Isobel pointed to her feet and then the backpack. "You can dig through it. I'm sure you'll know which one is for you. In fact, can you give everyone else their books? I think I'm going to sit here for awhile."

"I'm going back upstairs. If you see Hayden, tell her to come up."

"Thanks Vaughn, for helping me back home."

"Yep," was all he said as he left.

DISTRACTIONS

Vaughn would have recounted their adventure with more enthusiasm and creative license than Isobel but, as the other residents heard of her return and came to hear her recount it, she stuck to the truth. She even told them about the Barnes and Noble bum now that Vaughn was out of earshot. Her story was interesting enough, making embellishments unnecessary.

"You met someone else? All I got to meet was a dog. What was he like?" Molly asked. She hadn't seen any living people when she was forced to brave the outdoors.

"He was crazy, with a capital C. I don't know if he started that way or if the circumstances made him lose his mind."

"He could have hurt you," Ben said, putting his hand on hers.

"He wouldn't even let me in *his* bathroom."

"Still, what if he had a weapon?" Ben continued.

"I'm not a child Ben! I could have handled it," she pulled her hand out from under his. "Ahhh!" she screamed as she stood up, having forgotten about her ankle again. She sat back down, beaten by the injury.

"At any rate, we're happy you made it back," Moira said, "and thank you for the books!"

"I hope they were worth it," Isobel replied.

"I've already started mine!" Edward smiled, holding up his new novel, a bookmark snug in its first pages.

Even though Isobel brought back with her a terrible attitude toward the world, the new literature in the complex had helped to keep everyone distracted and happy.

ADMITTING DEFEAT

Rob had never been good about asking for help with raising Gabe. In fact, he had outright refused it from Gabe's mother's parents. They hadn't believed in Rob and they wanted to make sure that their daughter's child was reared correctly in her absence.

He was happy the phones didn't work; happy her parents lived in South Seattle and had a heavily populated, heavily infected city between them. He knew if they could see Gabe now, his behavior growing stranger by the day, they would turn to him and shake their heads. *You're doing it wrong! You're a failure as a father!* He could hear his mother-in-law's voice yell. The most difficult part of it was that he knew she would be right. Gabe's obsession with the dead was growing every day. It was time to ask for help.

"Hey Gabe, do you ever miss your school?" he asked his son at lunch.

"Not the school, just my friends," he said as he ate peanut butter and crackers.

"What about the learning? Because I was thinking we have a lot of smart people living around us and I bet they'd like to share their smartness with you. What do you think?"

"I guess. There's no choice."

"You have a choice, I'm asking you."

"I mean, there's nothing else to do."

"You're right about that."

"When do I go back?"

"Back?"

"To school, Dad!"

"Oh, um, tomorrow? That way you can enjoy your last day of summer vacation."

"It's not summer. It's fall. *You* need to go back to school too, Dad."

"All I meant was your last day of freedom. Anyway, I'll be right back. I'm going to talk to the first of your new teachers."

He'd heard Moira say that she'd raised three children. He hadn't met any of them and so he didn't know how they had turned out but Moira was a kind enough woman. She also felt like his only good option.

He found Moira in the common room looking out the window at the dead.

"Looks like you need some distraction too," he said.

"Oh! You startled me Rob!" Moira turned to him and he could see that she had been crying.

"Is something wrong, Moira?"

"I was just thinking about my family; how I might not see them again." In her hand she held a photo but Rob didn't recognize any of the faces.

"You can't think that way! You have to hold on to a little bit of hope," he said, hugging her.

"You said something about distraction? That is the only hope I have. It better not be drugs though, I don't do those." She tucked the photo back into a worn album and put it away with some other books.

"It's not drugs," Rob laughed. "Do you think, um, that you could spend some time with Gabe? Teach him something. He needs to focus on things other than zombies for at least part of a day."

Moira sighed. The boy had a lot more energy than she had to match. "I don't wake up very early and I could only keep up with him for about an hour."

"That's great! That's fine. I can bring him over right after lunch tomorrow." Rob hugged her and went back to his apartment before she could change her mind.

ANOTHER STAB IN THE HEART

The next morning Gabe was bouncing off the walls. He was excited to have somewhere to be and something to do. He picked his clothes out carefully and gulped down his oatmeal breakfast. He was ready to go at nine.

"Moira is still sleeping, dude. You'll have to wait a bit. Why don't you go see if Molly is awake?"

"Ooooookaaaaayy." Gabe left the apartment and went to find Molly. She was sitting in her living room reading a book and drinking coffee.

"What's up, Gabe?"

"Nothing. Moira is going to teach me stuff but she's old so she's still sleepin'. Can I try that?" He pointed to her coffee.

"Hmm, I'm not sure if your dad would like that."

"It's fine, let him try it but he doesn't need the sugar. He's been a little hard to contain this morning," Rob said as he invited himself into her apartment.

"Hi," Molly said. "What are you doing here?" she asked, hoping it was to see her.

"Actually, I sent Gabe here to kill some time and then I remembered that Isobel offered to give him a haircut. Come on Gabe."

"I like my hair. I don't want a haircut," Gabe protested as he plopped down onto Molly's couch and grabbed her coffee cup.

"We don't have a lot of time so let's go get it done."

"No!" He yelled, a few drops of coffee splashed over the edge of the mug.

Molly took the cup back from him. "Will you let me cut your hair?" she asked.

"Okay!" Gabe complied. He liked her way more than Isobel.

"Thanks Molly. You're the best," Rob said. "You be good for her!" He pointed a finger at his son and left.

Molly was disappointed. Rob wasn't unfriendly or mean to her but she expected so much more from him. A kiss on the cheek wouldn't hurt or a bit of company as she took scissors to his child's head.

"We'll do the haircut in the kitchen so your hair doesn't get on the carpet." She grabbed his hand and led him to a high stool.

"I want a Mohawk," he said, picking up his hair in the middle of his head.

Molly laughed and entertained the idea. It would be a good way to make a statement to Rob to lighten up or it may just drive him further away from her.

"Maybe next time?" she suggested. "Now sit still."

HOME SCHOOL

Three hours later, Moira sat Gabe down at their dining room table. She had lain out a notebook, a drawing pad and as many pens and markers as she could find. She sat down next to him to begin the lesson.

"You smell funny," Gabe said as he leaned away from her.

"Ha! What a straight shooter you are. It's moisturizer. I'm so old, if I don't wear it all the time I'd just crumble into dust." She fluttered her fingers in the air to mimic her dusted self blowing away in an imaginary wind.

"You could get a nicer smelling one."

"Nah. I'm too old for change."

"Me too!" Gabe smiled.

"You are a funny kid. What do you want to learn about today?"

"Mummies!" he exclaimed.

"Why mummies?" Moira asked with a laugh.

"They come back to life like the zombies 'cept they look nicer 'cause they're wrapped in toilet paper."

"Well that is true but they only came back to life in movies. The real ones stayed in tombs built by the Egyptians."

"Do you think the mummies will come out of the movies like the zombies did?"

"I'm not sure where you get your facts but you need to find a better source. The zombies didn't come out of the movies. We don't know where they came from."

"They had to come from somewhere."

"Let's keep our fingers crossed that somebody in the world is trying to figure that out right now! So do you want to learn about Egypt?"

"Ok!"

She talked for a half an hour on the subject and then they moved on to writing practice. Gabe carefully spelled out the names of the other residents with his misshapen letters. Moira found it easy to spend time with the child. It wasn't at all like she expected. Her children had been more poorly behaved than Gabe was.

When Rob came by after an hour to pick Gabe up both Moira and the boy weren't ready for "school" to be over. So he left them for a few more hours. Gabe drew a picture of his father and Moira played with his beloved Legos, though her arthritic hands could barely pull the plastic bricks apart.

Two more hours elapsed and dinnertime was nearing. Rob came a second time for his son and Moira reluctantly let the child leave.

"You let me know when you want to come over again, alright?" She hugged him.

Gabe pulled away from her and smiled. "You're alright for a girl, even if you smell."

"Gabe! That's not a kind thing to say," his dad scolded him.

"It's alright Rob. We already talked about it. And thank you Gabe, I'll take that as a compliment."

DEADBEAT DAD

Isobel did a lot of the group laundry herself. She had found a large bucket for soapy water and a few tools for scrubbing and dirt removal. On this day, Isobel thought it felt like a Sunday, she wasn't alone. Due to her slowly healing ankle injury she had to take a volunteer helper to carry the supplies to the roof and back and to help get through the massive pile of smelly clothes and bedding. Hayden volunteered without hesitation, eager to help in some small way to pay back the group for letting her in.

The day was windy and it could really be felt on the roof. The clotheslines they had strung up in the first week were whipping back and forth, a forgotten sweater waved like a flag. Hayden setup all the supplies and Isobel sat down in front of the large bucket. She would wash the clothes and Hayden would rinse and squeeze them out before hanging them to dry.

"Man it is really cold up here!" Hayden shivered and took the abandoned sweater off the line. "I don't know who this belongs to but I'm going to put it on to stay warm."

"I'm sure that's fine." Isobel said over her shoulder. She looked like a natural homemaker as she skillfully removed stains and laundered each piece of clothing with care.

"Have you ever wanted children, Isobel?" Hayden asked her as she took a few of Ben's plaid shirts and clipped them to the line with two multicolored clothespins.

"Me? No! Well, I guess I've never thought about it. Maybe if I fell in love with someone who wanted children then I would. Why do you ask?" She stopped focusing on the washing and turned her head to Hayden.

"Oh, no reason. You just look like you would make a good mom and I was thinking about those people, that family that died before I moved in."

"The Coopers," Isobel said and then turned her attention back to the laundry.

"Yeah, them. Did they seem scared to be bringing a child into a world like *this*?"

"A little, yes. But the world hasn't changed as much as everyone is going on about. It has always been full of bad people. Only now it's easier to tell the difference."

Hayden thought for a while on it and decided to press on with her questions. Her period hadn't come on time but her diet had been horrible as of late and she had missed a period in the past so she wasn't too concerned. She couldn't help but think that it was due to something other than malnutrition this time though so, she felt the need to inquire about Tom.

"Because you've known him a lot longer than I have, do you think that Tom would make a good dad?"

This time Isobel didn't stop her work, she just laughed loud enough for Hayden to hear her. "Sorry. That was a serious question wasn't it?"

"Yes. It was."

"You would think that a man who loves himself as much as Vaughn does would value his offspring. He has kids from a marriage that ended."

"And?"

"He never talks about them. So, there's your answer. I've never seen them here to visit him either."

"How do you know about them then? Tom isn't the sharing type."

"I saw their names on some rental paperwork in the office when Ben and I were there."

"He must pay child support or something." Hayden was starting to feel queasy. She wasn't sure if it was from her possible pregnancy or her nervousness about Tom's lack of responsibility.

"Well if he ever did he certainly doesn't have to anymore and I am willing to bet money that he is happy about it. My advice? Don't travel down that road with him. Inside, he's as dead as they are." Isobel pointed to the street where the dead were still walking in great numbers.

"I thought you guys were all buddy-buddy," Hayden said to her.

"Think of me as a diplomat. I'm just a group representative trying to keep things smooth with the evil dictator that could really fuck us over if he wanted to."

From then on Hayden hung laundry in silence. The only positive thought she could come up with was that there was already a lot of unused and unneeded baby stuff packed away upstairs.

A GLASS OF COURAGE

Jeff wasn't drunk or tired and the one glass of wine he'd consumed had left him feeling bold. Markus had downed a few glasses of wine, almost an entire bottle by himself. Jeff and he had made love and then Markus had passed out. It felt like the right time for Jeff to try to cover up one of the evil deeds he'd done. He was going to move the body of the dog.

He looked outside. The sun was on its way down but it still covered the lawn in a soft glow. He looked around his apartment until he found the baseball bat he'd been given by the others. With the utmost care he opened the slider to his balcony, stepped outside, and closed it behind him. Looking over the railing he could see the dog's remains, mostly because he knew they were there. It was fairly well hidden but to anyone who might climb down his own fire escape. There were heavier bushes just an apartment down and he made the plan to drag the decomposing animal to them in order to fully conceal the body.

Slowly, he climbed down the ladder. He reached the ground and took a moment to check for the dead. He knew nothing of how they found their prey. Could they smell or see him? Could they hear his heart pounding? Goosebumps formed on his arms and he made himself stop thinking on the matter. He set his baseball bat down and reached for the hind legs of the poodle.

Just moments before, he had envisioned himself pulling the body with ease and in one piece to its new resting place a few yards away. Instead the back legs pulled free of the hips with a wet sound. A smell rose in the air that made him vomit on the side of the building. He dropped the legs and looked at his hands. Bits of the fur and flesh remained there, clinging to his skin. He turned away from the carrion and crouched to wipe his hands on the grass.

Night was approaching and the world was quiet around him but for the sound of feet hitting the grass, growing closer with each step. His courage had left him and been replaced by embarrassment.

"Why didn't I bring gloves? And a bag? The dog's been out here far too long to stay in one piece." He wiped his brow with the back of one hand.

"Uuuuggghhhh."

Jeff stood back up and turned to the voice.

"Sheila?" His undead wife was walking quickly to him. "Sheila, you can't be here!" He stumbled backward and found the bat but not enough of the courage he'd lost to actually take a swing. She was much more terrifying to him in this new form. He chose to throw the bat at her and use the second it bought him to climb back to safety. On his balcony again, he sat with his back against the glass of the sliding door. Five minutes later the door moved behind him.

"What are you doing out there?" Markus asked through a yawn and a burp.

Jeff jumped to his feet. "I needed some air."

"You must be freezing cold. Come here and let me warm you up." Markus offered himself to Jeff.

"No, I, I need to use the bathroom first." He dodged Markus' open arms and went directly to the bathroom. He used bottled water and soap to scrub the fur and skin from his hands, making sure there wasn't one hint of curl or fleck of it left in the sink basin. Clean, he went to the couch in the living room.

"You shouldn't furrow your brow so much," Markus said as he sat down next to him. "You're going to get wrinkles."

SMOKE ON THE HORIZON

Vaughn had been out in the morning on the day the mall burned to the ground. A smell built in the air around ten, carried by a west-blowing breeze, a horrible mix of wood smoke and burning flesh. From that smell, he knew what was happening before he actually saw the smoke and flames rising beyond the freeway. He decided it best to not investigate; the smell would be impossible to get out of his clothes if he did and it wasn't like he could stop it from happening. There were no firemen to call, no first responders, nothing to save. He went back to Willow Brook, climbed the fire ladder onto his balcony and immediately headed upstairs to the roof for a better view. Isobel appeared at his side soon after and he silently handed his binoculars to her.

"The mall," She said softly. "Is this your work, Vaughn?" There was a hint of disgust in her voice.

"Is that a serious question, Isobel? I wouldn't waste a resource."

"Ha! You know, you're right about that. You saw Hayden and you just had to tap that oil reserve," Isobel said, smacking her hip for effect.

"If you came up here to start something with me then you are just as stupid as the other women; that or fond of the colors black and blue," Vaughn said in a low voice, his jaw clenching.

"Don't threaten me. That Hayden thing just came out, ok? I came up here because there is a man in the bookstore bathroom. He's going to die in that fire."

"Eddie can take care of himself and it's not him I'm worried about." Vaughn's eyes squinted into the distance looking for things Isobel couldn't see, even with the binoculars.

"We can't be talking about the same guy. The guy I met was starved and half-crazy; maybe all the way crazy."

"He's got a really curly beard, about five-foot-two and paranoid about eviction?" Vaughn used his hand to show Isobel how tall he remembered Eddie to be.

"Yep. Same guy. How do you know him?" Isobel pulled the binoculars from her eyes and looked to Vaughn for his explanation.

"I used to give him my leftover coffee out front of the coffee shop right by the bookstore. He'd always hang out there. I saw him once after the first day; he wouldn't let me near a trashcan he was sleeping in. He must have moved into Barnes and Noble when he found out it was still unlocked. So, like I said, he can take care of himself. He's been homeless for at least five years. He'll just move to Target if he gets burned out of his 'home'."

"That sort of makes me feel better." And it did, but Isobel felt guilty for not telling Vaughn at the bookstore.

"If you want we can invite him to move in." Vaughn nudged her, smiling and winking.

"Why? You want to sleep with him too?" she shot back.

Vaughn punched her arm. "You really can dish it out, Iz. That's why I like you."

"I'm going back inside. For the record, I still don't like you and this better not bruise," she said as she rubbed her arm. He took the binoculars back and resumed his watch over the disappearing mall.

Vaughn stayed on the roof for most of the early afternoon. Ash had begun to fall lightly on Willow Brook and the sky to the east was dark with smoke. *Who started the fire?* Vaughn thought over and over. He felt like a rat watching an exterminator get closer and closer to discovering his nest.

COMFORT IN CHAOS

At around noon a woman's voice could be heard across Northgate; carried by a megaphone and asking for survivors to come out. Her smooth voice and promises of food, water, and protection had everyone in the building curious. They still hadn't seen the source of the voice when Vaughn came to the second floor with a gun.

"Everyone," he whispered, "turn off any lights or radios you have. Move away from the windows. We don't know what we're dealing with just yet but I'm pretty sure those are our fire starters."

"She's offering a lot. Rations we haven't had in weeks," Markus said. "I'm not one to take women up on their offers but I might make an exception."

"Do what I say or regret it." Vaughn sounded deadly serious. So, as quietly as everyone could, they turned Willow Brook into a silent, dark, and seemingly empty shell.

Ten minutes passed and a truck rolled around the corner. It sat on giant wheels and was raised so high that someone could almost walk underneath it. Once white, it was now a dirty brown like the people it carried.

"There must be twelve people in the bed of that truck," Isobel gasped as she peeked out of the darkened room into the day lit street. She hoped the glare of the sun would make it hard for them to see her in the window.

"They look like crack addicts." Ben had braved a quick look outside to assess the group for himself.

"No. Anarchists," Vaughn said from the corner of the common room closest to the stairs. He crouched down and started double-checking the weapons he'd brought with him.

Isobel looked out the window again and she could see that what Vaughn said was true. A large "A" within a circle, the emblem for anarchy, was spray-painted with black paint on the driver's side door of the truck. She could see the people better too as the truck was driving slowly up the road and was now parallel with the building. They wore a lot of black and many of them had bandannas covering their faces up to their eyes. It had been unseasonably sunny and any skin that was exposed had been *over*-exposed; an unhealthy tan and on some, a peeling burn.

The woman on the megaphone, tall and blonde, stood at the center of the truck bed, leaning against the back of the cab in a relaxed pose as if she didn't really give a shit about the task she was performing. The sweet words coming from her mouth clashed horribly with her body language.

"I don't trust her," Isobel said.

"She's in charge," Vaughn whispered.

"Anarchists don't have leaders," Isobel thought aloud.

"Tell that to her," Vaughn laughed.

"They are attracting a lot of attention from the zombies but they don't seem to care," Ben said after looking again.

"You're right Ben. Good eye. You notice how they're not shooting any of 'em?" Vaughn responded. "Just pushing them away if necessary with those poles they have. Something's definitely up."

"What should we do?" Molly asked.

"Wait . . . someone is coming out of the office building across the street!" Isobel yelled, surprised to see that someone had been surviving over there this whole time.

"Shh!" Vaughn whispered. "Just watch."

The woman was tall and thin with closely cropped black hair, peppered with gray. She looked like a librarian and moved like a bird; many quick steps with a constantly moving head. She carried a gun with her, held in front of her body by shaking, outstretched arms. Other faces appeared in the windows of the entry to the building, watching as their volunteer canary flew deeper into the mine. Isobel thought she saw the woman's eyes flick in the direction of Willow Brook. She hoped the anarchists didn't see it. A zombie approached the bird-like woman and without hesitation she shot the thing down to keep the path ahead of her clear and safe.

"Wrong choice lady!" The blonde on the megaphone yelled, her voice now cold and unfriendly as it projected across the paved lot. She tossed the megaphone to another of her gang and was handed a sniper rifle by another. The anarchist leader laughed and aimed the gun at the office building survivor.

"No, please!" she begged. "What did I do wrong? We're starving in there." She gestured toward her family and friends, the building itself. "We need the help you offered."

"But you broke the rules of the game. You killed an ally."

The blonde pulled the trigger and sent a bullet into the woman in the parking lot. She fell backwards, the handgun clattering on the pavement. Blood began to seep from her chest and her breathing slowed and stopped.

"She'll get back up again. They shot her lung or something," Ben said.

Isobel had stopped looking and, like many of the others, she was trying not to freak out.

"I think that's the point," Rob spoke up. He hadn't seen any of it but from what he'd heard he could put the pieces together. "They don't want this plague to end. It has been the only thing to successfully bring down the American government. Chaos reigns and they are right at home in it. If it was my cup of tea I certainly wouldn't want it to end either."

"Crazy bastards," Vaughn shook his head but he couldn't help but admire the blonde's savageness. She wasn't bad to look at either.

The megaphone found its way to her hand again and she spoke more animatedly than before, as though the shooting had reinvigorated her. The dead swarmed the truck, following the sound of the bullet and the megaphone to their shared source.

"We are the future of this forgotten world. The establishment will never return! If you kill a zombie, we'll make you a zombie. That's the deal, an eye for an eye!"

The fallen office woman stood back up. Blood still oozed from the bullet hole in her chest. She walked toward her killers without one thought of revenge on her mind. When she made it to the truck they pushed her backward into the mix to fulfill her duty as one of the dead.

The faces in the office building windows had disappeared but it was too late for them.

"The rest of you come out here and make your choice. Join us or join the undead!" The blonde yelled into the megaphone.

"Daddy, I don't want us to go out there," Gabe was crying as he whispered to his dad.

"They aren't talking to us buddy. They don't know that we're here. We just have to stay very still and quiet so it stays that way; like playing hide and seek, except we don't want to be found. Ok?" Rob said in the steadiest voice he could find.

"I like that game!" Gabe whispered again, but with more happiness in his voice.

The blonde was getting impatient. She pressed a button on the megaphone to make it wail. Everyone in Willow Brook jumped.

"Make me come in there and you're dead. No choice," she threatened.

Two more women, a man, and a child emerged. They looked like skeletons after all this time stuck in the commercial building.

"Those people, they have to know we're in here," Isobel said. "How many of us have left the building? How much noise did we make when Hayden was stuck on the roof? Vaughn, we walked right through that parking lot to go to the mall!" Vaughn nodded in acknowledgement.

"All we can do is pray. Pray that they are God-fearing people who wouldn't betray us," Moira said.

"That doesn't leave me a lot of hope," Ben said. "They are desperate and desperation often throws the fear of God out the window."

Moira sadly knew that to be true.

"Those anarchists could have already scouted the area too. Don't forget about that possibility," Vaughn said.

The anarchists made the office skeletons stand in a line in part of the empty but filling parking lot. The man dropped to his knees and started to talk with the blonde. Isobel waited for his finger to point at Willow Brook. But instead his fingers came together in front of him like he was praying.

"See," Moira said, "God-fearing."

"No, he's begging for his life," Ben corrected her.

The anarchist leader slapped the man's face and pinched his deathly thin arms, kicked him in his hungry stomach. She wouldn't be sparing him or his family today. They were too close to death to save them from it. Four more shots were fired but never once into a brain.

"We're in the zombie making business, fellas!" the blonde roared to her motley following, not into the megaphone, but at the top of her lungs.

"They don't have room in that truck for anyone else. You see that?" Vaughn asked to the room, to everyone who dared look outside again. "They aren't taking on anymore mouths to feed, just drawing people out and killing 'em to keep the status quo."

"Those people will be able to get through the stairwell in fifteen minutes," Isobel said.

Moira had a bible out and she was reading it through tears. Everyone else had a weapon, even Jeff.

Vaughn was camped out at the top of the barricaded stairwell with an array of weapons. He looked eager for a fight. The possibility of urban warfare excited him. He clearly wanted to kill someone living, someone who was more of an adversary than a shuffling corpse. Molly watched him. It ran chills down her spine but surprisingly also sent a warm blanket of security over her. *He could kill us all with his experience and his small armory, propped up against the wall. Or, he could protect us from this group of tyrants.* She thought. She was confident that he could take down four of them before breaking a sweat. Her only doubt came from the fact that it was *his* choice and Vaughn wasn't exactly known for his *good* decisions.

The group drank room-temperature coffee to stay alert as they sat silent for ten hours, until they felt like the anarchists had left the area. They relied on their bullhorn a lot, which allowed Vaughn to track their general location.

"We are really fortunate that they didn't come by our building at night like Hayden did. We'd be dead now," Markus said as he finally took the risk to speak aloud.

Molly felt her loneliness ten-fold when she was surrounded by the others. Edward had Moira. Isobel and Ben had each other's company. Jeff and Markus were able to create something new together. Vaughn had Hayden, even though it was wrong. Rob had his son. Staring out the window after everyone else had crept back to their own apartments, still fearing her own death, she realized that she had no one. Would it matter if she lived? Would it matter if she died? She was so stunned by her depression she couldn't even cry.

"Hey," Rob said. She thought she was alone and his voice made her jump. "Are you alright?"

"Yeah, why?" Molly asked.

"You've been staring out that window for almost an hour."

"No, it hasn't been that long," she said, but she knew it had been. She could see that the light was different outside.

Rob held his arms out and Molly welcomed his attention and his embrace. "I know you're mad that I haven't spent any time with you."

"Did Hayden say something?" Molly fumed.

"No, no! You are easy to read. I want to tell you that I'm sorry. Gabe's mental health has become an all-consuming thing for me."

"What do you mean his 'mental health'?"

"Something is changing inside of him. He is a darker version of himself."

"Aren't we all?" Molly said solemnly.

Rob didn't answer, choosing instead to enjoy a quiet moment with her in his arms but mostly because he feared that she was right.

PERMISSION TO LEAVE

The whole building was asleep except for Vaughn. He was so distracted and antsy from the event with the anarchists earlier that he'd even pushed Hayden away. He spent an hour cleaning and reloading a handgun and shotgun. He sharpened his machete. He could have chosen to slip out quietly and return before the others woke up but he felt the need to let someone know he was leaving.

He went to the second floor and knocked on Isobel's apartment door. Ben answered with his eyes still closed.

"Isobel here?" Vaughn asked.

"Of course she is. Where else would she be. Don't think she'll want to see you at this hour. What hour is it anyway?"

"Three or so in the morning," Vaughn guessed.

"Jesus Christ. What do you want?"

"Isobel. I already said that."

At that moment Isobel came to the door. "Who are you talking to Ben?"

"Isobel, it's me, Vaughn. I just came by to tell you that I'm going out."

"That's all you had to tell her?" Ben asked, miffed. "I could have told her that."

"You always leave without telling anyone. Why now? Why me?" Isobel yawned.

"I don't know. It felt important."

"Ok. Well, have fun? Watch out for those asshole communists." She wasn't sure what he was looking for from her.

"They were *anarchists*, Isobel," Ben pointed out knowledgeably.

"I know. I'm tired. Anarchists. Watch out for *them.* I'm going to go back to bed. Bye Vaughn." Isobel waved half-heartedly and stumbled back to her bedroom.

"She doesn't like you," Ben felt the need to inform Vaughn.

"She doesn't like you either man." Vaughn shrugged and walked back to the stairwell.

FRESH FARE

The air outside still smelled of the burned out mall, which only fueled Vaughn's anger.

"Where did you go, you bastards?" Vaughn crept through the night, cursing the anarchists with every other breath. The loss of the mall was a heavy blow; a blow alone that he wouldn't overlook. But then they came nearly to his front yard, killed people on his street, put fear into the eyes of his neighbors. His hatred of the anarchists was very personal because their destructive entrance into his life felt equally so.

He knew they had traveled east down Northgate Way because they had listened earlier to the blonde leader's fading voice as it echoed off buildings in that direction. He picked up his pace to a light jog and found himself making good progress down the thoroughfare. Vaughn wanted to see the mall up close so he took a sharp right when he reached the parking lot of the bank on the corner of the shopping complex.

The middle of the mall had been opened up where the arched wooden roof had burned away. It was as though he was looking down another road lit by stars. He walked carefully through the hole where the North entrance had been and stood there for a while. All the clothing was gone and left in its place were the twisted metal skeletons of racks that used to hold it.

"No more new shoes then," Vaughn said in farewell as he exited the fallen structure and re-launched his pursuit of the blonde and her dirty cronies.

He was nearing more residential areas and the blanket of dead on the streets was growing heavier. It was almost so difficult to move forward without trouble that he was going to admit defeat in his search and turn home but then he heard a gunshot.

"Stupid fuckers. Lead me right to you."

He traveled the remaining five blocks and ended up at the back corner of the QFC grocery store lot. He could hear the anarchists on the other side of the building. A Jiffy Lube sat even with the front parking lot of the store. Vaughn let himself into the small office of the vehicle maintenance business to plan his next move. He sat on the dirty floor, out of sight of anarchists and zombies alike. The smell of the grease and engine oil gave Vaughn a sort of high. He missed his truck and would give a lot just to sit in its cab again and drive around the city. It sat parked and untouched in the small parking lot of Willow Brook. Shaking himself from his daydream, he looked for a way onto the roof and he found a narrow staircase behind the counter that led to it.

He army crawled to the edge and lay flat, overlooking the entire lot of the grocery store. The anarchists had somehow found keys for enough of the large abandoned vehicles to form a semi-circle of them in front of the entrance. It had proven effective in keeping the dead away from them.

"Like a fucking wagon train laager."

Vaughn laughed, mostly at the fact that he remembered the term for it.

From this vantage point Vaughn spotted one of the anarchists outside the protective half-circle. He was in the bushes, maybe urinating, and playing with a lighter. Vaughn watched as the man repeatedly flicked the lighter open and closed. It ticked him off. He climbed back down from the roof and made a large circle around the outside edge of the lot until he was right behind the man.

"You like to start fires, huh?" Vaughn spoke softly and the man jumped. "Don't say anything. I've got my shotgun pointed at your back. If you want to live, you'll stay quiet."

"Who the fuck are you?" the man asked in a whisper.

"What does it matter who I am? All I can figure is that lighter in your hand looks like it could burn down a mall. *My* mall."

The man turned around and came out of the bushes. Vaughn could just make out a large dirty beard on his face. "*Your* mall? Me and my friends own this fucking city now. We'll burn what we want," the bearded man said as he flicked open his lighter once again.

"No, you won't. Not after tonight," Vaughn said, his shotgun still trained on the man's core.

"Whatcha gonna do? Steal my lighter?" the bearded man giggled. Vaughn could smell the sweet scent of alcohol on his breath.

"Much worse than that," Vaughn said as he pulled his silenced handgun from his belt.

The man put his hands up like he was being arrested. "You got a lotta guts walking into this. What do you have that you are protectin'? A bitch? A family?" The man smiled and his eyes lit up at the thought of women.

"Neither of those. Just me. My right to live. Look, I'm tired of talking. I'm going to kill you now."

The smile disappeared from his face and fear took its place. He dropped to his knees. It reminded Vaughn of the survivor that the anarchists had killed earlier that day, the one who had begged for his own life.

"Please sir. I'm just trying to survive, just like you. I'm just like you," the man cried out.

"You're nothing like me."

Vaughn raised his silenced handgun to aim for the man's heart.

"See you soon."

"Ple-" the man tried one last time to save himself but Vaughn had already pulled the trigger passed the point of no return. The lighter fell from the man's hand and to the pavement with a clink. His body fell too, only quieter. Vaughn took a length of rope and tied one end around the man's neck to drag his body to the back of a nearby car. He tied the loose end of the rope to the bumper.

"Don't go anywhere. I'll be back," he said to the corpse that had yet to reanimate. "So will you."

A GUT FEELING

Hayden couldn't fall asleep. She'd been nauseous before breakfast and again after dinner that day. She didn't feel sick otherwise but she did feel different and she'd definitely missed her period. She had to accept the fact that she was pregnant and hope that the others would welcome the idea when she decided to share it. She lay awake on Tom's couch, waiting for him to return and cursing herself for coming to Willow Brook. Something felt wrong about the place but it was too late to leave. She couldn't be a single mother on the streets of an infected city, running from house to house with a hungry baby. Surely they would die the first time the child cried aloud.

SPECULATION

Isobel had tried to fall back to sleep but Vaughn's short visit had left her concerned. Ben saw Isobel's concern and wouldn't go back to bed while she was awake.

"Do you want some tea or something, Iz?" Ben asked, his hand resting on her shoulder as she sat in a chair in the living room.

"I don't like being called 'Iz'," Isobel said bluntly.

"Vaughn calls you 'Iz'," Ben said to prove a point as he removed his hand and went to turn on the camp stove on the balcony to boil water.

"I don't like it when he does it either," Isobel said out the open slider. "And can you close that door? It's freezing in here already."

Ben frowned at her but she wasn't looking at him to see it. He got the water set up and came back inside, closing the slider behind him. He sat across from her and waited for her to start a conversation. He was tired of trying to please her. After almost ten minutes of silence the water was boiling outside so Ben brought it in and made them both a cup of tea.

"Maybe Vaughn isn't coming back," Isobel said after she'd sipped her tea a few times.

"He didn't have a whole lot with him. In fact he looked kind of like Lara Croft equipped with only rope and weapons."

"She has nicer breasts," Isobel laughed.

"I believe Lara was better educated too," Ben laughed with her. "But seriously, he'll be back. I think he enjoys feeling like the guy in charge. You can't be a king without a court."

"Hmm. You're right. We'll just have to wait for him to return to us lowly commoners." Isobel blew on the surface of her hot tea and watched as the steam rose in delicate tendrils.

SNEAK ATTACK

Vaughn moved right up to the semi-circle of vehicles. He climbed into the bed of a truck that was parked dead center in front of the store entrance. The anarchists had lit the front of the building with two torches, highlighting their location and inviting the dead to join them. The blonde leader sat in a folding camp chair smoking a cigarette and taking swigs from what was probably a room-temperature beer. He was ready to take her out when she stood up and went inside the QFC. She came out less than a minute later with two men that looked a lot like the bearded man he'd already killed. He could hear her easily as she spoke to them.

"Dimitry went out to piss and he hasn't come back. One of you needs to go find him."

"I'll go," the skinnier bearded man volunteered. His arms were covered in tattoos that suggested a former membership with a gang.

"What about me?" the other man asked. He was fat and sweaty, like the pregnant woman Vaughn had wasted a rescue mission on some time ago.

"Brick, the dead will overwhelm us here if we don't do something about it. Take some of them out."

"On it," the fat man said as he pulled a machete from behind his back and lumbered off out of the glow of the torches and into the dark of the lot.

Vaughn was growing angrier the longer he was with the anarchists. He went to look for the skinny gangbanger but instead of following him he just went back to the body of 'Dimitry' and waited for the living to find the dead. Maybe they'd designated this area as the urinal. Dimitry had already returned from the dead and was struggling to get off the ground. Vaughn had tied the rope short though and the zombie was stuck in a kneeling position.

The gangbanger showed up a minute later and saw Dimitry but not Vaughn, who was hiding in the bushes.

"Oh shit, man. What happened to you?" the skinny man asked his undead friend. Vaughn stayed in the bushes and pulled the trigger again, killing the gangbanger. Another shot to the heart. Vaughn: 2, Anarchists: 0. He stepped out of concealment, smelling faintly of piss, and walked up to the body.

"You picked the wrong friends," he said as he tied a length of rope to his second catch. "As in life, so in death." He left the tattooed man there to rise beside the bearded man and went to find the fat one. He was starting to have fun.

"Here little piggies!" the fat man snorted, mocking the zombies. "All you do is eat, eat, eat." And then he hit one in the head with the machete. *Thunk*. Vaughn could see that he'd already successfully killed around twenty of the dead in the short time he'd been working at it.

As impressed as Vaughn was with Brick's ability to put down the corpses in one hit, he was boiling with rage. The anarchists weren't practicing what they preached. Their crowd control methods directly violated their zombie majority, no-kill policy.

"Fucking hypocrites," Vaughn whispered. He waited for Brick to kill a few more to make a clear path, then he pulled out a roll of duct tape from his cargo pants. He pulled slowly on the tape to keep the noise down. Selecting a length that he thought could wrap once around Brick's fat head, he cut it with a pocket knife and ran up behind the thick man. As quickly as he could he covered Brick's mouth with the tape and grabbed his wrists, forcing his arms behind his back. He used rope to tie the man's wrists together.

Brick bucked back and forth, giving Vaughn a workout as he pulled him around the back of the QFC. A semi-truck was still parked in the loading area. Vaughn tied Brick to its bumper and stood in front of him. Brick's eyes were wide in terror and he struggled to get loose but Vaughn's knots were tight and out of reach.

"You can hear me still, right?" Vaughn asked him.

"Fuuuuuhhh uuuuuuu," Brick managed through the tape on his mouth.

"You got a lotta meat on you big boy. And as you said, these zombies love to eat, eat, eat. Y'all want them to be well fed, don't you? So they stay majority, right?"

"Nuuuuuhhhhhho!" the man yelled through the duct tape.

"So you *don't* want them to stay the majority? That's why you were killing them? I'm really confused. Tell you what; I'm going to leave you here to sort it out." Vaughn smiled, picked up Brick's machete and threw it into a garbage bin. "It's time to go talk to the head bitch." Vaughn left Brick to die and walked the short distance back to the front of the grocery store.

"Brick! You dumbshit, where are you?" the blonde yelled from the safety of her semi-circle. "Guys?"

Vaughn could see that she was unarmed but he didn't know how many dirty, bearded men were hidden within the store. There were too many unknowns but Vaughn was growing impatient. He was ready to play with this mouse before killing it. He took out his bowie knife and walked the outside arc of the vehicles, puncturing the tires as he went. He waited for her to turn her back and then he slid underneath the truck, stood up and positioned himself directly in front of her.

"What the hell is that hissing noise?" she asked no one as she turned around and saw Vaughn.

"The air leaving all your outside tires. I hope you didn't plan on going anywhere."

"Who are *you*?" she asked, crossing her arms.

"Why does everyone need to know that?" Vaughn sighed. "I'm from a building on the other side of Northgate, from earlier."

"I thought we got all of you."

"You missed me," Vaughn smiled.

"Well, the offer has expired. We aren't taking any more people on so unless you want to die I'd recommend you leave before I get a gun in my hands." She uncrossed her arms, readying them for a weapon to appear.

"Call me a lone wolf if you like but I don't need your company unless it's for a fuck."

"I've got plenty of men if I need one. Speaking of men, what did you do to them?" the blonde accused and inquired in one breath. Her eyes looked beyond him, waiting for the shapes of the men to appear out of the dark.

"Gave them a new life; helped your majority out a little bit. You are *very* welcome." Vaughn bowed mockingly.

Just then three men came out of the store entrance, all armed and angry. One man carried an extra rifle.

"Rachel!" he yelled as he tossed the gun to her. Vaughn knew the war had begun. He hopped into the bed of the truck and back out of it on the other side of the circle. Two of the men walked closely together in his direction. As soon as they reached the truck and started over the bed he raised his shotgun and killed them both.

"They're as dumb as the fucking zombies!" Vaughn yelled. Seeing the undead coming from the other side of the lot he ran to an R.V. that was parked in the laager. The door to its inside was on the outside of the circle. He opened it and climbed inside. There wasn't a safe place to dodge bullets inside the vehicle's thin-walled living space but he could take one of them out if they followed him inside. The door handle moved and another brainless anarchist displayed his body for Vaughn to fill with bullets. The body fell on the hideaway bed and Vaughn exited the camper.

While inside he hadn't seen if more men had come out of the grocery store. The leader, Rachel, was nowhere in sight. He could see movement in the aisles of the store, torches being carried back and forth. He was reluctant to go into the building. He didn't know the layout very well and there were too many places to hide, but he wanted a victory.

Vaughn walked slowly to the front door of the darkened store. He opened it and the smell of rotten food hit him unexpectedly. He coughed and a bullet whizzed by his head. Dropping to a crouch he made his way to the checkout lanes at the front and waited for someone to make a poor decision. A soft glow was approaching from the back of the store. Someone with a torch was coming for him. He took out the silenced handgun and aimed for their head. He didn't need any zombies in the enclosed space. The body dropped and the torch fell against a shelf full of chips. The plastic, engulfed in flames, melted and filled the air with thick smoke. Vaughn could hear coughing from the next aisle to the right of the fire. He moved to his right and lay on the floor, dragging his body on the smooth surface of the market. An anarchist sat in the aisle, his back against the shelf, coughing and wiping his eyes. Vaughn took him out with another silenced bullet. The man's head slumped on his chest and a tear fell from his eye.

A man dressed in a hastily buttoned white shirt and dirty khaki pants emerged from the depths of the deli department on the left side of the store. His arms were up in surrender. "I'm not with them. I've been held prisoner. Please, take me with you," the clean-cut man said.

"Take off your shirt." Vaughn said.

"What?"

"Do you want to live? Take off your fucking shirt!" Vaughn said with more force.

The man looked behind him for a second, as though he was taking commands from a hidden individual. He started to unbutton his shirt and just as Vaughn saw the beginning ink of a large chest tattoo he heard footsteps running up behind him. Still on the floor, Vaughn pulled his bowie knife out and flipped onto his back. A teenager in combat boots and a wife-beater jumped on top of him and onto the large blade of the knife. Vaughn rolled the teen off of him and withdrew the knife from the boy's chest. The boy put a hand to the wound. Vaughn put the silenced gun to the teen's head and shortened his dying time.

"He was my only son! You killed him!" The man with the khakis had removed the white shirt altogether and a large Mexican gang tattoo covered his chest. "Rachel, where's my gun?" the man yelled.

A golden handgun slid across the floor and the man bent down to pick it up. Vaughn got to his feet and ran back behind the registers. A bullet grazed his shoulder.

"You can't aim very well with that bedazzled thing; *looks* better than it works," Vaughn taunted the shooter. He put his handgun away and took his shotgun from his back holster. "I've got some extra gems if you want to decorate it some more. Forgot my glue gun though." Vaughn heard no response from the man so he moved back carefully to where he'd left the body of the boy. There he found the khaki pants man, holding his son and crying. His golden gun lay on the ground and he didn't move to grab it.

"Kill me. I want to be with my boy. I'm not staying in this world without him."

"I'm not going to waste my bullets on someone who wants to die. Kill yourself," Vaughn pointed to the golden gun on the floor.

"I won't go to Heaven."

"You think your son is there?" Vaughn scoffed.

"He was a good boy. You didn't know him," the man cried more over his son whose white tank top had become red with his blood.

"I'm going to shoot you now. But only because I hate hearing men cry. I don't believe in Heaven." Vaughn withdrew his silenced gun once again and ended the man's life.

"I'm tired and I'm ready to go home. Can you all just come out and we can get this wrapped up?" Vaughn yelled into the aisles of the store. He heard the blonde leader laugh somewhere near the back.

"Lower your weapons," she yelled back. "I'm coming up there.

"Lower yours," Vaughn said as he saw her coming out of the soup aisle.

"They are. You're outnumbered anyway so I only see one end to this affair." Rachel wore a smirk on her face. It didn't matter to her that so many of her men died. She was still breathing.

"I'm not sure of the count. Maybe I still have a chance." Vaughn packed his guns away and shrugged.

"Everyone out!" Rachel yelled at the top of her lungs. A giant blonde-haired man appeared from behind the floral department counter, he had a crossbow and he looked like he could be Rachel's brother. He came to join her at her side. No one else appeared.

"How many goons did you have? 'Cause I killed, like, ten of 'em."

Rachel's face turned white. The man at her side raised his crossbow. She placed a hand on it and made him lower the weapon. "You killed them all?" she said quietly. "Are you special forces or something?"

"Nope, just special. Now, can we end this?" Vaughn asked.

"I can't let you walk out of here after tearing apart everything I've created. You'll have to fight Hans. No weapons, man vs. man, hand to hand combat."

Vaughn laughed at the man's cliché of a name. "Like in the movies?"

"Just like in the movies. Otherwise we'll be here all night dodging each other's bullets."

"Let's go outside then, shall we?" Vaughn said as he backed up towards the entrance. Once outside he bent down to set his guns on the ground. Hans did the same with his crossbow, taking an extra moment to tuck his long blonde hair back behind his ears. Vaughn didn't have time for games like this. He pulled a grenade he'd stowed in a pocket of his cargo pants out and pulled the pin, chucking the small explosive at Hans as he was still standing back up. Vaughn prayed it worked and prepared for the explosion by running to the pickup truck one final time to slide underneath it. The explosion rocked every vehicle in the semi-circle and shattered the windows of the grocery. Vaughn dared to raise his head above the truck to look for Hans but he could only find a few harmless pieces.

Rachel had been blown backward against the hard cement of the building's front wall. Her gun had landed too far away for her to reach before Vaughn was in her lap. She was screaming.

"I come here armed to the teeth and you want me to punch a guy? Come on!"

"But, that's . . . not fair," Rachel managed to spit the words out with blood and a few teeth.

"All is fair in love and war and this certainly isn't love, blondie." He pulled his handgun out.

"Really, though, who are you?" She coughed up more blood.

"Let's just say that I'm kind of an important guy to miss," Vaughn answered. He removed the silencer from his gun and placed the barrel against Rachel's head.

"Ooops," she said weakly.

"Ooops," Vaughn said as he moved the gun from her head to her heart.

ROLE PLAYING

If Vaughn could do things like leave the building without telling her why or where he was going, Hayden was going to do what she wanted to as well. She went downstairs to the common area in her skimpiest tank top and shortest shorts and lay on the couch, pretending to read a book, waiting for a man to find her there. She didn't care which man it was as long as he was willing to play along. She heard an apartment door open and soon Ben had joined her in the room.

"Hayden," he said, acknowledging her as he went to sit in an armchair across the room from her.

"You look tired," she said to him, sitting up slightly to make her breasts hang and appear larger.

"It's not from a lack of sleep," he said with a sigh.

"What do you mean?" she asked as she closed her book.

"You don't want to hear about an old man's pangs of the heart," he smiled.

"You are *not* old, Ben."

"Then what is it? Why doesn't Isobel care for me?" he asked her with every expectation of hearing the answer.

"She doesn't know how to have fun. She is caught up in all the details and controlling every moment. There's no spontaneousness."

"The word is *spontaneity*," Ben corrected.

"Oh, professor! I do believe I am in love," she laughed as she threw a hand across her forehead dramatically.

"But you are right about her. She's too high-strung." Ben turned to look out the dark window. "I wonder where Vaughn is right now."

"I don't," Hayden said.

"It's nice to get away from him for a minute, isn't it?" He smiled knowingly.

"He won't be back for awhile if I know him at all. Do you want to come upstairs with me? Keep me company?" she smiled coyly.

"Are you asking me to bed?" Ben asked her, wide-eyed.

"Exercise a little *spontaneity* and come play a game. Can you get the keys to the Cooper's apartment?" Hayden got up off the couch and walked toward Ben. She held a hand out to him and he grabbed it. His palms were sweating and he felt like a teenager again, walking to a dark room with a girl, not knowing what to expect.

"Yeah. But why there?" Ben asked.

"Let's pretend we're starting a family."

Ben snuck back into his and Isobel's apartment quietly and found the key ring from the office. He took the key to 305 and walked with Hayden upstairs.

"I've never role played before," he whispered.

"It's not hard. Pretend I'm someone else."

"Isobel?"

"Sure."

"This is only for tonight. I don't ever want her to know about this."

"It's my secret," Hayden said and kissed him as he unlocked the apartment door. She led him past the nursery where she could see the crib and changing table in one corner and into the master bedroom. They lay down on the bed together and started to undress.

"Tell me how beautiful our baby will be."

"She'll be gorgeous, Isobel."

"Don't say her name," Hayden hissed and smacked his arm.

"I have to; it's part of the fantasy."

"Ok, well I'm going to call you Tom then."

"I'm alright with that. We're Vaughn and Isobel and we're making love and having a baby together," Ben said aloud to try and make it more real.

"Oh, Tom! I want you in me!" Hayden whined.

Ben took a second to think about his response. "Will I hurt the baby?" he asked with concern in his voice.

"That's good, that's good," Hayden said. "Don't worry. The baby will be fine."

"I'm going to enter you now."

"Ew, don't narrate it! Just do it! Fuck me, Tom!" Hayden yelled.

Ben's hands were softer than Vaughn's. Hayden liked the difference even if it took away from the fantasy. She felt like she could be loved by his hands and, for a half an hour, she was.

PROOF OF DEATH

When Vaughn got back to Willow Brook he had a smile on his face, a graze mark on his shoulder and a gift for Isobel. He had wanted to do something bigger, like bring some of the zombies back with him to show the group but it was too much work and too many blocks to cover. He knocked on her door but no one answered, not even Ben. He tried the knob and it was unlocked. Inside, Isobel had fallen asleep in the living room. Two cups of cold tea sat on the coffee table. *Where's Ben?* Vaughn wondered. The man usually followed Isobel like a loyal dog. He had to be there somewhere.

"Oh well. I'm not here to see you anyway," he said to the room. Isobel moved in her sleep from the noise. He didn't want to wake her so he set down his gift, a lock of beautiful but dirty blonde hair, on the table along with a note bearing three words: *we are safe*. He left her apartment and made his way back to his own on the third floor. Upstairs, he passed Ben in the hallway.

"I was just getting a snack," Ben hurried to explain his being on the third floor. He couldn't stop smiling though. He looked guilty of something.

"Do you want me to tell you when I take a shit? I don't care why you are here," Vaughn said as he kept walking to his door. Hayden opened the door to the Cooper's and stood in the doorway, she was wrapped in a bed sheet.

"Goodnight Ben!" She waved at him, making him blush as he continued to the stairs.

"Don't you mean 'hi Vaughn'? And why are you sleeping in there?" Vaughn asked her as he grabbed her face, forcing her to look at him.

"Don't touch me like that." She pulled his hand from her jaw.

He slapped her cheek. "I'll touch you how I want. Are you coming over?"

After being hit she didn't feel like she had the choice to say no. She followed him to his cold apartment and let his rough hands undo the soft work of Ben's.

CURIOSITY

Isobel finally woke around noon that day. Ben sat on the couch across from her, reading a book. Two new cups of steaming tea sat on the coffee table next to something else.

"What is that?" Isobel pointed at but didn't touch the bunch of hair. "Or, whose is that?"

"Vaughn left it here. Ask him," Ben said quickly before he returned to reading his book. "Don't waste this tea too. Take it with you."

Isobel gulped the hot tea, burning her tongue and throat a little. She stood up to the pain of her ankle and hobbled slowly to her bedroom to change clothes. She dug in a kitchen drawer for a Ziploc bag to put the hair in.

"I'll be back," she said to Ben, who didn't respond. On her way to the stairs she passed Rob and Gabe in the hallway. They were playing with toys and talking in whispers. Hayden was in the common area writing in a notebook and staying out of view of the windows. Isobel nodded to her when she looked up.

"Do you need help up the stairs?" Hayden asked.

"No, that's alright. I think I can do it. Thank you though." Isobel smiled at the teen. She took each stair one at a time and she could feel Hayden watching her the entire five minutes it took her to make it up the first flight of them.

PLAY TIME

As soon as Isobel was making her way up the second flight of stairs, Hayden jumped up from the chair she was on and ran down the hall to Isobel's apartment.

"Isobel just left," Rob called out to her. "Didn't you see her?"

"Um, yeah. I wanted to ask Ben if I could borrow a book." Hayden lied as she let herself into the unlocked apartment and closed and locked the door behind her.

"I see," Rob said.

"Ben doesn't like Vampire books," Gabe said.

"That is exactly what I was thinking," Rob said to his son. "Let's go have some lunch, what do you say?"

"Yum!" Gabe jumped to his feet from the hall floor.

"Bring your toys."

Gabe harrumphed and picked them up. "You should help 'cause you played with them too."

"Which ones did I play with?" Rob joked.

"You touched this one and this one," Gabe said as he pointed to toys he was leaving for his dad to clean up. "Oh and this one too!" He dropped one of the toys he'd already picked up.

"Gabe! How about we each pick up half?"

Hayden watched them through the peephole of Isobel's apartment door. Behind her Ben had closed his book and started towards her.

"Isobel will kill us if she knows you were in here. Vaughn probably will too. Do you *want* to die?"

"Shh! Rob and Gabe are leaving now." She watched them finish picking up their mess and disappear from view. Once she was satisfied that they had left, she turned to Ben in the dark entry and kissed him. Ben pulled her from him.

"Why are you here?" he asked her.

She replied by unclasping his belt and unzipping his pants. "I want more."

"Ok, well, it's not that I don't want more, it's just, we are going to get caught. It's the middle of the day." Ben was trying to pry the girl off of him but she was making it difficult. "This is Isobel's apartment! Not mine, not an empty one, definitely not yours! We can't do this!" Ben succeeded in pushing her away.

"Fine!" she yelled. "Maybe someone else wants to play!"

"You're not a toy, Hayden," Ben said quietly as he kissed her forehead. "And there are other ways to show love." He caressed her cheek lovingly. She turned away to unlock and open the door.

"Not in my world," she said before running down the hall.

Ben stood for a moment in the doorway thinking about the choices he had made and the ones he had yet to make. Life was becoming difficult when right and wrong were becoming similar shades of grey.

KILLING AS KINDNESS

"What did you do, Vaughn?" Isobel asked, holding up the bag containing his 'gift' of Rachel's hair and wincing from the pain in her ankle.

"Do you really want to know?" He tried to read her face.

"I know you didn't go out at three in the morning to give free haircuts," Isobel said as she lowered herself onto Vaughn's couch.

"I killed the anarchists." He smiled like a proud child.

"All of them?" She looked amazed.

"Every. Last. One."

"That was fifteen people." She counted on her fingers everyone she could remember on the truck yesterday.

"Twelve," he corrected her. "But I could have handled fifteen easily."

Isobel threw the bag at him. "Keep it. It's your trophy."

"Why'd you put it in a bag?" he laughed as he looked through the plastic at her.

"I don't know. It's gross," Isobel said as she looked at it again.

"It's just dirty hair. We all have it." Vaughn ran his fingers through his own greasy locks.

"It belongs to a dead woman!" she screeched.

"She wasn't dead when I cut it off."

"Ok, stop there. I don't want to know the details. As long as we are safe and they won't be coming back here, I'm good."

"They won't be coming back; not here anyway." Vaughn smiled.

"Thank you," Isobel said, standing up and forcing herself to hug Vaughn. "Even though you may have just done it for your own safety, we did benefit from your murderous rampage."

"The 'thank you' would have been enough."

"A note *without* a pile of a dead woman's hair would have been enough too," Isobel said and then made her way slowly back down to her apartment.

Ben awaited her nervously. He had his book in his hands but he wasn't reading it, only staring at the blank paper between the lines. Isobel entered the apartment and Ben stood up.

"I'm not the pope," Isobel said.

"What?" Ben asked, confused.

"You don't need to stand when I come into the room. You can sit," she assured him.

"Oh," he said as he sat back down, not really realizing that he had stood to begin with.

"Your fly is down," Isobel pointed out.

Ben's face flashed red as he zipped it up. He'd remembered to redo his belt but not his pants.

"We shouldn't have taken in Hayden," Ben blurted out.

"She just offered to help me up the stairs. What could *you* have against her?" Isobel asked, thinking it strange that Ben suddenly cared either way about Hayden.

Ben chose his words carefully. "She . . . came onto me."

"She's confused. She has all those teenage hormones racing around in her and Vaughn treats her like shit so, you are the obvious next choice."

"What do I do?"

"You do the right thing, the adult thing. You deny her. She's underage," Isobel said.

Ben's chest hurt a little. He hadn't done the right thing. He'd followed her upstairs and entered her and he had liked it.

"But Vaughn didn't," he said, looking for some sort of redemption.

"If we based our moral standards off of Vaughn's, well, we'd be truly fucked."

"Didn't you go upstairs to thank him profusely for being our savior?" Ben teased.

"I've never been a fan of him but you have to admit that it was a pretty nice thing he did for all of us."

"He's a wolf in sheep's clothing. I just hope that last night he got his fill of shooting the living."

FRIENDSHIPS FORGED . . .

Three days had passed since the anarchists tried to take over the neighborhood. The group had warmed only slightly towards Vaughn when they'd all heard of what he'd done. But life was brighter and louder again inside of Willow Brook, now that everyone could make noise again without fear of alerting an enemy.

Gabe was running sprints down the second floor hallway for exercise and when he was done he grabbed some toys and camped out on the floor in a bit of sunshine to play.

While he was there he thought he heard a voice, not unlike his own; a child's voice calling for his help. It was coming through the chairs, lamps, and bedside tables tossed into the stairwell to keep the dead people away. For a moment Gabe was terrified. He thought it might be a zombie trying to eat him. But then his brain caught up with his imagination, reminding him that zombies didn't use words like regular people did.

"Hello?" Gabe whispered. He turned away from the apartments down the hallway so the adults wouldn't butt in. He pretended to keep playing with his toys but he waited anxiously for the child to respond. "Are you there?"

"Can you help me? I need help. And food and I'm stuck," a weak voice responded.

"How did you get in there? They hammered everything downstairs."

"They did a bad job 'cause the dead people opened it up again. There is a lot of 'em so I had to squish into here and hide. But I'm hungry now and I can't climb up anymore."

"Where are you in there?" Gabe asked. The child grunted and pushed a hand through the debris. Gabe reached out and grabbed it. "I'm Gabe, nice to meet you."

"I'm Charlie. I'm hungry! Can you give me some food?"

Gabe ran to his room and grabbed some peanut butter stuffed cheese crackers that were still unopened; he'd been saving them for later but Charlie needed them more. The plastic crinkled in Charlie's hand as he pulled apart the wrapping and consumed the crackers in no more than a minute.

"Do you have anything to drink?" Charlie's voice was thicker sounding from the peanut butter. Gabe had thought ahead and brought a juice box too and he handed it to the outstretched and crumb-covered arm. The box disappeared into the furniture and he heard slurping shortly thereafter.

"Ahhhhhhh. That was good. Got anymore?"

"Not right now. I can try to sneak some stuff from dinner for you. How old are you Charlie?"

"Six."

"Stick your hand back out."

Charlie poked his arm through the opening one more time and Gabe stuck a matchbox car into his hand.

"You can keep that. I'll bring you some more food in a little bit." Charlie didn't respond but Gabe could hear car noises and he knew that, because of him, Charlie was happier; if only temporarily.

"Who were you talking to Gabe?" Rob asked as they walked to dinner. He'd seen Gabe in the hall but didn't want to disturb him.

"Um . . . nobody." Gabe didn't want to share Charlie with anyone else and he was scared that his dad would make Charlie go back to his own house.

"Do you have a friend that you can't see?" Rob knew imaginary friends were a common occurrence and not an unhealthy development. It was probably just another way that Gabe had found to cope with the craziness and his lack of playmates his own age.

"How did you know?" Gabe was amazed at his dad. He knew everything. "His name is Charlie and all I can see is his arm."

Rob laughed. He was expecting purple hair or silly clothes but an imaginary arm? "That's strange."

"And he likes peanut butter and juice."

"How does he eat and drink with just an arm?"

"He takes the food and puts it in his mouth. Duh."

At dinner, which was in Molly's apartment that night, Gabe couldn't stop talking about Charlie.

" . . . and he likes matchbox cars and he wants me to bring him some food and he's my friend."

"Jeez, Charlie sounds real," Molly leaned over to Rob and whispered. She'd gotten to know Gabe and she didn't see him as the imaginary friend type.

Moira didn't think the boy was imaginary either. "How could a child survive out there for this long?" Moira asked.

"Hayden did it," Ben said.

"She is almost an adult. Charlie is supposedly six. He isn't real," Markus tried to reason.

Isobel laughed. "Real or not, at least I don't have to play with Legos anymore."

"You never did! It was either me or Molly," Moira frowned at her. "My hands still hurt from trying to pry those blocks apart."

"Gabe," Edward said to the boy, "does your friend like to draw or read?"

"I don't know yet. I just met him."

"That's strange," Rob whispered to Molly. "Usually when children have imaginary friends, they know all about them. There is no 'getting to know you' stage."

"He isn't imaginary! He's real!" Gabe yelled.

"Calm down, Gabe. Let's focus on eating dinner right now. No more talk about Charlie."

Dinner was uneventful after Gabe's small explosion of emotion and when everyone was finished, Gabe jumped back to the topic of Charlie.

"Can I bring him some food . . . please?" Gabe was begging as Molly and the others cleaned their plates from the table.

"You have to promise to eat it if 'he' doesn't, ok?" Rob said.

"Oh he'll eat it!" Gabe's eyes lit up.

"Gabe?" Rob wanted to hear two words from his son.

"I promise."

Rob made a small plate of leftovers and handed it to Gabe.

"Bring the plate back to Molly when you're done," he told the boy as he ran off.

. . . AND LOST

Gabe carried the plate to the top step and called out to his friend.

"Are you there Charlie? I brought you dinner." Gabe leaned forward, straining to see any movement in the barricade. He could hear muffled crying but no response. "Are you ok?"

"They got me. My leg," Charlie sobbed louder.

"What do you mean? How could they get you?"

"They climbed up in the hole I made. They bit my leg and now it hurts and it's wet."

Gabe knew that a bite was a bad thing. His dad had kept a lot of things from him to "protect" him, he was told, but Rob had taught his son that bites were bad.

"I'll get help then. I'll get my dad."

"I don't wanna be a monster." Charlie cried much louder.

"Here, reach out your hand and take this food." Charlie's tiny hand accepted the leftovers and Gabe ran down the hall to his father.

"Dad! Charlie needs help! They got him!"

"That's not funny Gabe. You shouldn't joke about it. Charlie will be fine. He can't get the infection."

"Why not? He's just a boy like me."

"He's not real so he can't get sick, that's why."

"He is too real and he's stuck in the stairs and he needs help!" Gabe started to cry and Rob knew then that his son did not have an imaginary friend. Charlie was actually real. He followed his son to the end of the hall and sat next to him on the top step.

"Charlie, are you there? Can you show me your hand?"

Again a tiny hand, this time slightly green from smashed dinner peas, emerged from a gap in the debris. Rob gasped.

"I told you he was real."

"We're going to get you out of there, ok?" Rob reassured the little boy. It took thirty minutes to remove enough furniture to see the child's face and thin upper body. He was barely alive, even before any injury he may have acquired, weighing just above nothing. "Gabe, go get more help. Find Ben and Isobel and tell them to come here. Then I want you to go to Molly and stay with her."

Gabe made no move to leave. "I want to stay with Charlie."

"He's in bad shape kiddo. I don't think you want to see him like that."

"I don't. But, he needs a friend."

Rob couldn't think of anymore to say to spare his son the tragedy of the situation. "Ok. Get Ben and Isobel and bring them back." Gabe smiled, nodded, and sprinted away. He was still brimming with youthful hope that his dad and the others could save his new friend.

Ben and Isobel were as stunned as Rob.

"How'd he get that far up the stairwell?" Ben was warily eyeing the mess of chair and table legs, books, clothing, and other items there.

"He is so tiny and it was his only choice." Isobel was teary-eyed and holding Charlie's hand. She could see and feel the life fading from the child.

"It didn't do him much good. Gabe says he was bitten," Rob added.

"We have to get him out of there whether that is true or not. If he was bitten, before he turns. If he wasn't, before he dies from something we could save him from." Ben was starting to formulate a plan of object removal as he spoke.

A thought occurred to Isobel that she shared with the men. "He'll spread disease if he dies and we leave him there. We'd be forced to abandon Willow Brook."

"Let's stop talking and get to it then. Step back Gabe."

Gabe stood across the hall in the common area as the adults slowly moved one household object after another from the pile that was tightly packed around Charlie. Every so often he would see Charlie's hands flinch and his face grimace in pain as items shifted and settled over his body. It was when Ben moved a large framed mirror from atop the child that they saw the bites and the blood.

"Gabe, go to Molly," Rob said without looking at his son. "Now!" he yelled more forcefully when he sensed that Gabe hadn't moved. Isobel went to him, placed her hands on his shoulders and guided him away.

"Goodbye Charlie!" Gabe whispered as they walked down the hall. He knew if he spoke any louder that he would start to cry. His dad had been right. He really didn't want to see his friend like that, all messy and ripped up. He could feel his chest get heavy with sobs and his eyes filled with tears as he reached blindly in front of him for the doorknob of Molly's apartment. He couldn't find it so Isobel took over, finally getting the door open. Gabe ran to Molly, who was seated on the couch reading, and took shelter close beside her.

MOVERS

"I don't want to get dirty," Markus was unenthusiastic about being recruited to get Charlie out.

"Too bad. I need someone to hold this table out of the way while two others gently ease him out," Rob said.

"I'll hold the table then," Markus quickly volunteered. "That sounds like the cleanest job."

"Someone should have a gun. In the event that something does crawl up through the opening he made," Ben suggested. "I'll grab mine."

"Jeff that leaves you and me to free him. Can you help me do that?" Rob asked.

Jeff had come out with Markus but was aimlessly wandering around, looking out the windows of the common area and picking food out of his teeth, disinterested in the goings on of the stairwell. "Huh?"

"Get over here and help please. You'll support his shoulders while I lift what's left of his legs," Rob explained.

"Why do I have to hold the teeth end of his body?"

"He isn't dead yet, Jeff." Rob looked daggers at him.

"It could happen at any moment," Jeff hypothesized.

"All the more reason we should get him out now!"

Ben had returned with his gun and a thick wool blanket to wrap Charlie in. "I'm ready when you are." He tossed the blanket over the back of a chair and had his handgun trained on the hole in the debris, his finger positioned to quickly slide down onto the trigger.

"On three then. One. Two. Three!" Rob yelled.

Markus pulled the table up with all of his strength. Jeff and Rob grabbed the boy's body and gently freed him from the barricade. Ben set his gun down for a second to spread the blanket across a couch in the common area. They placed the child on top of the blanket to inspect his wounds.

"There's something crawling up the hole already!" Markus yelled as he dropped the table and ran for safety into Jeff's apartment.

"Ben, get your gun back on that hole! Jeff, watch Charlie! I'm going to repack the barricade," Rob directed.

Ben shot the zombie as its head appeared in the small hole. The shot made everyone jump. The pile of furniture in the stairwell was pulsing; moving up and down as though it had a heart beat. The hallway downstairs was filled to capacity with the dead and they were piling on one another trying to push their way through the blockade. Charlie's living flesh and spilled blood had put a strong scent in the air around the stairwell. The sound of the bullet had only encouraged their pursuit.

Isobel ran to her apartment and dragged her couch out into the hall. Jeff left Charlie's side to help her move it faster. Molly and Gabe came into the hall.

"Was that Charlie? Is he dead?" Gabe asked, looking around for answers.

Isobel was out of breath from pulling on the couch. All she could do was shake her head. Gabe squeezed past the couch and ran ahead to check on Charlie. Rob was busy repacking the debris for the tightest, most secure fit.

"What's going on?" Molly asked.

"They're trying to get through. The whole barricade is moving. We have to stop them. Grab something heavy."

Once at the top of the stairs, Jeff and Isobel tipped the couch up onto its side and pushed it on top of the pile. Rob stood back to see if the weight was helping.

"A second couch should do it," Molly suggested. "We can use Angela's. It's uncomfortable anyway and really heavy. It'll take everyone to move it."

Jeff returned to his apartment to check on Markus while Rob, Molly, Isobel and Ben walked quickly to Molly's apartment for the couch, leaving Gabe alone to find out what had happened to his friend.

Gabe found Charlie on the couch as he breathed his last breath. The amount of infected saliva that had entered his body made for a quick turn upon death and a few seconds after dying, the boy stood up. Gabe couldn't tell the difference.

"You should stay on the couch. Your leg doesn't look so good. But don't worry. My dad could probably fix it," Gabe said as his friend stumbled toward him. He ran forward to help Charlie stay upright and to give him a hug. Gabe was incredibly happy that his new friend was free from the stairwell.

"You're really cold Charlie. I can warm you up!" Gabe laughed and started rubbing the boys back briskly. "This is what my dad does if I'm cold."

"Gabe, no!" Rob yelled as he and the others returned to the common area, a heavy couch in tow.

Charlie's mouth was almost closed on Gabe's neck. Rob dropped his corner of the couch and ran forward to tear his child from the beast's arms. He pushed Charlie away with a force that made the boy's head slam against the wall. It wasn't enough to stop the zombie child. He stood back up.

Ben had dropped his corner of the couch as well and grabbed his gun. He shot without hesitation, which didn't leave Rob any time to cover Gabe's eyes. Blood and brain hit the wall. Isobel and Molly had dropped the couch altogether, unable to hold up the massive piece on their own. They ran to Rob and Gabe.

Gabe cried hysterically, hitting his dad. "Why'd you guys do that to Charlie? He was gonna play with me!"

"He was a monster and daddy had to protect you from him. He was going to hurt you. I couldn't let that happen," Rob said as he took the beating from his son.

"I hate you. I hate you!" Gabe yelled as he pried himself from his father's arms and ran down the hallway to his room. Rob stood in the common area staring at the spot on the wall where Charlie's life had ended for good.

"Let's get this couch on top of the other one first and then we can clean up this mess," Ben said to Molly and Isobel, realizing they had little time at the moment to dwell on the emotional impact of what had just transpired.

"Can you help us finish the couch, Rob?" Molly asked the pale and shaken man gently, knowing the couch was too heavy for only three people. "Rob?"

"Sure," Rob said, snapping out of the trance that had taken him. He picked the blanket up off the couch and tossed it over Charlie's body, wiped the sweat from his palms and grabbed his corner of the couch once again.

PICKING UP THE PIECES

Hayden hadn't watched as Charlie was rescued or killed. She had heard the gunshot and waited to come downstairs, Vaughn in tow, to find out what had happened. It was an hour, maybe more, after she'd heard the gun when she stepped into the second floor common area. No one was in the living room and it looked quite different than it ever had to her.

"There's more furniture on the barricade," Vaughn noticed as he touched the couches, one after the other, shaking them to test their stability. "Do you think something tried to get through?"

"Something did." Hayden pointed at the person-shaped blanket against the common room wall and the bloodstain above it. She could tell by its small size that it was a child and it brought her to tears.

"Why are you crying, you don't even know who it was!" Vaughn said. He approached the blanket and kicked it roughly to make sure whoever it used to be was dead. Satisfied with its deadness when it didn't move in response, Vaughn gripped a corner of the blanket and pulled it off.

"Whoa."

There was little left of the child's head. Hayden, unable to stomach the sight, ran back upstairs leaving Vaughn with the body.

"It was a little kid zombie," Vaughn said to himself. "Tough little motherfuckers, those ones."

He went to Isobel's and knocked. She answered the door soon after. Her face was weary.

"So, were you going to do something with the half child out there under the blanket?"

"Yeah, we were getting to it. We needed some time to . . . decompress."

"Well while you are decompressing, that thing is out there *decomposing.* Time to get rid of it. Put your big girl pants back on and help me."

Isobel groaned and asked Ben to grab a sheet, some rubber gloves, spray cleaner and a few hand towels. When they got to the common room, Isobel remembered there was another body in the stairwell debris.

"We have to pull one out of the furniture there." She said pointing through the stacked couches. "Quietly though; the hallway downstairs is still probably full of them."

"Can we put them in the same sheet?" Ben asked, hoping he wouldn't have to go find another one.

"I don't think they'll mind." Vaughn laughed.

By candlelight they gathered the bits of the boy into the linen. Isobel scrubbed the wall and carpet as best she could. Ben and Vaughn removed the couches and a few pieces of small furniture to uncover the other body. It took five sharp tugs to pull the large male out of the barricade. His body, not so recently turned, was covered in oozing pustules. As they pulled him onto the sheet, Isobel set to work cleaning the snail's trail of pus he'd left behind. The smell of him was enough to drive Vaughn to vomit. He barfed on the body so they wouldn't have to clean up more dirty carpet.

"Let's wrap this up!" he said as he wiped his chin with the top of his forearm, laughing at the double meaning. He grabbed a side of the sheet and folded it over the bodies. Ben took the other side and placed it over the top of that.

"These windows don't open," Isobel said. "I didn't notice that until now. I guess we'll have to toss them from my balcony."

Ben and Vaughn did just that while Isobel decided on the best way to sanitize her body. She was paranoid that the pus of the man had gotten on her, into her. She pulled off her shoes, socks, shirt and pants, leaving only her bra and panties on and she walked to the balcony. Ben and Vaughn stared at her as she threw her clothes off the edge and walked back inside.

"She should do dirty work more often," Vaughn said.

Normally Ben would have been disgusted but he had seen her beautiful body as well.

"Yep," he agreed.

A ROUGH NIGHT

SELFISHNESS

Three hours after the event, Gabe had fallen asleep from emotional exhaustion. He'd cried in his room for at least two of those hours before passing out. Rob sat in their living room in the dark, listening to his son the entire time, doing nothing but cry along with him. He was sick of feeling helpless, sick of watching his son's rationality slip further away every day, still reeling from the thought that his son had nearly become one of *them*. He couldn't think about Gabe anymore at that moment. He had to think of his own sanity, his own happiness. He left his apartment to find Molly.

A DIFFICULT DECISION

Moira's hands were shaking as she held the weightless pill bottle in them. She had been taking medication for a heart condition for the last five years and it had kept her alive. She counted her pharmacist as a close friend and that friend had refilled her prescription just before the infection hit Northgate. It was only twenty or so pills and she had to take them twice a day. To make them last, she'd been taking doses of half a pill. After dinner, as she readied herself for bed, she opened the bottle and stared down at a lone half of a blue pill; all that was left and no way to get more, no way to even know if the pharmacist was still alive herself. Even if the pill monger lived, she would be unreachable as the pharmacy was across town some thirty blocks through heavily infected areas.

On the half doses she was able to stay active for the most part. Her appetite was sometimes weak but her humor was always at its peak. The forced rationing was slowly doing its damage inside her body; damage that no one could see. The doctor had warned her that her heart could stop at any time without the medication. Looking back, she should have asked for more pills or at least broken them into smaller pieces but she hadn't thought the world would be broken into so many tiny pieces of its own. She took the half dose with a swig of water. *Edward can't find out about this*, she thought. He'd march outside and down the street to get more pills to keep his wife breathing, her heart beating; risking his own life in the process.

Moira climbed into bed and turned to her husband of over fifty years. "I love you Edward," she said one last time before turning off the lamp on her bedside table but her husband was already asleep.

COLD FEET

Markus lay awake. He was unable to stop thinking about the barricade. He'd watched as a corpse clawed its way toward him. *It has to be better somewhere else.* He thought to himself. He didn't feel safe at Willow Brook anymore and Jeff was starting to get on his nerves. He had become clingy and the feeling was tenfold since they couldn't leave the building. He rolled over and looked at Jeff in the dark. The moon was large outside so he could just make out his face and his furrowed brow. *What is he dreaming about?* Markus wondered as he reached out and gently rubbed Jeff's forehead until it relaxed.

TO THE POINT

Molly, contrary to what Rob was expecting, was not happy to see him.

"Do you know how many times I've needed someone and you weren't there for me? And now this one traumatic experience has you running to my door?"

"Molly, I just need some sanity. Can we please forget about everything that is going on right now? We both need to relax."

Molly knew she would give in to him eventually. She felt love for him even if she wasn't *in* love. "Where's your son?" she asked.

"Asleep. He'll be out until morning. Can I *please* come in?" Rob begged her.

"You're here for sex?" Molly asked directly.

"Yes," Rob said so quietly it was barely audible.

Molly smiled. She'd been waiting to be with him for a long time and he looked cute in a messy-haired, broken down kind of way. She walked into the apartment, allowing him to follow her.

"I'm assuming Hayden's not here," Rob asked as he started towards Molly's bedroom.

"She's with Vaughn. She's always with Vaughn," Molly said, pulling her shirt off.

PROMISE OR PRAYER

Ben and Isobel too were having trouble finding sleep. It seemed the whole of Willow Brook, save for Edward and Gabe, was awake with thoughts of sex, death, love and leaving. Isobel had put on clean clothes and she sat cuddled in a heavy comforter in a chair in her living room, talking with Ben by candlelight.

"You look tired," Ben said to her.

"I am, believe me. But I'm scared about what I'll see in my dreams so I'm staying awake. You can go to sleep if you want. I'll be quiet." She reached out for the candle on the coffee table, ready to blow it out.

"No, leave it lit. Let's talk for a while longer. Tell me, were you seeing anyone?" he asked her. "Before this?"

"I was seeing a guy but we only talked once every couple of weeks. I don't think he would have tried to call me when things started happening. He has a cabin up in the Cascades. He's probably there now; sitting by a fire, listening to owls and watching the stars come out. Not a care in his mind."

"Is the cabin hard to get to?" Ben asked with genuine interest.

"I don't know. He'd only ever *told* me about it. I never got a chance to go."

"Damn," Ben said and smacked his knee with an open palm.

"We aren't going anywhere if that's what you were getting at." She shook her head. "In the movies, anytime the survivors try to travel, people die. Look at me, I sprained my ankle and I only went to the mall and back. We'd die before making it out of the city."

"People are dying anyway!" Ben exclaimed as he gestured toward a wall of Isobel's apartment, toward the common area where Charlie had been put down by Ben's own gun, his own hands.

"No one else is going to die," Isobel said in a much calmer voice than him, trying to convince herself as the words came out.

"That promise sounds suspiciously like a prayer," Ben said.

THE BEST WAY TO GO

Moira lay there, thinking how happy she was to have lived a full life with the man next to her. They had raised three children and been through both tough and wonderful times alike. She prayed in the dark for one more day of life with him. But, at three in the morning, her body could no longer support itself. Her heart stopped as her doctor had promised and she died in her sleep. Most people would say that it's the best way to go. But, as the dead were doing these days she didn't stay gone.

"Wha- What are you doing?" Edward awoke startled by the cold touch of his wife. It wasn't like her to be so physical, especially late in the night. Something felt wrong to him; different in an unsettling way. Moira was being very rough and she was scrambling closer to him underneath the blankets. He reached for the chain of his bedside lamp and gave it a quick tug. The sudden brightness stole his vision for a moment and when it returned he was staring into the undead eyes and biting mouth of Moira. She had somehow died and come back without humor but with an appetite more voracious than ever.

"Oh, Moira. Not you, not us," he sobbed. She had climbed on top of him, something she wouldn't have asked her body to do in life at her age. He tried to hold her at a distance but his elderly arms lacked the strength to continue, especially when they didn't have the support of his own heart. He had said he'd fight for his life. He just didn't imagine he'd have to fight Moira for it. He wasn't afraid to die. He was almost happy that it would be her that would end his life. She was moving in closer toward his neck, toward anything that she could consume.

He closed his eyes, prayed for the safety of their friends beyond the apartment walls, released his grip on her body and focused on the light scent of her perfume. It was the same perfume she was wearing on the day they first met.

A ROUGHER DAY

BABY BLUES

Hayden left Tom's apartment after another sleepless, sex-filled night. It was still too early in the pregnancy for any of the noticeable body changes that would eventually expose her secret but she knew she'd have to tell him soon. She almost had, as they lay in bed the night before. Tom was always kind and gentle after he'd been satisfied but still she couldn't find the courage.

She tried the doorknob of the Cooper's old apartment and found it still unlocked from her time with Ben. Closing the door quietly and locking it behind her she exhaled and started looking for the boxes of baby stuff.

"I hope it's a girl," she said as she felt the softness of the pink bedding of the crib in the nursery. Feeling suddenly energized she began to organize the room, readying it for her and her child. She found a box of baby clothes and took each item out individually, folding onesies and infant shirts and placing them neatly into the shallow drawers in the dresser next to the changing table.

"I think everything is going to be ok, little baby," she said to her belly. "Tom will take care of us."

A DIFFERENT APPROACH

Rob had made it back to his own apartment just as Gabe was waking up. His son looked terrible and just as sad as when he'd put him to bed.

"Hey champ. Are you ready for breakfast? I heard Moira say the other day that she'd have hot chocolate for you," he said, trying to start the morning off pleasantly.

"Will she have enough for Charlie?" Gabe asked with a small bit of hope in his eyes.

Rob sighed. Had his son been so traumatized that he'd become delusional overnight? "Charlie's gone, remember?" he reminded him.

"He can't be gone!" Gabe yelled. "He was the only friend I had! You stupid grownups killed him." Gabe picked up a wooden train he'd left on the floor and threw it at his father.

The train hit Rob in the face. Rage grew in him and he ran at the boy, grabbing his shoulders and shaking him.

"I'm doing the best I can! The best I can!" he yelled.

"Do better!" Gabe yelled back with defiance.

Rob raised his hand open-palmed and slapped Gabe hard on his cheek.

"Don't ever talk to me like that again," Rob said through gritted teeth as anger rippled through his body. "Now get dressed and ready to eat."

Gabe broke into tears as his skin grew red from the impact.

DEATH WITHOUT DIGNITY

"Where are we having breakfast today?" Ben asked Isobel after he'd finished brushing his teeth with bottled water. The residents of Willow Brook had taken to having weekly group breakfasts to create a better sense of community.

Isobel took a moment to think to herself who'd hosted the last breakfast. "At Edward and Moira's place," she said as she stretched in front of the living room window, "though I could easily have slept a few more hours."

"Don't go back to sleep, I'm hungry!" Ben said.

Isobel grabbed a sweater and opened the door to the hallway. Markus and Jeff had just arrived at the door of 206 and Markus was knocking on it.

"Normally they have their door unlocked if they are hosting breakfast," Isobel said as she pointed to the doorknob.

Jeff reached out and tried it. "Locked," he said.

Markus knocked again, this time harder and louder. A moment later they could hear growling within the apartment. The growling became pounding and clawing as Moira and Edward reached the other side of the door. They sounded desperate to get out; like wild animals trapped in a cage.

"Not them." Ben burst into tears and collapsed, hitting the floor heavily.

"What's going on?" Rob asked as he and Gabe approached the four a bit late. He'd had to wait for the redness on Gabe's cheek to diminish before leaving their apartment. His son stood a small distance from him, still slightly terrified of his father.

"Something happened to the Cabels. They are infected," Isobel said flatly. She was shocked.

"Gabe, go to Molly," Rob told his son. He didn't want the boy seeing anything more that would traumatize him.

"But I'm hungry," Gabe whined quietly and without making eye contact with his dad.

"Breakfast is going to be a bit *delayed.* Go to her!" Rob yelled at him. The others were surprised at the interaction. It wasn't like Rob to be so severe with his son. Gabe ran next door to find Molly while the others decided what to do.

"It was only a matter of time before this would happen. We just didn't know when or to whom," Jeff said.

"That doesn't make this easier," Isobel replied shortly. She sat down next to Ben. "We need to deal with this," she whispered to him.

"I know," Ben responded just as quietly.

"We should get Vaughn," Isobel suggested.

"No!" Ben said. "He'll turn it into a show. These are our people, not his. We'll kill them ourselves."

"Come with me to get some weapons then, Ben," Rob said. "The sooner we get this over with the better we'll feel."

Ben stood and led Rob into Isobel's apartment where he had a few unused weapons kept. Molly came from her place to get more information.

"Gabe said something happened to Edwar . . ." she stopped mid-sentence when she heard the wood of the door being torn apart and a wild shriek from within the Cabel's apartment. She shook her head in disbelief and walked back stunned to her apartment and Gabe.

Ready with weapons the group stood in a half-circle around the door.

"I never thought I'd be trying to get *into* a room with zombies," Markus laughed faintly. He was scared to death about what he was about to see.

"We can't leave them in there. They'll get out and infect us or they'll rot," Isobel reasoned.

Two swift kicks with Ben's steel toe boots and the door broke inward pushing the corpses deeper into the apartment. They instantly started back towards the hallway. The semi-circle of residents expanded as the Cabels approached. Moira's mouth and neck were covered in dried blood. One strap of her thin, blue nightgown had fallen from her shoulder, leaving a flat gray breast exposed. Isobel wanted to pull the strap back up to cover her nakedness but Moira wasn't concerned with her partial nudity. Rob shot first but he only hit Moira in her neck, which did nothing but absorb the bullet.

"Shit!" he said nervously. He aimed again and hit her in the forehead, just left of center. She fell near the doorway.

"No no no no no no," Markus repeated as he held his head and stepped backwards, further away from the scene. He couldn't take what he was seeing. He would never be able to forget it. He nearly backed into Isobel's gun.

"If you can't help, get out of the way!" she yelled at him. Markus did as he was told and went back to Jeff's apartment.

Edward was disgusting. His face was unrecognizable as it was one open wound. Moira had eaten the skin and chunks of muscle tissue from his cheeks and nose. One eyeball was missing. A gentleman in his life who had prided himself on being clean and well groomed, it was devastating to see that he had wet and soiled his striped pajama pants before he passed. The smell was overwhelming.

"Oh Edward, I'm sorry," Ben pulled his gun up with heavy arms and took out Edward's other eyeball and brain, causing his body to fall in the hallway.

Hayden and Vaughn had come down to investigate the source of the gunshots. Hayden's hand went up to her mouth in surprise and Vaughn leaned in to get a closer look. They didn't say anything, only gawked and left.

Ben and Rob donned gloves and wrapped the bodies of the Cabels in their bloodied bed linens and then dumped them off the balcony. The dead surrounded the two concealed bodies, doing their routine investigation for food but, finding no life left, they dispersed.

The men spent midday with gloves and masks on cleaning and disinfecting each lamp, side table, and every inch of carpet in 206. They couldn't afford to lose another apartment on the second floor to the gore of violent death. Every last speck of blood and body matter was gone by three p.m.

"What happened here?" Isobel asked as they finished the job.

"Moira didn't have any wounds so I'm guessing that she died somehow, came back and then killed Edward," Ben said as sweat dripped from his brow.

"Why do the dead come back even if they aren't bitten? How did she get the infection?" Isobel wondered aloud. "That bicyclist did, now that I think of it."

"Maybe it's airborne too. Maybe we are all hosts and the processes of death set off the disease," Rob suggested.

"You can die from a bite and then the disease takes hold of you or you can die naturally but it will end the same. We're all doomed to be monsters."

"Have you been thinking about this a lot? Maybe you could give the CDC a hand. You sound like one of them," Ben said.

"It's all Gabe talks about so I've been thinking a bit on the subject," Rob replied.

Isobel went into the bathroom. The rest of the apartment had been covered in blood. The bathroom was spotless but for an empty pill bottle in the trash.

the infection exists in the entire population.

HONOR THE DEAD

The residents ate dinner together that night. It felt much better to be a group than to be lonely individuals, especially after losing Edward and Moira to the infection. Ben, Isobel, Rob and Gabe, Molly, Jeff and Markus all found a place at the makeshift table setup in the common area of the second floor. Even Hayden came to eat and to offer her condolences but she hadn't been able to convince Vaughn to join.

"On the menu tonight," Ben announced, "is Edward's apocalypse favorite."

"What's that?" Gabe asked with an equal mix of caution and curiosity. He didn't want his dad to hit him again.

"Hmm, I know," Isobel smiled. "Cream of chicken soup, green beans, and crumbled crackers all mixed up together."

"Sounds gross," Gabe said.

"Gabe," Rob said. "Be polite."

"Sounds like the poorest excuse for a casserole I ever heard of." Markus shook his head.

"Taste it, Markus. You may change your mind. You too, Gabe," Ben suggested.

They drank the last of Moira's tea stash with dinner and chatted softly in the candlelight as they ate. Ben stood up part way through eating to read a paragraph from one of Edward's favorite classics: Grapes of Wrath.

"'They's a time of change, an' when that comes, dyin' is a piece of all dyin', and bearin' is a piece of all bearin', an' bearin' an' dyin' is two pieces of the same thing. An' then things ain't so lonely anymore. An' then a hurt don't hurt so bad.'"

"I wish I could agree. This hurt doesn't feel any different though. In fact, it feels worse," Molly sighed.

Ben closed the book. Dust was forced from its pages and, rising, it brought to his nostrils the smell of Edward, a comforting mix of tobacco, paper, and pomade. He sat down heavily, enveloped in the smell.

"I liked them," Gabe said.

"I did too, Gabe," his father said. "They were good people."

"We all liked them a lot. They would be happy that we are thinking of them," Isobel added.

"We're going to die too and come back, aren't we?" Gabe asked, directing the question at Molly. Rob was too taken aback by his son's complete understanding of the situation to answer. Besides, he had asked Molly so Rob waited for her to address Gabe's question.

"Not for a long time, ok?" Molly smiled gently at him. "So we don't have to worry about it."

"Do you think Mommy came back somewhere?" he asked his father.

Rob answered quickly. "No, she didn't. She's been gone for too long. We talked about that already."

"But it would have been nice to see her though, don't you think?"

"We can look at her pictures." Rob tousled his son's hair lovingly.

"You can show us all a picture of your mom, Gabe. I think it would be nice for us to see her," Hayden said.

"But it would be nice to see her for *real* again," he countered.

"Gabe, it wouldn't be mom!" Rob was clenching his fist on the table, holding his fork tightly in the grip; suffering the old pains of his lost love.

"But . . ." Gabe's eyes had started to tear up.

Molly put a hand onto Rob's clenched fist.

"Yeah, ok, you are right. It would be nice to see her again," Rob admitted solemnly, his hand relaxing under the warmth of Molly's. There was no point in arguing with a child that his mother wouldn't be beautiful, or loving, or even clean. She would be just another of the walking dead on the lawn, covered in her own gore, rotting away with no love in her heart.

"Ben, you were right," Markus said after licking his paper plate clean. "That was delicious."

"Well you can't have the recipe," Ben said playfully.

"It has three ingredients!" Markus held three fingers up.

Rob was happy for the change of topic and he'd try to thank Markus and Ben for that later.

"Hey everyone, I think it would be fantastic if we went around the table and each of us could say something that reminds us of the Cabels. I'll start! A tobacco pipe," Isobel chimed.

"That's too easy!" Rob yelled. He thought for a moment. "Talk radio. Edward always had that thing on."

"Mummies!" Gabe exclaimed. His answer made everyone laugh uncomfortably until Rob explained how Moira and Gabe had talked about them in "school".

Hayden closed her eyes and thought for a second. "I didn't know them very well," she said. "I guess maybe knitting needles."

"Nice one, Hayden," Jeff said.

"Books, of course," Ben held up the novel.

"I'm going to have to say religious conviction. It may have been questionable these past few weeks but they went to church *every* Sunday and every Wednesday evening as well," Markus added thoughtfully.

"How do you know that?" Jeff asked.

"Hello, I'm gay. I don't know how many times they invited me to go with them." Markus silently counted on his fingers for added affect.

"They tried to 'save' you?" Rob asked incredulously.

"Informally, yes. I don't hold it against them," Markus said holding his hands up.

Vaughn appeared at the head of the table. He had been listening from the top of the stairs and had finally come down to join the group. "Blue, blood-soaked night gowns," he said with a smile. Stunned silence fell over the diners.

"What did you just say?" Ben asked angrily.

"Blu-" Vaughn began to repeat himself.

"Don't say it again." Ben pounded a fist on the table. Rob had pulled Gabe's chair closer to his side. Vaughn sauntered over to Hayden, paying no more attention to the rest of the group.

"Come on, girlie! Now that we've said our goodbyes to the old folks let's ditch this somber party and go have some fun!"

He took one of Isobel's extra crackers and chomped it messily, getting crumbs on his shirt. He reached his hand forward again but this time he was aiming for Hayden's breasts. He didn't see the horrified look on Markus' face. He didn't see Jeff rest his own face in his hands. He didn't see Ben's right hand set down his fork and disappear under the table to grab his gun from its holster. Vaughn was looking only at Hayden but she didn't want to go with him. She tried to pull his groping hand from her body but he grabbed her hand and pulled her from her seat. Her chair toppled backwards.

"Hey!" Molly stood up and yelled at him. "Can't you see she doesn't want to go with you? Have some respect and leave her alone!"

Vaughn had turned to face Molly and just as she finished her berating, he punched her. She fell back into her chair and blood started to fall from her nose. Ben was out of his chair with his gun pulled on Vaughn. Vaughn saw the gun and Gabe's wide eyes full of fear. He saw the blood on Molly's face, the tears on Hayden's. He released his grip on Hayden without a word; no muttered apology, nothing and he went back upstairs to his porn and his bottle.

"What the *fuck* was that?" Isobel asked.

"Inhuman," Ben said as he holstered his gun with shaking hands. "He would have shot me if he'd had a gun with him!" Ben walked weakly to Hayden's side. He picked up her chair and sat her back down in it. "Are you ok?" He asked her, stroking her hair. Hayden didn't respond. She only brushed his hand away and continued eating what was left on her plate.

"Unfortunately the night is still young," Markus said eerily. "I'm going to bed before anything else happens."

"Ditto," Jeff said as he picked up his trash and threw it in a garbage bag. "Night everyone, don't forget to lock your doors." He waved a farewell as they walked back to his apartment.

Rob picked up his son who had been crying into his side and carried him off to bed.

"Are you going to be ok, Molly?" Ben was looking at her nose, trying to be helpful, but anything he did only made her flinch more.

"Can you just walk me to my couch?" she asked in pain.

"I can take you," Isobel offered.

"I'll stay here until you get back, Isobel. I'm going to watch for Vaughn," Ben said.

It was now only Hayden and Ben at the table. Ben returned to his chair and sat back down. He collected dirty paper plates within his reach and stacked them in a pile, ready to be thrown away. He waited for Hayden to say something, anything at all. But she was embarrassed beyond belief at being publicly groped. She especially didn't want to talk to Ben, who she'd shared a bed with. She carried what food she still had to finish and sought refuge in the apartment she shared with Molly.

EVICTED

Later that night Molly still lay on her couch with a cold washcloth pressed to her face, wondering if her nose might be broken. Hayden walked by her without a word and out of the apartment to climb the stairs to Vaughn. When Hayden came back three hours later, Molly was still on the couch.

"You've got to move out of here." Three hours had been plenty of time for Molly to decide that her nose was definitely broken and that she no longer wanted to hold the title of caregiver. Hayden refused to make eye contact and that was infuriating to Molly who had taken her in; convinced the others to let Hayden stay in Willow Brook.

"Did you hear me? I want you out of this apartment. I can't *believe* you went to see him after he did this to me! Let alone after the way he treated you! I defended you for nothing? Did your parents raise you to be an ungrateful bitch?"

"They taught me how to eat properly which is more than I can say about yours!" Hayden finally raised her voice and eyes to meet Molly's.

"At least I can go to therapy for my problem. I don't think there's any hope for *you*!" Molly shot back.

"Well that's one thing we can agree on. I'm hopeless," Hayden shrugged.

"We took you in, Hayden! We've fed you and sheltered you. Everything you do still matters here. It matters to all of us," Molly pled with the teen. She was tired, her nose ached and throbbed, she was done. "But if you don't see it that way, get out."

Hayden said nothing more as she packed her things and left 204. Molly slept peacefully that night, despite her injury, with the weight of another person's welfare off of her back. Now she could focus on herself again even if the loneliness was bittersweet.

ALTERNATE ENDING

Hayden stood at the top of the stairs to the first floor. She could hear the dead beyond the couches and through the spindly legs of office desks and dining room chairs. The zombies never stopped moving, never stopped searching. Without another option, she moved into 305 for good. Vaughn was passed out across the hall and she wanted him to stay that way for now. A light knock came on the Cooper's door and she answered it.

"Hi," Ben said shyly. "I knew you'd be here."

"Where else can I go?" Hayden laughed weakly.

"I completely agree. We're all just kind of stuck and it gets crazier every day."

"I actually have *nowhere* else to go in the building. Molly kicked me out," Hayden explained.

"Oh. I'm sorry. I'd let you stay with me but I'm not in the position to offer such accommodations. Can I come in?"

"Sure." Hayden allowed him to pass the threshold. She started walking to the bedroom but he put a hand on her shoulder.

"We can talk for a while. Just as Ben and Hayden. No role playing." He sat on the couch in the living room.

"About that . . ." Hayden began.

"What do you mean?" Ben leaned forward.

"I'm pregnant."

"I'm not the father, am I?" Ben turned white at the thought of Vaughn finding out that he and Hayden had slept together.

Hayden considered lying to Ben and telling him the child was his but then she'd be just as bad a person as Tom.

"No! I was pregnant then! That night! The baby is Tom's," she admitted.

Ben relaxed. "What are you going to do? You have to tell him."

"I know but it's never the right time and I'm scared that he won't want the baby."

"Yeah, for some reason I just can't picture the guy pushing a stroller and it has nothing to do with the fact that we can't take leisurely strolls outside anymore."

Hayden laughed but inside she panicked each time someone told her Vaughn wasn't dad material.

Ben could see the trouble in her eyes. He stood up and hugged her. He kissed her head and came to a decision.

"If he doesn't want you and that baby, I do," he said and he meant it. "I'd be a good dad."

"Don't tell anyone. I'm not ready," Hayden cried.

Ben nodded and led her to the bedroom where they fell asleep, his hand resting gently on her slowly growing belly.

VERSIONS OF THE TRUTH

Isobel wasn't used to waking up in an empty apartment. Ben wasn't around and she was certain he hadn't spent the night on her couch. She made herself coffee and lazed about. She was not religious but she found herself talking to God, asking for just one uneventful day. Just as Isobel was finishing her cup of coffee, Ben returned home.

"Hey," he said as he used the remaining hot water that Isobel had heated to make a cup of tea for himself.

Normally Ben talked to Isobel a lot. So much so that it seemed he liked the sound of his own voice but he said nothing more. He sat down on the couch and picked up a book to busy himself.

"So, where've you been?" Isobel asked, the curiosity overwhelming her. "By process of elimination I have decided your answer will either be 'with Molly' or 'with Hayden'."

"Does it matter either way?" Ben answered her question with a question of his own. "You and I aren't together in any form or fashion so I don't see how it concerns you."

"Molly would be the more suitable answer but she has a thing for Rob. So what were you doing with Hayden?" Isobel continued her questioning. "Nothing illegal I hope."

"Well sheriff, no. I did spend the night with her but we didn't do anything. She needed a friend, a listening ear. She has a lot more going on with her than you know."

"We can't be a team, Ben, if you are keeping secrets from me."

"I won't be pressured into discussing her issues," Ben growled from over the brim of his mug.

"Fine!" Isobel huffed. "Just don't sleep with the girl. God knows what diseases Vaughn's given to her!"

STREET VIEW

Rob knew that Molly had kicked Hayden out. He'd checked on Molly after Gabe had fallen asleep the night before. In the morning, once he'd fed himself and his son, he went to her apartment with a pair of binoculars hanging around his neck.

"Want to go bird watching?" he said cheerfully.

"You don't watch birds. There aren't even birds around to watch anymore. What are you really asking? You're not here for more sex are you?" she asked with accusation.

"No! Do you want to come to the roof to see if anyone else is out there? I've been thinking how crazy it is that we didn't know there were survivors across the street. We haven't been paying much attention to our surroundings."

"Maybe they were just as good as we are at staying hidden," Molly suggested.

"Do you want to go or not?" Rob asked impatiently.

"Alright, let's go." The weather had grown even colder so Molly looked around for a thick jacket, hat and gloves.

They took turns with the binoculars, pointing out anything interesting they saw. There wasn't much to make them smile but they were happy in one another's company.

"Look over there!" Molly gasped. "The mall is completely destroyed. The whole thing is gone!"

"Do you see anything up the road near the hospital?" Rob asked as he strained to make sense of the shapes in the distance without the aid of the binoculars.

"There are a lot of abandoned cars. Bodies are lying in between them. The road is covered with them."

"Let me see." Rob took the binoculars from her and raised them to his eyes. "They are all dead. I mean *completely* dead. Someone must have killed them when they turned. That might mean there are survivors up there in one of the houses."

"We couldn't risk that trip. There aren't enough of us left and we're all weak."

"I wasn't suggesting we try to make contact. But the undead are growing weaker too. Look at that one over by the crosswalk button." He gave Molly the binoculars back.

The zombie was trying to walk but his rotten legs made it difficult to achieve any sort of progress. "He doesn't look too good." Molly turned the binoculars on others to see if they were all having as much trouble. One of the zombies stood out to her.

"Isn't that Sheila?" she asked, pointing to one of the dead.

"Where?" Rob asked. His heart started to pound and he tried to get the binoculars back from her. "It can't be. Jeff said she was out of town."

"No, that's her! I'm sure of it. That is the same outfit she wore to work all the time and that giant diamond on her finger is unmistakable. Jeff must have paid a fortune for that thing," Molly said as she followed the shuffling corpse moving down the street. "That is so strange."

"Hmm?" Rob asked half-heartedly, hoping she would drop the conversation.

"It doesn't look like she has any wounds. She wasn't bitten."

"Maybe she took some pills?" Rob suggested.

"Come on! She wouldn't have come back here just to kill herself! And if she never went out of town and did it here, why would Jeff keep that from us?"

Rob could see the gears turning in Molly's head. She was doing the math and any moment she would have the answer. He decided to give it to her.

"He killed her," Rob blurted out.

"No, Jeff's a good man. We shouldn't assume that," Molly replied.

"I'm not making an assumption. He strangled her. He admitted it."

"How long have you known this?" Molly's voice was rising as she uncovered the extent of the lie.

"We've known since the second day when we went door-to-door."

"We? The others know too? How could you not tell me this, Rob?" Rob walked toward her but she backed away. She was growing more agitated.

"Listen, Molly. We wanted to give him a second chance," Rob said.

"Murderers don't get second chances!" Molly threw the binoculars hard onto the rooftop, breaking a piece off of the plastic frame. She ran back inside, leaving Rob alone.

CARELESS CONFRONTATION

Markus and Jeff were looking over a map of the city that was unfolded on their coffee table. They had an address book out and they were going page by page marking the locations of all of his friends. It was important to be prepared to find death and therefore ready to move to the next house if they were to set out on their own.

"Someone has to be alive. It isn't that difficult to survive, is it?" Markus said. He was worried about his friends, some of them ex-lovers.

"They'll be fine," Jeff said comfortingly. "But more importantly, we'll be fine."

Markus leaned across the table and kissed him. "If we stick together, I'm sure everything will work out.

Jeff sighed happily, relishing the comment. Suddenly Molly barged into the apartment without knocking. Markus and Jeff jumped to their feet, ready to fight if necessary.

"You fucking MURDERER!" Molly screamed.

"Molly, calm down," Markus said. He looked to Jeff for an explanation.

"I don't know what she's talking about," Jeff feigned ignorance.

"How's your wife, Jeff?" Molly asked. "Tell me! Lie to my face!" She ran up to him to meet his eyes.

"You can't just barge into someone's apartment and start accusing them of murder." Markus stepped into the small space between Molly and Jeff, ready to protect his boyfriend. "Well you can't just strangle your wife, dump her body, and start fucking a man either! Playing homosexual HOUSE like everything is normal!"

"It's not your business what I do, Molly," Jeff said, his face turning red with anger, "or what I've done."

"Hold on. Jeff, is she telling the truth? Because that would be *my* fucking business!" Markus yelled.

"She's outside right now, Markus. Walking around like the rest of the DEAD PEOPLE but without a single bite wound," Molly said.

Markus left the apartment. He wanted to see for himself if what Molly said was true.

"You bitch!" Jeff yelled at Molly. He tried to grab her but she stepped into the kitchen, putting the island in between them. Jeff looked for the baseball bat but the wall where it normally sat was empty. He'd left it outside when he'd tried to move the dog.

Molly could see him looking for a weapon. "Don't come near me!" she screamed.

"You ruined EVERYTHING!" he snapped at her as he ran out of the apartment.

OUT OF THE BAG

Jeff's heart hurt. He hadn't felt pain when Sheila died but he was feeling it now. Not because his wife was dead but because all the wrong people now knew it. His body shook with tension as he stormed down the second floor hallway to apartment 205. *No need to knock*, he thought to himself, *there is no privacy here anyway.* He turned the doorknob and let himself in.

Isobel was in her kitchen, still in pajamas and eating cereal with rehydrated powdered milk. She almost dropped the bowl when Jeff let himself in.

"Why'd you do it?" Jeff yelled.

There was a machete propped inside its sheath behind the door. He wrapped his fingers around the handle and slid it easily from the cover. He tried to swing the blade at her but the entry to the kitchen was lower than he realized and the machete hit the top of the frame with a thud. Bits of paint and plaster fell to the carpet. Isobel dropped her bowl of cereal. Jeff was about to try again when someone, he guessed it to be Ben, grabbed him from behind and dragged him into the living room.

"What are you trying to do? You could have split her skull," Ben said as he grabbed the machete handle and wrestled it away from Jeff.

"Fuck you!" he yelled as he took a swing with a fist. "Who told her? Who was it?"

Ben tossed the machete onto the couch and punched Jeff just to get his attention. "What are you talking about? Why are you acting like this?" he asked Jeff as he nursed his knuckles, which were virgin to fist fights.

"Who. The fuck. Told Molly. About Sheila?" he asked in response, his nose bleeding lightly from Ben's massive bear paw of a hand.

"No one told me!" Molly yelled. She stood in the doorway with the apartment door propped open, ready to run if she needed to. "I saw her in the binoculars. No bite marks, no blood, just bruising on her neck."

Isobel was cleaning up the spilt milk when Rob and Markus appeared behind Molly in the hallway. Markus was crying. Jeff, upon seeing the tears, lowered his head into his hands in defeat.

"I'm not a murderer," he whined. "It's different than that. She was taunting me and her damn dog wouldn't shut up!"

"That doesn't make it ok!" Molly yelled, still extremely upset about being left out of the loop.

"You're anorexic and kept it from us!" Jeff argued back.

"Bulimic," Molly said more quietly. "And that was different. Not knowing this about you could have gotten any one of us killed!"

"And starving to death wouldn't?" Jeff shot back.

Molly gave him a hurt look, scowled at Rob and left. Markus followed behind her. Rob shook his head and entered the apartment to sit on Isobel's couch. He touched the machete. Isobel closed her apartment door.

"She confronted me in front of Markus. He doesn't want anything to do with me now." Jeff was crying so heavily he was having trouble breathing.

"I'm sorry Jeff. I thought it would be better if people didn't know," Isobel said, stepping closer. Jeff no longer seemed dangerous, just depressed.

"The dead aren't keeping secrets anymore," Rob said. He too was sad about the fact. Just as Markus wasn't likely to forgive Jeff, Molly wasn't likely to forgive him.

SCREW THIS

The group was falling apart and Markus had been ready to leave them for at least a week. Now it had become a solo journey. He cared for Jeff, a lot, but he couldn't love a killer or live with people who would cover for one. Markus packed a few of his things into a backpack, grabbed some food and climbed down the fire escape of 201. At the bottom he saw the rotting body of Jeff's dog behind a bush, tufts of its curly coat moving gently in an almost indistinguishable breeze, reinforcing his decision to walk away from it all. He saw Jeff's baseball bat and took it with him.

His friends, spread throughout the city, would welcome him with open arms if they were still alive. Willow Brook was a sinking ship with few decent people left on it to die with.

STRUGGLE WITHIN

Ben walked Jeff back to his apartment. Jeff said nothing as he closed the door and realized his worst fear had quickly become a reality. Markus, his address book, the city map they'd been working on were all gone. Jeff sat on the floor next to the coffee table. He touched his hands to the cool wood and closed his eyes. *If it stays quiet and I concentrate,* he thought, *I can remember some of the places he might be going.*

"But what would I do if I found him?" he asked himself out loud.

I'll kill him for leaving me. His mind said.

"No! I love him!" he yelled and opened his eyes. Jeff formed two fists with his hands and punched the table. Left. Right. Left. Until his knuckles bled and the rage left his body.

MOLLY MATHAY, ALONE

When Molly was moving into Willow Brook, the office lady went on and on about how *nice* the residents were. *They'll do just about anything for each other,* she had said. Molly had believed that and it was one of the reasons why she decided to stay after her lease was up about a year before the infection came. Now she was sitting in her cold apartment remembering all that those residents had done for her.

Jill had killed herself and her baby after Molly's kindness and care. Hayden had gone back to the man who'd punched Molly in the face and who'd molested her in the third floor hallway. Rob, the only man she'd let into her bedroom, had kept a secret for a killer, as had the others. But *she*, with her eating disorder, was such a threat and needed to be punished. She didn't know if Markus had left but she assumed it was likely. She felt like high-tailing it out of Willow Brook too only she had no one to run to.

The only thing she could come up with that they'd actually done for her was keep her from focusing on her eating disorder. Besides all the dying and deception, life actually felt more normal for her than it had in a very long time. She couldn't remember the last time she'd binged and purged but, as she sat alone, she could feel the familiar need growing inside of her. Stealing from the others was out of the question. She would have to resort to more wild and dangerous efforts to get the food she so desperately needed.

PUNISHMENT, BANISHMENT, OR DEATH

"He'll have to pay for what he's done," Isobel said to Ben and Rob. "It's only fair. Molly had to."

"An eye for an eye? Molly had to get food for stealing food. Does that mean we have to kill Jeff?" Ben asked with worry in his voice.

"We aren't killing anyone. There's been enough of that," Rob said.

"It seems a bit too late to try to create a justice system here. We should have done that when we made the rationing one," Ben said. "Or when we found out he killed someone."

"We can't let this fall apart. We have to do something," Isobel said as she looked out the window at another day passing by. "I'm going to talk to Molly."

GOSSIP MILL

Rob left Ben and Isobel's after she did. Ben left shortly after and headed upstairs to the Cooper's apartment to tell Hayden of all that had transpired that day.

". . . and then Jeff came in to attack Isobel, thinking she told everyone," Ben recounted the event to Hayden.

"Wow. It's like a soap opera. I knew that Jeff guy was a creep. He always gives me nasty looks."

"Why didn't you say something to me?" Ben asked with concern in his voice.

"I didn't want to bother you with it. I just think he doesn't like teenagers."

"Yeah, you're too loud," Ben laughed and Hayden hit him playfully.

"Can we talk about baby names?" Hayden asked with hope in her eyes.

Ben wasn't in the mood for baby talk. He wanted to touch Hayden intimately again. He'd tried to tell himself it wasn't right but her youth and beauty were intoxicating to him.

"In a second," he said as he kissed her and lowered her gently onto the bed.

HINDSIGHT

Molly didn't get up to answer the knock at her door, not even when it grew loud and irritated. Only when she knew it wouldn't stop did she make the decision to see who it was.

"Look, I know you're a little pissed off," Isobel said.

"A little pissed off?" Molly laughed sarcastically, allowing Isobel into the entry of her apartment but no further.

"What would you have done?" Isobel queried.

"First, I would have tried to call the police," Molly said matter-of-factly.

"They wouldn't have come," Isobel shook her head. "Can I come in?"

"No. Second, I would have gathered everyone and informed them of his wrongdoing."

"We didn't really know each other yet," Isobel reasoned.

"You gathered everyone together anyway. You just forgot to leave out the bit about Jeff being a murderer. You also helped to sell his lie."

"We could have handled it differently," Isobel agreed.

"Third, I would have kicked him out."

"You want us to ask him to leave Willow Brook?" Isobel asked, dumbfounded. "Where would he go?"

Molly shrugged. "I don't see another option." She pushed Isobel out of her apartment and closed the door on her.

UNLIKELY ADVISOR

Jeff grew sick of his empty apartment and he knew that the others were going to try to appease Molly with some form of punishment for him. He needed someone on his side, someone who would understand his position, and someone who seemed to hate women as much as he now did. The hallway of the second floor was quiet but he'd seen Ben through the peephole, walking by, so he waited for a few minutes to be sure that no one saw him go to the third floor.

He paced back and forth in front of Vaughn's door a couple of times digging deep within himself to face the monster of a man and ask for help. He was also trying to determine if Hayden was with Vaughn. He didn't really want to deal with the immature teen. He heard her voice but it was coming from the apartment behind him, the one the Coopers used to live in. He leaned against the cool wood of the door and listened for a moment.

"Oh, Ben!" Hayden yelled from inside.

Jeff was shocked and confused. Ben didn't seem like the kind of guy who'd fuck a teen and he was certain that Ben had a thing for Isobel. He stood there a minute longer until he heard Ben's voice and he knew it to be true.

"Oh man, this is too good." Jeff smiled to himself. He'd hold onto this newly found knowledge until it suited him to play the card. Now satisfied that Vaughn was alone he turned back around, reached out and knocked once, firmly, to hide his fear.

Vaughn opened the door, a bottle of beer in his hand, shirtless and smiling. He must have been feeling good because his smile didn't disappear when he saw that it was Jeff.

"What a surprise! How's the wife? I mean . . . the boyfriend? I mean . . ." Vaughn laughed maniacally. The look of pain on Jeff's face was priceless. Jeff turned to walk away but Vaughn grabbed his shoulder roughly and pulled him into his apartment before he could even protest.

"It's like you have an informant. You know everything that goes on in this place," Jeff said as he rubbed his shoulder where Vaughn had grabbed him.

"No one informs me of anything. I've seen your wife a few times, outside, thought about taking care of your little problem. Can't really tell you why I decided not to."

You know exactly why you didn't, Vaughn! His mind yelled but he had to stay calm. Vaughn was the only person who could help him. "How did you know about Markus?"

"I saw him leave. He looked really sad. That's not a good look for a man. Hopefully the world out there will toughen his gay ass up a bit." Vaughn punched Jeff in the shoulder in a manner that was meant to be gentle but it wasn't. "I'm sure there's got to be a thing or two that I am not aware of. Like why *you're* here." Vaughn pointed at him and waited for his explanation.

"I need your help. The group is after me. They want revenge or something. I know they are planning against me. You didn't get sucked into all their crap so can you just give me some advice?" Jeff pleaded.

Vaughn thought Jeff sounded a little nuts but he wasn't scared of him. He knew Jeff wouldn't try to hurt him since he wasn't a part of the gang downstairs. "Get a gun and assert yourself. The apartment is yours, right? They can't take it from you," he suggested.

"They have an extra key. They can come in whenever they want. I think they are going to kill me in my sleep."

"Get the key then. Simple," Vaughn said.

"Can I have one of your guns?"

Even though Vaughn didn't think Jeff capable of killing him he didn't want to risk it. He could take the man in a fistfight but he couldn't outrun a bullet. "No. You'll have to take one of theirs by force. It will be a louder statement if you do it that way."

"Really? That's all you've got? I thought you were some wise man, sitting up here in the clouds."

"Nope, I'm just the angry drunk on the third floor," Vaughn said, taking a swig from his beer.

"They're going to have a meeting, I know it. They love meetings. Maybe I can get a gun then, when they are all busy talking about me."

"Whatever you say. The details are yours to figure out. Now, I've got some business to attend to if you don't mind moving along."

"Yeah, ok," Jeff said weakly and left.

SLEEP

Rob prepared his son for bed. He wasn't sure what the next day would bring for them. The fissures in the group had grown to be crevasses, too deep and wide to cross or bring together again. It wouldn't be all that much different from before the plague, when neighbors didn't talk to one another.

Maybe everyone would be all right if they just stayed out of one another's way.

Gabe rolled over under his covers as his dad was leaving his bedroom. "Can you stay here until I fall asleep?" he asked in a small voice.

"There's nothing to be afraid of," Rob said from the doorway.

"There're monsters everywhere," Gabe whined.

"The walls will protect us," Rob said as he made his way back to his child in the darkened room.

"Can the monsters turn doorknobs?"

"No. Now try to sleep." Rob tucked Gabe's blankets in tighter and lay next to him on the bed, waiting for his breathing to slow and sleep to take him. He felt a small bit of happiness that he might be getting his fragile and sensitive boy back.

TORRENTIAL

The next morning it was pouring down rain. Isobel woke early due to the noise and was never able to fall back to sleep. Ben wasn't home when she'd been pushed from Molly's apartment the day before and he still wasn't back.

The sheet of water falling on the world outside made her feel more trapped than usual. She took in a deep breath, let it out and got herself ready for what promised to be another long day. She ate breakfast alone; stale crackers with canned tuna fish and a fruit cup.

She knew Ben was with Hayden again, she just didn't know where. She wanted to talk to Vaughn as well but thought it best to seek out the secret couple before him. Isobel went to the third floor with the ring of keys in her hand and started opening apartments, only to find them all empty until the Coopers'.

She turned the key in the doorknob and opened the door. "*Ben!*" She whispered. "*I know you're here.*" She started into the apartment but Ben quickly appeared and disallowed her from further intrusion.

"Hey, um, I was just checking up on he-" he started but was cut off by Isobel.

"I know you're screwing so drop the act, ok?" she said. "We need to gather up everyone and figure out what to do about Jeff. Molly won't let this go. Get some pants on!"

Ben and Hayden dressed and went with Isobel to Vaughn's door. Isobel knocked instead of using the key.

"I don't wake up this early," Vaughn yawned in the entryway, nude. "I may come down in a bit but feel free to start without me." He closed the door and wondered if Jeff was planning to act on his paranoia during the meeting but was uninterested in showing up to find out.

Molly, as expected, was much harder to convince to leave her apartment.

"I don't really want to be in the same room with him," she said as Ben, Hayden and Isobel stood in the hallway pleading with her to come out.

Ben gave up and went to get Rob who was already awake and ready to get it over with.

"Do you need someone to watch Gabe?" Ben asked.

"No, he'll be ok. I gave him a book about Egyptians to look at. Found it when we were cleaning up the Cabels apartment. It'll keep him occupied."

When the men left Rob's apartment they found the others, including Molly, gathered in the common area. Everyone was silent and most were looking out the windows at the still pouring rain.

"I'm going to make some tea," Isobel said to the somber group.

"I'd like some," Molly said.

"Me too," added Ben.

Isobel came back ten minutes later with three steaming mugs and they began.

THE TRIAL OF JEFF BROWN

"I'm not interested in hearing apologies from any of you," Molly started. "I wanted to make that clear. I just want to feel ok at night knowing that we haven't turned a blind eye to murder."

"He killed her in the heat of the moment," Ben said. "He isn't a dangerous person to be locked up or let out."

"He strangled her to *death*! Have you even considered how much hatred and evil it takes to commit to that? It isn't a quick process!" Molly cried out. "Unlike a bullet, you have time to reconsider!"

"Well, no, I hadn't thought about the time it took him to do it," Ben said, slightly more confused about his own position on the event.

"So, no one has any suggestions? Let me start. I say we kick him out of here," Molly said.

"Are you kidding? You've seen the guy. He wouldn't have any chance out there. He'd die!" Rob said, shaking his head in disagreement.

"Exactly the plan," Molly said with a smile. "We certainly can't kill him ourselves but it is what he deserves for taking a life."

It was then that Jeff emerged from his apartment. His fists were clenched and the knuckles were scabbed and covered in dried blood. He looked like he might kill again.

"Hi . . . Jeff. Care to join us?" Isobel asked slowly, carefully.

"A meeting," Jeff said brightly, "how nice. I seemed to have misplaced my invitation."

"It's been a rough few days. We just forgot to wake you up," Ben said with a forced smile.

"Yeah," Hayden played along, "sorry about that."

"It's kind of unfair not being invited to my own trial, don't you think? Kind of unfair not to ask for my suggestions," Jeff said, still standing at a distance from the group.

"It isn't like that, Jeff. We were going to talk to you," Isobel said.

"**WHEN?!**" he roared and Isobel flinched from the shock of it.

"Finally, some fucking *drama*!" Vaughn clapped his hands together with excitement as he walked down the stairs into the charged room wearing only dirty jeans.

The anger this brought up in Isobel temporarily outweighed the fear she felt from Jeff's anger. "Where were *you* Vaughn, when we had to slaughter The Cabels in the hallway? Or how about when we risked our lives to bring your felony in from the cold? And where *the fuck* were you when Ben had to pull his gun on you at dinner two nights ago?" Isobel screamed at him. "I had a door frame save my head from a machete for Christ's sake!"

"That dinner thing was just a big misunderstanding," Vaughn laughed as he walked up to Jeff and threw an arm around him jovially.

"No Vaughn **THAT WAS DRAMA!** And the only one who doesn't understand *a thing* is you," Isobel ended her tirade and took a gulp of her tea which had thankfully cooled significantly.

Jeff pushed Vaughn's arm off of him and put about three feet between them. "You want to punish me for killing my wife and yet you all stay quiet while Vaughn and Ben fuck Hayden like bunny rabbits? Last time I checked it was illegal to screw a minor."

"Whoa there," Vaughn broke in, "for the record there was *never* a threesome. I don't do men."

It hurt Hayden a little that Vaughn didn't care that she and Ben had been together but it felt good to have it out in the open. They wouldn't have to sneak around anymore.

Isobel looked at Ben for his reaction to be outed in front of everyone. Ben couldn't raise his eyes.

Jeff wasn't done with the finger pointing and he began again, his eyes growing wilder as he spoke. "Molly and Ben are thieves. They've taken other people's belongings for themselves! There are no rules anymore. I did what I had to do! You can hate me for it but you can't kick me out!"

"I haven't done anything wrong, Jeff," Isobel pointed out.

"Whose shoes are those? Huh? And what about the books? I know you didn't swipe your visa for any of it. You're a looter, a thief just like Molly and Ben, Vaughn too. You are the worst, Tom," he said, staring Vaughn down.

"We are *surviving*, Jeff," Isobel explained. "We need shoes, we need books to feel human and we kill to *stay* human."

"I was traumatized by her. I had nothing of myself left. No life or choice to speak of. I killed to stay human too. It was the only thing I had left. How is it that no one sees that?" he cried.

"Our crimes are smaller than yours and I don't feel safe with you here, Jeff," Molly said, ignoring his words.

"*I* make you feel unsafe? **ME?** Do I have to point out that you are sitting next to someone with an alcohol problem, a penchant for hitting women, and a gun collection larger than Sports Authority? How's that nose of yours?" Jeff asked, waiting to hear what he suspected to be true.

Molly hung her head. "Broken."

"That's right. Broken! Like our sense of right and wrong. I'm sick of these double standards. I'll be in *my* apartment, the one on *my* rental agreement. I'm not leaving and I'm not eating dinner with you hypocritical fucks anymore!" Jeff yelled and then retreated back to his apartment.

It was as though everyone had been holding their breath for when he was gone they all exhaled. Ben wiped his sweaty palms on the sides of the chair he sat in. Isobel tried to hug Molly, who was trembling, but she pushed her away and went back to her own place.

Unfazed by Jeff's speech and the overall mood in the room, Vaughn laughed. "Meeting adjourned then!" he said and went back upstairs. In all honesty he was underwhelmed by Jeff's performance. He hadn't demanded weapons or keys and his eyes had started to tear up. Maybe he didn't have it in him. *Such a pussy,* Vaughn thought, *such a pussy.*

ON THE OUTSIDE

Markus was soaking wet, shivering and second-guessing himself. His right hand ached from gripping the baseball bat for hours. He had managed to get as far as the burned out mall, though even that short journey had taken him all night and all of his physical and emotional strength. *What was I thinking, leaving that fortress to walk the streets with the dead?* He thought as he watched the crowd of corpses gathering in the south parking lot. They not only disgusted him, they truly terrified him.

His hideout was secure as far as he could tell. He had found a large tunnel running underneath the mall, used by semi-trucks for delivering consumer goods for the shops above. It was closed on either end with seven-foot high chain link fences (one of which he'd had to climb over). It wasn't the best place to stop as it was pitch dark within ten feet of the opening; anything could be hiding in it, but he'd made the quick decision to take shelter there. Markus didn't plan on staying long and he made a point to stay as near the fence as he dared without tempting the undead on the other side of it.

He sat on the floor of the tunnel. Runoff from the parking lot had seeped in and wet the ground but it didn't matter to him; he was already drenched. He pulled the map from his backpack and carefully unfolded it. The map too was wet with rainwater and its paper in danger of tearing. It was not the closest house he was looking for but the easiest to get to from his current location.

"There's no way that I'm heading toward Lake City," he said as he studied the map.

"Anthony was always a jerk anyway. Or maybe *I* was the jerk? I can't recall," Markus said aloud, his voice echoing into the darkest depths of the tunnel at a much louder volume than he felt he spoke the words. He listened a moment for any response from possible inhabitants but heard nothing but droplets of water breaking on the surface of the puddles surrounding him.

He returned to the map to look for better possibilities. He had a friend in Green Lake, actually *many* friends, but one that he'd met in college and whose house was perched on a hill above the lake. The entire first floor of the house was a garage and the only two entrances were up narrow stairs that he felt certain could easily be blocked to keep the dead away. With a finger he traced a route. It would require him to double back to the freeway and travel along it for a few miles, leaving him exposed to the world.

He folded the map and stowed it in his backpack, pulled himself from the floor and turned to climb back over the fence but more than thirty dead people waited for him on the other side.

A FOR EFFORT

Jeff was also underwhelmed with his performance. He had meant to make demands but when he was faced with so many people at the meeting he'd lost the nerve to go big. He looked outside to the falling rain and wondered about Markus. Was he staying dry? Had he made it any distance yet? Would he survive to find a better place? Jeff made himself stop the painful train of thought and focus on the next step on his journey. He had to gain the upper hand to control his own fate again.

NORMALCY

Rob had been right about the change in Gabe. His interest in darker things had passed and he was returning to his smart and silly self. He witnessed more evidence of this as Gabe pulled his Legos out once again, creating an impassable, foot-injuring pile in the middle of the hallway of their apartment.

"Who's this guy?" Rob asked as he sat down on the carpet and chose a miniature figure with a red baseball cap on.

"Just a regular guy. He sells bikes," Gabe said, pointing to a crude shop he'd built. Two plastic bicycles sat inside the display window.

"What about her?" Rob pointed to a lady figure on the street.

"That's his mom and she's bringing him lunch."

Rob smiled because he hadn't heard the word *zombie* once. He *did* hear Gabe's stomach growl and he knew he needed his own lunch.

"What do you say we eat something and if the rain stops we haul your bike up to the roof and ride around?"

"Yippee!" Gabe jumped to his feet.

"But you have to pick up your toys first, remember?"

"Will you help?" Gabe asked pleadingly.

"Absolutely, I will."

TUNNEL VISION

"You can do it, Markus! You can either climb the fence or walk into the dark, scary tunnel armed with nothing but a bat and a mini flashlight." Markus was having difficulty deciding which would be worse and any pep talk he gave himself to bring him over the chain link was unsuccessful. He turned back toward the darkness, shone the small beam of light into it and forced his feet to move him forward under the mall.

He had never spent much time at the mall before the trouble started so he could not estimate its length with confidence but he did know it was extremely long and that the tunnel would be equal to its length. His journey was slow as he took the time to shine the flashlight on every inch of both of the sidewalls, the floor and the high ceiling before pressing on to the next section. He'd never seen rats in Northgate, maybe not even in Seattle, but he knew they were there and he swore every time he heard the tiny feet running across his path, somehow avoiding the beam of the flashlight. There were many doors and shipping platforms, each identical to the next but for a small label with the names of the individual stores printed on them. He considered trying a few of the doors to see if they were unlocked but he didn't fancy climbing through a burned out landscape. He was wet but he was still clean and he wanted that to last.

A half hour passed and he could see the light of the other end. He felt no elation at making it through the underground passage because from where he stood he could easily see that a vehicle had driven through the fence. It had not happened recently, he knew, because he couldn't hear an engine or voices and he smelled no exhaust. The crashed vehicle, a Jeep of some kind, sat still and empty. A door was left open on the passenger side. Half of its body jutted out into the light. The other half was eaten by the darkness.

"Hello?" Markus yelled. He could hear the trepidation in his voice. "I'm not here to hurt you." He added just in case someone was hiding inside of it where he couldn't see them.

From the darkness a noise began to grow. It started first as a whisper and then rose to become noisier than a mob. No words were spoken, only moans emitted. He could feel a presence there in the dark, coming closer to him. He knew it was them and that he would never reach the light at the end.

MIND GAMES

Hayden felt lighter on her feet – even with the occasional nausea from her pregnancy – because Vaughn knew that she'd shared a bed with Ben and he seemed to be all right with the fact. She was back in the Cooper's apartment, her apartment now, and reading through a book that Jill Cooper had purchased in expectation of her child called *What to Expect When You're Expecting.* It was a long book and some of the information scared her but she knew that nine months would fly by. She needed the book, even the scary parts, to prepare for motherhood.

Maybe he didn't knock or maybe she was too absorbed in her reading; suddenly Vaughn was in the living room with her. He pulled the book from her hands, threw it across the room, grabbed her and pulled her into the nursery, which he mistook for the bedroom. As soon as he saw the baby stuff, which turned him off, he pulled her back into the living room and pushed her onto the couch.

"What are you doing here?" Hayden yelled at him, trying to push him away but he was too strong.

"I was just curious what a guy like Ben could do for you that I can't," Vaughn answered as he opened his pants and took off hers.

It was immature of Hayden to think that he would ignore her having cheated on him. "A lot," was all she could cry out as Vaughn forced his way into her.

"I'm more of a man than he is and you know it. I fill you up. He probably has extra room." Vaughn finished quickly, due to his excitement over the tension during the meeting and to the frightened look on Hayden's face. She didn't have the energy to yell at him, defend her or Ben's actions, or to tell him about the baby. She redressed herself without looking at Vaughn.

Ben came in as Vaughn was zipping up his pants. "She's all yours," Vaughn said to him as they passed in the entry of the apartment.

DISORDER

If Markus can leave, I can leave. I've been out there before. I know what it takes to survive, Molly thought. She'd taken stock of her food and even gone to take an extra ration from the third floor but it still wasn't enough. It would only last her a few days with her new plan to stop fighting the bulimia. She was going to check the houses near the hospital. Someone over there had killed the people in the street. That someone had to have food if they were still alive.

She left as the sun was going down, hoping she wouldn't run into Vaughn. If he found her alone no one would be there to rescue her. There were few dead on the street in front of Willow Brook and she attributed it to the fact that last night and today Markus had been making his presence known to them, drawing them away from the building and toward wherever he was running to.

It took some nerve for her to walk by the cemetery. It was large, covering over 144 acres, and she had seen movies where the dead had clawed their way out of their graves. She looked through a hole in the hedge that surrounded it and saw that save for a few vandalized headstones, the grounds were undisturbed. Maybe Rob was right about the infection. People caught it when they were alive and then when they died, whether from a super-infected bite or natural cause, it took over. The people in the cemetery died before they could catch it, whatever it was. They were still at peace. Molly did notice some undead wandering through the burial grounds but they hadn't been buried, she could see the wounds.

She made it to the vehicles she'd seen from the roof. All of them empty of people but still holding personal belongings; none of them loaded with anything edible unless moldy coffee and sandwiches were suddenly safe to consume. As she moved among the cars she stayed low to the ground. She still was unsure whether or not there was anyone alive in the houses she was about to break into. *They could be watching me, training their guns on my head,* she thought. It was at that moment, when she was thinking of being killed, that she realized she hadn't brought a weapon with her, only a flashlight and an empty bag to carry food.

"It's too late to go back home," a voice said behind her. A man, looking close to sixty in age and pointing a shotgun at her, walked into the street. "What'cha looking for anyway?"

"Um . . ." was all she could get out on her first attempt to speak.

"Nothing but a bunch of dead folk out here and I know you aren't looking for them." He smiled, exposing his yellowed teeth.

"Food," she managed to say. Her body was jittery with nerves. Who was this man and why hadn't he shot her yet?

"Well you don't look hungry but I've got plenty of it. If you come inside I'll share some with you."

It would have been a nice offer if he weren't still pointing the shotgun at her. The polished wood of the stock and the flawless barrel told her that the man spent hours keeping it clean. He had it low, against one of his hips, and he held it comfortably, like an old friend. She knew she couldn't refuse his offer or she would end up lying on the street amongst the other bodies.

He moved the shotgun to signal her to walk in front of him, like a captive. He led her to a gated home just up the road. She assumed it was his house but he could have taken it from someone else. It was made of brick and had two levels. It looked like an old English house; with its small windows and steep roof. Inside it lacked the benefits of natural light and the man quickly went room-to-room lighting candles. It smelled like mothballs, which made Molly want to gag. She was about to make a run for it when the man came back into the foyer.

"The food is this way." He gestured to his right. She followed him through a library and into a formal dining room. The tabletop was covered with canned food. A smile crept across her face. She opened her bag and started dumping food into it. When it was full she made toward the front door. The man was in front of her with his shotgun before she knew it.

"Not even a thank you? Can't you stay awhile?" he asked, blocking the only exit she knew of. "I've been rather lonely."

"No, I really can't. I have to get back to my family," she lied, hoping that he had a compassionate bone in his body that wouldn't kill a mother or that he might think they'd come looking for her if she didn't turn up.

"The food isn't free," the man said, again showing his yellow teeth in a grin. He took one hand off of the shotgun and started to undo his pants.

EXIT STAGE LEFT

Markus was not ready to die. He wanted to run for the Jeep in the distance but he'd have to run through the dead and he couldn't tell how large the group was. The vehicle was also abandoned and that surely meant it was in some way unusable, out of gas or damaged from the crash. He pulled himself up on to one of the raised cement platforms. From there he felt he might be able to fight off a few of them instead of the horde that was approaching down the road of the tunnel. Hugging the wall he moved toward the noise; he would not return to the fence on the other side for he knew the dead awaited him there. Using the darkness to his advantage he made it another thirty feet before the platform ended and he was forced to climb down.

He could smell them now and that meant they were closer, by how much he wasn't sure but he knew he had to get out of the tunnel as fast as possible. Markus walked with the bat parallel in front of him as a barrier. With his fingertips he felt in the darkness for the start of another platform. He reached the cool surface of one and he began to pull himself up. A hand, so cold he could feel it through his pants, grabbed his right ankle. A sharp tug nearly brought him back to the ground but he kicked and fought with such energy brought on by sheer terror that he managed to break free. Safely on top of the platform he made for the first door he could feel. Locked. He continued on but each door was locked like the first.

Ahead of him he could see that some of the zombies had made it onto the next platform. They were everywhere now and he had only one more door on the zombie-free platform to try. To his surprise, the door pushed open easily and he stumbled inside. He was in a room full of shipping boxes and he was able to pull some of the heavier ones in front of the door to block it from opening again. The smell of burned materials was strong and he was unsure where the room would let out but he had to move forward, there was nothing but death behind him. He stopped to catch his breath and gather his thoughts. Escaping the dead had filled him with new energy to press on.

He could see an open door on the other side of the room and he ran for it. The moment he made it through the door a piercing, sharp pain erupted in his stomach. He dropped the bat and his hands went to hold the pain but they found what felt like a kitchen knife stuck into his belly. Blood poured from the wound and he sank to his knees.

"I found this place! You can't have it! Go away! Go away!" a man yelled at him in the darkness.

"I . . ." Markus started to speak but found it difficult. He couldn't see the source of the voice but he could smell it. Urine and old food, dirty feet and body odor.

"Go away! Go away! Go away." The man kept yelling over and over. Markus wanted to explain that he was only passing through but no words came, only blood. He wondered if he would die and come back, he wondered if Jeff had come looking for him, he thought of his friends that he'd never see again. Markus lay down on his side as he listened to the lunatic's lullaby and the sound of undead hands hitting the door in the other room. He lost consciousness and bled to death.

MOLLY FIGHTS BACK

"I'm not a whore!" Molly yelled and backed away.

"We all have needs, lady. I was only suggesting we barter with them. All the food you want for just a little companionship."

"I'm done with 'companionship'," Molly said with disgust.

"I wasn't giving you a choice," he said as he backed her all the way into the dining room, pushing her up against the dining table. He kissed her neck and chest, making her squirm. Just like the house his breath smelled like mothballs, like he'd eaten them and she was gagging uncontrollably now. Her hands searched behind her for the heaviest jar of food she could find. She brought the jar down hard on his head once, twice, a third time before the glass broke and cut into his skin. He fell to the ground, covered in pickle juice. The smell wafted up into her nostrils and filled the room, an improvement on the mothballs. Molly was not sure if he was already dead, just unconscious or if he might bleed to death so she moved with purpose. Pulling up the corners of the tablecloth and bringing them together in a knot over the food, she hefted it off the table. She dragged the load out of the front door, along with her previously loaded food bag, into the darkening evening. Still the dead were spread out near Willow Brook and it was easy for her to make it back to the building.

She managed to climb her fire escape, pushed onward by the adrenaline coursing through her. The moment she made it safely into her apartment she burst into tears. She cried for at least twenty minutes as she scrubbed her skin raw where his mothballed mouth had touched her.

Was he my first kill? Molly thought with horror. She didn't' want to be a murderer but she had no other option. She had killed to survive.

LIARS NOT WELCOME

Rob wasn't expecting much in the way of forgiveness from Molly. He didn't want to spend the rest of his life, however long or short that may be, knowing he hadn't tried to mend things between them. He knocked on the door of 204 and waited.

"Go away Isobel!" Molly yelled from within. Isobel was the only person she thought had the nerve to still come visit her. She didn't even check the peephole.

"It's Rob. Can we talk?" he asked as he pressed his ear to the door to discern what she might be doing inside.

"That's even worse. No, we can't talk. I'm busy," Molly said, and she was. Finally feeling like herself again after all the scrubbing, she had started to sort the food she'd found.

"What can you possibly be busy with?" Rob asked, annoyed that she was avoiding him.

Molly stood up from her place on the floor and went to the door. She opened it a crack, leaving the chain in place. "I'm eating dinner and then I'm going to bed."

"It's so good to see you," Rob smiled.

"So now that I want nothing to do with you I have become irresistible? Maybe Hayden wants some company or have you already been in her bed?"

"I haven't touched that girl, nor do I want to."

"Well maybe it's time to start because you aren't sleeping with me anymore," Molly said and then closed the door.

"Molly!" Rob yelled. "Molly, open up!"

"She needs time, Rob. Leave her alone," Isobel said softly. "Besides, it's too late to be yelling in the hall."

BOTCHED

Molly gorged herself that night. Twenty cans of food later she was feeling full but disgusted. Everything she'd learned in her group therapy came flooding into her mind. How she was beautiful, worth more than this, and damaging her body if she continued. She looked down at the empty cans, some of which were badly dented, some even expired, and she became convinced that she'd done something very wrong. She was in the kitchen then, digging under the sink for a garbage bag. She shoved a finger in her throat but nothing came up. She'd had problems vomiting before treatment but she was able to do it just weeks ago, why not now?

"This isn't the disease! I need to get this food out of me!" she yelled at herself. She'd remembered what Vaughn had said when they were in the kitchen of the hoarder, digging through her pantry. *"If you can't find a date or if the can is damaged leave it, or it might kill you . . ."*

"I don't want to die!" she cried out. Sitting on the floor, tears running down her cheeks she kept forcing more fingers in. After four fingers to no avail, she gave up. Her stomach was cramping, or maybe she was imagining it, and she was growing tired.

She fell asleep on cool linoleum, an empty garbage bag clutched in one hand.

TOM VAUGHN'S NEW PLAN

It was late evening. What evening, Vaughn didn't know. He might have known earlier what week they were in, what day of it he was living. But now he had lost count of the beers he had downed and with them, the days. He didn't usually keep track of either of those things anyway.

He was making plans to leave the complex for good. In fact, he had readied Dead Lawn, the house down the road with the dog, over a few days' time. Tom was sick of the group downstairs. They had become a hassle and he was gladly trading their company for that of Cheddar the Golden Retriever. He'd rather put up with Cheddar's constant need to have his paw held than any of the other tenants. It wasn't just the people though. His apartment, which was small before the outbreak, had taken on a coffin-like feel, stifling and claustrophobic. It was definitely time for a change.

He was packing the second of two large duffel bags and going over the plan in his head when Hayden let herself in to the apartment.

"Hey," was all Hayden said. When Tom heard the word 'hey' it told him that she was bored and he hated that. He wasn't her entertainer.

"Don't you knock girl?" Tom turned around on unsteady feet. She was playing with her hair and looking around. Her eyes came to meet his and he watched them scan down to the duffel bags.

"What are you doing?" she asked, though Tom was unsure if she was asking specifically about the bags.

"Not much, just hanging out." All his words came out slurred but he was sober enough to decide not to explain the travel gear. Hayden too had become a hassle and she wasn't invited over to his new place. He wanted to disappear.

"Don't you drink something other than beer? Ever heard of water?" she laughed, but Vaughn didn't think it was funny, just annoying. His anger and impatience with her were beginning to rise and he wanted her to leave.

"Are we going to screw or are you going to get out of here?" His impatience had won and now he was in full jerk mode.

"You shouldn't talk to me like that. You should treat me better, like Ben does."

"Ben is a pussy of a man and I don't have to do anything for you Hayden. If you let him touch you it just goes to show what a slut you truly are. Go away. We're done." He tried to push her towards the door so he could continue his packing. She pushed back and smacked his face. He hit her back, almost knocking her to the ground.

"I'm pregnant, Tom!" she yelled; the pain of his slap and his rejection registering and bringing tears to her eyes. Vaughn was too drunk and dumbfounded to figure out what that meant for him. He grabbed his cigarettes and a lighter and went for the balcony. Hayden followed so he climbed down the fire escape, something he knew she wouldn't do.

ARMED . . .

Jeff had to look out for himself again. He was happy he'd removed himself from the group and been able to return to the solitude of his apartment. He found only one issue with his idea of paradise, his food was very low but Isobel would try to convince him to rejoin the social structure of the group if he approached her in need. He wouldn't ask for sustenance, he would take it. But first he would take a gun and he knew just where to get one.

Feeling more empowered than usual, something similar to the feeling he felt when he'd killed his wife, he walked upstairs to Tom's apartment to arm himself. When he knocked Tom didn't answer, Hayden did.

"Hi, um, Jeff," she said as she held a hand to her face where it still burned from the impact of Vaughn's hand.

"Hey, is Tom here?" He looked around the living room.

"No, he went out for a little bit. Can I do something for you?"

Jeff didn't know if she was trying to come on to him but he didn't care either way. "I just need a gun."

"He won't like that," Hayden shook her head.

"But you won't tell him," Jeff grabbed her throat. His hand gripped her small neck hard enough to let her know that he wasn't there to screw around. "He has so much crap in here he won't notice."

Hayden nodded her head as much as she could in his grasp and he let go. She moved out of his way. Jeff picked a handgun; it would do the job he needed it to.

"Knowing how psychotic he is, I bet you he'll notice the gun is gone. You should think about leaving before he comes back," Jeff suggested. Hayden thought it semi-psychotic of Jeff to choke her and look out for her well being in the same visit.

"No, we were talking about something and we weren't finished."

"Well, I should go then. Thanks for the gun."

. . . AND DANGEROUS

"I'm going to bed soon. I feel super drained. Maybe things will look up tomorrow," Isobel yawned and waited for Ben's reply but he was already snoozing. She blew out the last lit candle and made her way to her bedroom in the dark. Not twenty minutes later Ben was shaking her awake.

"Isobel, get up. Jeff is here."

"Tell him we can talk tomorrow," Isobel said as she rolled over in bed.

"Isob- " Ben started.

The beam of a flashlight hit her in the face. The brightness blinded her temporarily.

"Get out of bed. Now." It was Jeff, his meek voice sounding strong and scary to her.

"Can't this *wait*? Whatever this is?"

"I have a gun, Isobel. I don't need it to kill you but don't make me use it." His allusion to strangling as an option made him smile and Isobel cringe.

She was out of bed at the word *gun*, leading the way into the living room, followed by Ben with Jeff and his mysteriously acquired handgun bringing up the rear. Isobel lit a few candles for some light that would be softer than the glare of the flashlight. She discreetly looked around the table and side tables for Ben's handgun. Jeff saw it at the same time she did. He picked it up and tossed it behind the couch.

"I defended you to *everyone*, Jeff. Why are you doing this?" Her teeth chattered from nervousness and the nighttime cold of the room. Isobel didn't want to die but she couldn't think of a reason why Jeff would actually kill her. Still, a gun in her face had her on edge.

"I just want to live like everyone else and to do that I have to eat. I need you to give me the key to the rations apartment."

"But . . ." Isobel began to argue. Jeff cocked the gun.

"Are you going to tell me something stupid like 'you found it first?' Because I don't fucking care. No one elected you supreme leader. I'll bring the key back when I take what I need."

"Then why the gun? Why are you scaring the hell out of me to take something you are going to return anyway? Borrowing hardly seems like a good reason to threaten a life."

"I want the extra key to my apartment too," Jeff explained. He didn't want to talk to her he just wanted to get the keys and leave. "Don't say anything else. Just do it."

Isobel found the key ring and relinquished the requested keys to him. Jeff left backwards, the gun aimed at Isobel and Ben as he disappeared into the darkened hallway and back upstairs.

GAME CHANGER

Vaughn had never been outside with the dead while so intoxicated. It was a trip that messed with his head in a way he didn't like. Vaughn was stubborn though and refused to climb back upstairs before he finished a cigarette. The sky was dark; it was later than he'd thought. He had to keep walking or the dead would catch him. The more he moved the more tired he felt, the slower he became, like the alcohol hadn't been fully absorbed until this escapist expedition. He had to go back; this wasn't working. He would have to deal with Hayden, the girl he'd invited into his life, and face the mistake he had made by doing so.

He reached for the lowest ladder rung. A huge woman came around the corner of the building. Vaughn was struck by her size. She smelled absolutely putrid. Near five hundred pounds alive, all of that mass was rotting. He couldn't stop looking at her. She seemed to be coming for him in slow motion but slow was as fast as she could move. In the darkness her face looked like his mother.

"I don't want to raise a baby. I don't want to. I just wanted the retarded dog." He was talking to the thing, hoping for some understanding, looking for a little unconditional love. The alcohol was making him emotional and the tears started falling. They blurred his vision more than the beer; making the monster look even more like his mother. She had her arms open like a hug, an invitation. Vaughn put his arms out in front of him, ready for the embrace. The woman almost had him enveloped when she turned her head ever so slightly and took a giant bite out of Tom's left forearm.

The pain raced through his arm and into his head, clearing it in an instant. He'd had twelve beers, Hayden was knocked up, and this woman, who was *not* his mother and not really even a woman had just infected him. He fought his way out of the clutches of the beast and pulled himself up the ladder. Hayden was kneeling on the floor, unpacking his duffel bags and crying. She could see the wound on his arm.

"You bitch! You fucking bitch! Come here!" Vaughn pulled her from the floor by her hair and threw her face down on the couch. He ripped her clothes off and entered her without mercy.

OFF

Jeff's hands were shaking as he stood at the doorway to the apartment upstairs were the food was stored. He couldn't believe he'd held a gun to two people's faces! He felt incredible, in control and as badass as Vaughn. Just as he was about to turn the key to unlock the door he heard Hayden screaming from Vaughn's apartment. He crept to the door of Vaughn's place and pressed an ear to it. From the noises he heard the two of them were fucking again. Jeff was surprised to be turned on by the sound. Since Markus had left he was unmotivated to please himself but the grunting of Vaughn and the begging of Hayden was far too much for him to handle. He unzipped his pants in the darkness of the end of the hall and attempted to find a heaven similar to the one he'd found with Markus.

UNHAPPY ENDING

"How fast do you think the infection can spread through my *entire* body? Consider it a gift to you and the baby to show how much I care about you both," Vaughn whispered into Hayden's ear. His arm looked like shit and it was dripping blood on Hayden's back. She was screaming and struggling to get away from him but he was too strong and too determined to see it through to the end. He wondered if he'd have time to find Molly and be with her too before he turned.

"Do you see what you did to me? Huh?" Vaughn only knew anger now. His plans were ruined, his life ending.

"You brought me here!" she screamed. "You did this to yourself!"

As though he hadn't harmed her enough, when he was finished he flicked on some porn, something he knew Hayden despised, and went to grab another beer.

"Let me go. Let me leave," she was whimpering on the floor, naked and terrified that Vaughn would turn at any moment into a zombie and try to eat her.

"Oh, you want to go *now*? I was trying to kick you out earlier but you wouldn't leave. You know where the fucking door is, whore."

Hayden picked up her clothes and started for the exit. She saw a handgun on the side table near the couch. She reached for it as she heard the beer bottle drop.

"It's happening. I can't believe it. I'm going fucking numb!" Vaughn yelled as he looked at his arms.

She pulled the trigger but her shaking hands and lack of any real firearms skills made for a lousy shot. The bullet hit wall. She ran for the door. She had to get away before the change was complete.

SPENT

Jeff had finished and was sitting in the dark enjoying the afterglow when he heard a *pop* from Vaughn's apartment. He was still processing the noise when the door was ripped open. He lifted his gun, fearing it was Vaughn himself but Hayden's nude silhouette stood in the light of the doorway.

She saw Jeff sitting with his pants open in the corner of the hallway. "*Help me*," she had just enough time to whisper to him.

BANG

Molly was jarred from sleep by the sound of gunshots. Her body was stiff from lying on the kitchen floor for hours. She felt her forehead with the back of her hand, searching for fever but finding it cool and dry. She stood up slowly, holding onto the edge of the counter for support, expecting to be dizzy and nauseous. She found her feet steady, her vision acute and her stomach still holding its contents.

"Oh, thank the fucking Lord. That was close," she said, overwhelmed with relief that she hadn't poisoned herself with bad food. Then she remembered the noise she'd heard and wondered if it had been real. If she wasn't sick, it must have been.

Isobel too was startled from her sleep. The gunshots sounded as though it had come from within the building. Her watch said that it was only an hour after Jeff's gun-accompanied visit. She already had clothes and shoes on but she stumbled around to find a fleece jacket because the air inside was freezing.

Ben was awake in the living room, wrapped in a thick bathrobe, and sitting upright listening for some further disturbance.

"Who do you think that was?" Isobel asked.

"I don't know. Jeff, maybe? I don't hear screaming or running or anything," Ben answered.

"You think he took his life?" Isobel hoped that was the case. It would solve a few problems.

"Like I said, I don't know." Ben shrugged.

"Let's go find out." Isobel unlocked her apartment door to find everyone else, the small group that they were, in the second floor hall already. They all looked just as bewildered; no one had answers.

"Who are we missing?" Ben asked. He had his gun, recovered from behind Isobel's couch, and a flashlight, one in each hand. He shone the light over the bleary-eyed group, trying to recognize the shadowy faces of those surrounding him.

Jeff wasn't in the hallway with the others. Rob had Gabe wrapped up in a quilt. Molly stood alone, looking stressed and tired.

"What's wrong with your face, Molly?" Rob asked her, noticing strange markings across her left cheek.

"What?" She raised a hand to her skin and felt shallow, long, and strangely geometric indentations there. "Oh. I fell asleep on the linoleum."

Rob didn't ask for further clarification. It was an answer that made sense for the marks but why would she be on the floor? Molly saw him thinking over her response.

"I felt hot and it was the only cool place I could find," she added.

"Are you feeling better now?" Isobel asked her with motherly concern in her voice.

"Much better. Thank you," Molly answered only to end the conversation. She hated it when Isobel talked to her like a child.

"Has anyone seen Jeff?" Isobel inquired. She didn't know if he'd asserted himself with anyone else in the time since he had threatened her.

"I already tried to check his place but the door was locked and if he was in there he didn't answer," Rob said.

"Hayden's not here," Ben said, his heartbeat growing more rapid.

"Only one place it could have come from then. Ben, can you lead the way to the third floor?" Isobel asked expectantly. Ben said nothing but walked to the front of the group to take point.

"I think Gabe and I will stay here, if that's alright? If Vaughn has a gun I don't want it pointed at my son."

Isobel turned to him in the dark of the hallway. "We could really use your help, Rob." Isobel didn't feel safe with just Molly, who'd turned against everyone, and Ben whose attachment to Hayden might lead him to angering Vaughn. She needed another stable person with her and Rob was the only option.

"Gabe, can you promise to stay in the apartment until I come back?" Rob asked as he rubbed his son's shoulders through the blanket that enveloped him.

"I'm scared, dad. What if you don't come back?"

"I'll come back. I pinky promise."

"But what if you *don't* come back," Gabe worried.

"I will but, if I don't, someone else will come. Maybe Molly." Rob looked at Molly and she nodded lightly.

With Gabe safe in 203, Rob followed the others up the stairs with heavy feet and foreboding. It was dark on the third floor except for Ben's flashlight and the light coming through the open doorway of Vaughn's apartment at the end of the hall. A nude form was lying on the floor, halfway in the apartment, and halfway in the hall. In the corner opposite,

Ben could see Jeff sitting, clutching his knees to his chest. When the flashlight hit him he drew his legs in tighter and tucked his head deeper out of view, like he was hiding.

"Oh!" Molly cried out but then covered her mouth. It was difficult to tell if it was Hayden but the body on the floor couldn't be anyone else.

"Jeff! What happened? Is Hayden ok?" Isobel asked as they all moved forward. From their new position, just one apartment away from the body, they could tell for certain that it was the teen.

"Is she alive, Jeff? Is she breathing?" Ben asked with growing worry in his voice.

Jeff lifted his head slowly. "Shut up!" he whispered. "He'll hear you!" A strange growling noise came from Vaughn's apartment. Everyone turned to the doorway, expecting Vaughn to emerge but nothing happened.

"What the hell was that noise?" Isobel asked Jeff as quietly as she could with still being audible to him.

"Vaughn has . . . turned," Jeff whispered back.

"Can you crawl this way, slowly?" Rob asked him. As much as he despised Jeff for his poor choices, he didn't want anyone else to die.

"Get the flashlight off of me! He'll notice." Jeff needed darkness to button his pants and conceal the handgun that tied him to Hayden's murder. Ben did as Jeff said and lowered the light to his own feet. Once Jeff had the gun tucked in the back of his fastened jeans he started to move along the wall towards the others. As he did, Molly got onto her knees and crawled by him.

"Molly, get back here!" Isobel ordered. "What are you doing?"

"Hayden!" Molly whispered, her voice trembling a bit as she crawled closer to the girl. "Hayden, come on, we have to get you out of here."

Another growl emitted from the unit and Hayden's body was pulled in entirely. A trail of blood appeared in its place. The blood drove Molly to stand up and run forward to the light of the door. Something inside, something only she could see, made her scream. She turned to run back as Vaughn's half-naked self came lunging out of 306. Ben aimed and pulled the trigger of his handgun. The bullet hit Vaughn in the head above his left ear. Vaughn fell forward, onto Molly, pinning her to the ground.

"Get him off! Get him off!" she shrieked over and over. Ben and Isobel pulled Vaughn off of Molly, careful to not get his blood on them. He reeked of beer and there was a baseball–sized bite wound on his left forearm. He had jeans on but his cock was hanging out of the open fly. Some of his semen had leaked onto Molly's pajama pants. She screamed as she ripped them off, sitting in the cold in her underwear she began to cry. Jeff watched, and as he did a smile grew on his face. He had fallen into the deep end of the pool of insanity. He had killed his wife and enjoyed it. He had pulled a gun on friends and wanted more. He had masturbated to a rape in progress and wished for it to go on forever and he had shot a girl. As the group of residents flooded Vaughn's apartment to check on Hayden, he crawled back to the end of the hall and touched the pool of Hayden's blood on the carpet. This time he wouldn't be admitting anything to anyone.

IT ALL ADDS UP

Hayden was lying where Vaughn had left her and Ben knelt at her side. The teen was completely naked, her panties lay nearby. A pile of the rest of her clothes lay deeper in the apartment. Porn played on the television, as usual. Inside the light of the apartment it was obvious that Hayden was dead. In her forehead was the bullet that had torn all of Willow Brook from its sleep.

He looked over the soft skin of Hayden's body and found no bite wounds. "She wasn't infected. What happened?" he cried at Jeff who was back in the hall, in the light of the doorway.

"I don't know. Maybe Vaughn shot her when she was trying to leave? I think he was drunk again," Jeff explained as if the reason was simple and clear as day. He didn't point out the position of the entry wound, which faced him and not Vaughn. He hoped no one else would notice that bullet-sized hole in his story.

"He used her and then he killed her before she could get away from what he was about to become. Maybe if I hadn't kicked her out . . ." Molly was barely able to breathe.

"Yep," Jeff said.

"Fuck you, you're no help. What's wrong with you?" Isobel yelled at him.

"That is a good question," Jeff responded as he got up off the floor. "As soon as I figure it out I'll be sure to check in at a group powwow." He walked away out of sight of the doorway and back to the second floor, stopping first to get the food he had come for. He grabbed a bottle of wine too, to celebrate getting away with murder.

"Don't listen to Jeff, Molly. It isn't your fault. Vaughn was unstable, drunk. Hayden was . . . pregnant," Ben said as he placed a gentle hand on her belly.

"What?" Isobel was genuinely shocked.

"I think she may have finally told him and he lost it," Ben said, his tears falling on her body.

"But who bit the *amazing* Vaughn?" Isobel asked sarcastically, "and how?"

"Can we turn that shit off?" Ben yelled when he finally realized the porn was playing. Isobel found the remote and stopped the immortal porn stars in mid-moan. Rob brought Hayden's clothes over to her body and he and Ben redressed her. Isobel found a clean sheet to wrap her in.

"Why did you have to see him tonight? Why didn't you come to me?" Ben asked her as he carried Hayden's swaddled body to the balcony's edge. He let go and it dropped into the dark of early morning with a thud on the frosty ground.

Molly rushed to the bathroom as vomit was rising in her throat. Isobel could hear her heaving into the toilet and then crying; the sound of something being dumped on the tile, and a small scream.

"Molly, what is it?" Isobel pushed the door open. Molly was crumpled on the floor in front of the toilet, a box full of prescription drugs had been emptied all around her. Two pill bottles were clutched in her hands.

"This is the heart medication that Moira ran out of! He has at least six bottles of it in here. That man is a fucking monster."

Isobel took the bottles from her hands, set them on the countertop, pulled her from the floor and held her close. They cried for a while together, for Moira and Edward and for Hayden, for the group's ignorance and Vaughn's selfishness. Molly needed the affection and she held the hug longer than Isobel expected her to. When they came out of the bathroom, Ben and Rob were struggling with Vaughn's dead body.

"Tuck it in. I don't want that shit touching me," Ben yelled at Rob.

"So *I* have to touch it?" Rob shot back.

"Nobody has to touch his dick. Dump him over how he is!" Isobel yelled at them both.

"He doesn't deserve special treatment," Molly added.

Without a sheet or farewell, they threw Vaughn's body over the railing to join Hayden and their unborn child. Ben went back into the apartment and gathered up all the porn DVDs he could find and, one by one, chucked them at Vaughn's body as the sun slowly rose.

"You fucking ASSHOLE! You could have had a FAMILY and *her*, you could have had her but you don't value ANYTHING!" Ben screamed. He closed his eyes in sorrow but continued to throw DVD cases onto the ground below. The dead were gathering from the sound of his voice. Ben opened his eyes to see them stepping on the cases, breaking the plastic and it made him smile the smallest of smiles. He dumped the rest of them onto the heads of the undead and let the empty cardboard box fall as well.

Through tears, the group went through Vaughn's apartment and took anything they wanted: weapons, wine, toothpaste and the last issue of Rolling Stone to ever be published. Ben was close in size to Vaughn so he took all the clean shirts he could carry, which wasn't a lot (of *clean* ones).

SELF WORTH

Before Isobel closed the door to 306, Molly paused, looking into the bloody, ransacked apartment. She thought back to when Hayden said she was using Vaughn too, that there were mutual benefits to their agreement. Vaughn left this life happy, drunk, and satisfied, if a little numb from the infection.

"Was it worth it?" Molly asked the empty room. Isobel stood behind her but didn't say anything. She knew Molly wasn't talking to her; that she needed this moment with her ghosts.

"What do stolen designer clothes even mean when you spend your time naked and on your back? Whore!" Molly yelled.

This shocked Isobel to hear, but she understood Molly's anger and how it stemmed from regret. She was painting Hayden as doubly wicked in life so that she could be more easily forgotten in death.

"And he would have fucked you no matter what your perfume smelled like!"

Isobel knew this to be true. Vaughn was the dirtiest, horniest man she'd known. He could find beauty in a worn out, elderly barmaid if it meant he'd get laid.

"You can't even read those stupid books he got you now! You can't sell yourself for your own happiness, Hayden."

"Because when you do that," Isobel interrupted, "in the end there isn't any bit of *you* left."

SEPARATE WAYS

Willow Brook was dead quiet for the rest of the day. After the difficult morning, everyone went back to his or her own apartments and beds. It was early evening before anyone rose from slumber but even when they did, they kept to themselves.

THE GOOD OLD DAYS

No one came to the group breakfast the following day at Isobel's other than Ben and her. What group were they anymore? She and Ben had canned pears, granola bars and some re-hydrated eggs that they found in the food stash. They sat quietly, looking out the window. There were many more dead outside than Isobel had ever seen before, as though they were flooding into the area. She finished her food and went to her balcony. From there she began to pick through the crowd, searching for people she recognized from around Northgate, wondering if she might see Markus but hoping that she wouldn't.

The first zombie she recognized was a kid that had worked at the McDonald's counter up the block. He still had his uniform on. She imagined he smelled like a mix of fryer grease and decay. Next she saw a woman that she remembered from her QFC shopping trip on the first day. They had shared a laugh when they'd both wanted to go down the coffee aisle but beans covered the floor. It was almost impassable. The woman hadn't purchased much food that day and by the looks of it, it hadn't lasted. She'd been forced outside and the gamble had not paid off.

"I think that's my bank teller," Isobel said as she pointed to an angry looking corpse in a ratted negligee. Ben joined her on the balcony to see whom she was referring to.

"Yeah, I know her too," Ben commented but then went back inside.

"So many kids," Isobel said to herself. She said it very quietly, afraid that Ben might hear and be reminded of the loss of Hayden and her unborn child. There were so many of them in the street today. "School let out," she said louder.

"Huh?" Ben asked.

"Nothing, just talking to myself," Isobel replied.

"Don't make that a habit. Some might call that crazy."

Isobel sat on a deck chair, away from the railing, and closed her eyes. She tried to think of life when it had been more normal. Days when she could go on a walk outside without looking over her shoulder or ride her bike without fear of being chased. She daydreamed of long hot showers, fresh food and fresh air. It filled her with regret for all the things she didn't do. When life had been normal, she barely took walks outside. She sat at home on her computer in her stuffy apartment. Her bike knew storage more than it ever knew the streets. She'd always taken her car everywhere. She'd hated the chore of showers and so took hers quick and her food came more often from a frozen box than a field. She opened her eyes again, faced with all the time in the world but she couldn't do any of it. She went back inside and sat next to Ben on the couch.

"Living has become the chore. If we don't work hard at it, put it on our checklist to mark it off, we wouldn't make it through the day. I would give anything to lay outside on some grass, undisturbed, unthreatened by walking death, with the sweet smell of nothing in my nose!" Isobel said, almost poetic in her comment.

"Me too," was all Ben had in response, partly because he was surprised at Isobel's show of such sensitive emotions. The other half of him was gripped by sadness over Hayden's death. She had been an unexpected bright point in his dismal existence. Her news of the child that could be his, if he wanted it to be, was even greater still. Needing time alone and wanting to properly grieve, he left Isobel's and went upstairs to 305.

PAGES

Ben broke down as soon as the door closed behind him. He had been unable to keep both Anna and Hayden safe. On the coffee table he found the pregnancy book that Hayden had been reading and that had belonged to Jill previously. Many of its pages had been earmarked in anticipation that the knowledge would be needed. He took the book to the kitchen and tossed it into the sink. He dug through the drawers until he found a box of matches. The first three didn't strike but the fourth match caught fire easily. Ben touched the tiny torch to a corner of the book and watched as the pages blackened and curled. The smoke was heavy and it hurt his lungs but he didn't care. All he wanted was for the memories and the guilt to leave. The smoke became so thick that he had to sit on the linoleum and wait out the fire. He traced the lines of the flooring, remembered that Molly had said she'd slept on it, and he lay down. As his skin touched the cool surface an alarm rang out but he didn't move. It felt so good to him to be far away from the world above that pained him.

REVENGE

Molly had been thinking a lot about the day before. Vaughn's mysterious bite wound and Hayden's death. She could come up with multiple theories as to how Vaughn had found himself with a set of undead teeth on his arm. And Ben had given a plausible reason – the pregnancy – as to why Vaughn might be angry with Hayden. But two things nagged at Molly's head. Why would he kill her over that and what the hell was Jeff doing in the third floor hallway?

As she crawled passed him in the dim hallway she could see the gun tucked into his pants. After seeing the wound in Hayden's head, she knew it had been Jeff but she didn't want anyone to know. Jeff would kill more if confronted and now that he had a weapon it would be difficult to ever deal with him again.

Molly's confidence had grown as well though. After beating a man to death for food she felt like she could take on Jeff. The drawstring of her food bag pulled out easily; she checked it for strength and practiced looping it around a bag of flour, pulling it tight. She heard a smoke alarm going off in the building, somewhere above her head. She watched out the peephole of 204 while Isobel ran upstairs to investigate. Less than a minute later, Rob exited his apartment across the hall to follow. It was an unplanned and perfect coincidence. She only hoped that Jeff didn't struggle and make too much noise with Gabe in the apartment next door.

FIRE AND RESCUE

Ben looked up to the ceiling and the stormy, cloud-filled sky that he'd created there. Isobel was there now, above him. She'd found him and the fire and she was yelling at him.

"Get out of here, Ben! Get up!" she screamed. In her hand something red and round was killing the fire he'd made.

He sat up and he could see that the flames had grown to touch the cabinets. She was losing and it made him happy that the fire would win the battle.

"It's all got to go," he said as he lay back down.

"Shit, shit, shit!" Rob yelled. He'd heard the smoke alarm and run upstairs. In the kitchen of the Cooper's old apartment he found Isobel trying to suppress the flames. He went to the hall to turn off the blaring alarm. Back in the kitchen he attempted to drag Ben to the living room. "Isobel, he passed out. What the hell am I supposed to do?"

"Make sure he's still breathing. I don't know how much smoke he inhaled," she answered, still battling the flames but now in control of the fire.

"What's burning?" Rob asked as he pulled Ben a few inches closer to safety.

"The cabinets but it started with a book," Isobel responded, coughing from the smoke.

"Which one?"

"I don't know! I just want to know if he meant to burn the place down," she said as she set down the extinguisher and wiped sweat from her brow.

"That would be a problem."

"A problem I wouldn't even began to know how to handle," she sighed.

OPTIONS

Somewhere the building was burning, the air filling with smoke, but it felt as though the air of 201 had changed for the better. Jeff was looking to the future. With a gun, food and no way – beyond breaking down the door – for the others to enter his apartment, he finally had options. The only one he actually felt like pursuing was to find Markus. It was easy, in Willow Brook, to take sides when people driven by fear surrounded you. *But maybe*, Jeff thought, *if I find him and we're alone I can convince Markus to take me back*. And if that didn't work, he always had the gun.

He was packing a light bag for traveling as the muted wailing of the smoke alarm stopped. He finished folding a sweater and a change of socks into the bag and was standing up to leave when he heard a knock on his door.

MOLLY MATHAY, ACTRESS

Molly stood outside Jeff's apartment, the rope behind her back, a lonely look upon her face. Jeff wasn't going to let her in but he felt the need to brag about his mission to rescue Markus and Molly could tell him how to survive outside. *Hell, she'll be happy I'm leaving*, he told himself.

"Molly, to what do I owe the pleasure?" Jeff said with happiness that she knew was false.

"I'm really sorry about everything that has happened. I was feeling alone and we haven't talked much beyond fighting more recently. If you had a second, I was thinking maybe we could spend some . . . time together," she said with enough flirt to confuse and intrigue the man.

"Yeah, things have gotten pretty bad between us. I was planning a trip outside. Maybe you can help me with that?"

"I think I can, you know, since I've been out there before," Molly nodded and smiled.

"Great, great. Come in then. Have a seat. Do you want anything to drink? I have wine." Jeff allowed her in and took off his backpack, setting it down inside the doorframe.

"Wine would be wonderful, thank you." Molly looked around for the gun but she didn't see it. *The bag,* Molly determined. She watched his every move. With her back facing away from him to conceal the rope and her body between him and the bag she waited for the moment. He turned to the cabinets to find two wine glasses.

Now! She yelled at herself. *Do it now!* She lunged at him, threw the rope around his neck and tightened it with everything she had. Jeff dropped the glasses and brought his hands to the rope that was taking his life. She imagined a similar scene, only with Jeff's hands around his wife's neck. *Don't let go,* she thought.

"I know you killed Hayden. She could have lived but you wouldn't let her," Molly whispered in his ear. "Well I'm not going to let you get away with it!"

Jeff's body went limp and heavy. Molly checked for a pulse and found that his heart was still beating. She couldn't shoot him with the gun he'd taken. It would make noise; bring the others to his apartment. She lowered him to the floor of the kitchen and continued the pressure to his neck until her arms grew weak. When she checked for a pulse again she felt nothing. With tired arms she pulled his body to the balcony and pulled and pushed it over the edge.

"I told you I'd help you with your trip outside," she said to the corpse. "Say hello to Sheila for me!" Minutes passed before his body came back to life. Molly stayed and watched as Jeff Brown stood up and walked out of her life.

RIPPLE EFFECT

Isobel stood in the third floor hallway looking down at Rob as he in turn looked down at Ben. They'd dragged him out of the apartment while the smoke aired out.

"Hey, are you ok?" Rob asked as he shook Ben's shoulders gently, trying to rouse him back to consciousness. Ben coughed loudly, his eyes still shut, as he curled into a tight ball. "None of that! You've got to get up!" Rob shook him with more force.

"Why didn't you just let me die?" Ben cried out.

"Were you trying to kill yourself? You could have killed the rest of us too with that stunt! If you want to die, please do it in a more considerate manner." Rob pulled himself from the floor and started to walk away from Ben, who he determined to be hopeless.

"I wasn't trying to die. But I wouldn't be hurting so much if I had," Ben said. "Things would be better."

"The problem with this place, all along, is that everyone's been thinking about what they could do for themselves. Things might be better for you if you were dead but what would it mean to everyone who's left?" Rob asked him.

"Selfishness. It's the American way," Ben laughed.

"Well it sure as hell hasn't done us one bit of good. Now get off the goddamn floor and stop trying to ruin things for the group."

SHUT IN

Three days had passed since Hayden and Vaughn's death. Isobel hadn't seen Molly for that entire time. Ben and Rob confirmed that she hadn't left her apartment to their knowledge. They feared the worst but they couldn't deal with another zombie in the building to kill or an even smaller group, so Isobel was determined to find out if she was all right. She grabbed the ring of keys and went to Molly's door.

Pounding on it she yelled at Molly. "You have to let me know if you are still alive in there!"

Molly was still full of anger that she'd been lied to by everyone, forced into punishment for her own acts while Jeff had been given little more than a warning. And while she had taken care of that she was still traumatized over the event with Vaughn and Hayden. And even though they'd shared a moment in Vaughn's apartment, she had nothing to say to Isobel. In fact, she was happy to see Isobel losing control. It was getting hard to concentrate on the book she was reading with Isobel nearly breaking down her door. Molly looked around her apartment for something to slide under the door. She found a piece of printer paper and drew an unhappy face on it. She had considered leaving it blank but that would look like a white flag of surrender and she was not surrendering.

She slid the paper under the door.

"What is this? Proof of life?" Isobel shot angrily through the door, her words overwhelming Molly with sadness. "I want to see your face!"

Molly didn't want to open her door. Isobel would force her way in beyond the entry and see all the food she'd stolen. "Maybe tomorrow," she said through the door. In the entry sat Jeff's backpack, in the backpack the gun. No matter what tomorrow might bring, Molly was ready.

Rob appeared behind Isobel. "Looks like she still needs that 'time' you were telling me about."

"Can you blame her? She's lost everyone; the baby, Jill and Hayden," Isobel said.

"Me," Rob added.

Isobel patted him on the back. "I'm not going to tell you that things will be ok because that would be stupid at this point."

"Yeah. How's Ben?" Rob asked her.

"Almost back to his usual self. He's been reading a lot."

"I thought he hated books with a fiery passion," Rob laughed.

"Not funny, Rob. Hey, have you seen Jeff?"

"I checked on him yesterday but I couldn't find him. He left. Maybe to find Markus?"

"That's probably for the best."

NOTHING TO DO LIST

Back in her apartment she found Ben staring at the coffee table.

"What are you doing?" she asked warily.

"I thought 'killing any undead' would be the most difficult," Ben said. He was reading a piece of paper on the table.

"What are you saying?" Isobel rubbed her eyes from tiredness.

"Our checklist. I thought number three was going to be hardest." He slid the paper across the coffee table. Isobel recognized her handwriting, remembered the feelings of being organized, in control, sane.

"It was so easy. We checked it off like we were shopping for vegetables. This one is where all the trouble lies," she said as she pointed at number eight.

8. Wait it out until the end

"I fear we won't survive to check it off the list," Ben agreed.

Isobel stood up and went once again to her balcony to watch the dead, the street so full of them, her life so empty. Only this time she wasn't looking for the dead she knew, she was looking for the ones she hated. She sought in the undead crowd all the citizens that had driven her crazy while they were alive. She looked for the people that couldn't figure out how to function at a four way stop. She looked for the folks that would stand in the middle of a grocery store aisle, unmoving as she tried to squeeze by. She looked for the parents of noisy, uncontrolled children. She looked for the people who littered, continued shopping from the checkout line, parked crooked, and talked too loud at restaurants, and the ones who didn't use their turn signals. In the writhing crowd of the undead she saw reflections of the downfalls of their group, the weakness of the Cabels, the desperation of families trying to stay together like the Coopers and the selfish lives of the city – so close to that of Vaughn's existence. Isobel found every last one of the failing, fragile, and hopeless and then she didn't care that they were all dead. She was *happy* they were.

Dead (ded) adj. 1. . . 2. . .
3. Lacking feeling or sensitivity.

All this waiting and she was finally dead.

OUT FOR REPAIRS

Rob and his son were coloring in the common area. He'd stopped looking outside every day because the view no longer changed. The clouds rained and the dead filled the streets.

"Dad, do you think the 'copters are gonna come?" Gabe asked.

"I haven't heard any for a long time, so I don't think so."

"Maybe a tank?" his son continued.

"No, Gabe. A tank would have come already too if it could."

"Maybe it broke from driving over all the people and they just hafta fix it."

"I bet you're right," was all that Rob could say. He had little hope left for rescue. And if someone did come, how could they know it was all right to trust them? The world was full of horrible monsters, dead and alive both.

the infection has shown resistance to all treatments. all host subjects have died and no patient zero has been found.

WHEN THE DEAD . . .

When the dead come back even if you don't get bitten there are other infections that will do you in. Infections of the mind and heart like hatred, paranoia, greed, anger, and depression.

All of these diseases spread like wildfire in Willow Brook. The building itself still stands. The barricades have held firm. But inside the building, life crumbles as the remaining tenants lose hope and the will to live on. In times of duress, *we* are the biggest threat to our survival.

When the dead come back you are forced to choose only the lesser of two evils: cabin fever over the zombie plague.

They can't get in and you can't get out.

END

ABOUT THE AUTHOR

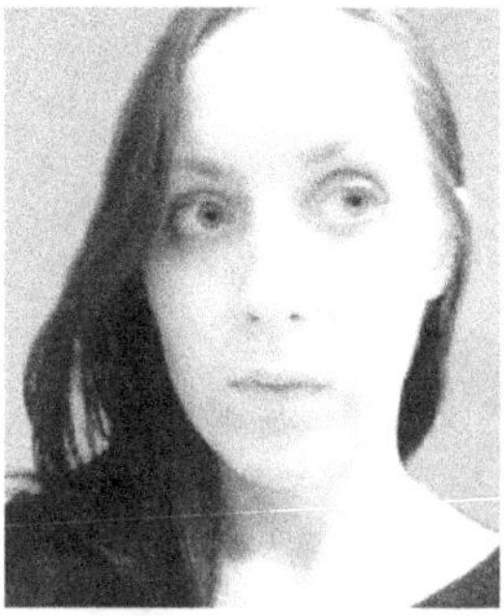

Michelle Kilmer is a fan of the macabre, especially zombies.

When she isn't writing zombie novels, she enjoys sewing, playing guitar, gaming and daydreaming about owning a Pomeranian.

Michelle is co-owner/designer at KILMERHANSEN Business Branding and Web Design; her day job and dream job.

She currently resides in a secured-access apartment in Seattle, WA that is uncomfortably close to a cemetery, two hospitals and a police station. Basically she won't survive the zombie apocalypse.

She lives with her husband, a machete, two baseball bats and a fear of the dark.

If you have questions, comments on the book or would like to learn more about upcoming releases, you can email Michelle at **michelle@whenthedead.com**

www.ingramcontent.com/pod-product-compliance
Lightning Source LLC
Chambersburg PA
CBHW061304170626
46817CB00001B/39
* 9 7 8 0 9 8 8 2 5 2 2 4 0 *